CLIMBING OUT
OF THE
FIRE

Lyndal Hennell

Published in Australia in 2024 by Lyndal Hennell

Website: www.lyndalhennell.com
Email: lyndalhennell@outlook.com

ISBN 9780645261820 (paperback)
ISBN 9780645261837 (ebook)

 A catalogue record for this book is available from the National Library of Australia

Typesetting and cover design – Brisbane Self Publishing Service

Disclaimer

This is a work of fiction. Names, characters, places, incidents and events, other than those clearly in the public domain, are fictitious and any resemblance to actual persons, living or dead, is entirely coincidental.

This book is for Jordan and Brodie – I love you guys.

The Legend of the Phoenix

Both the ancient Greeks and Egyptians had stories of a mythical bird called the Phoenix. It was a magnificent creature, with brilliant gold and red plumage, and like the sun that rose every morning, the Phoenix was a symbol of renewal and rebirth.

According to the legends, the Phoenix lived for five hundred years, and only one Phoenix lived at a time. When it knew it was about to die, the Phoenix built a nest and set itself on fire. A new Phoenix then rose from the ashes of its predecessor, climbing out of the fire.

1

Today

Fear rode through my body like a familiar but unwelcome acquaintance. I stood at the window and looked out. Fidgeting. Waiting. Breathing.

Fourteen stories below, the people on the beach resembled Lego minifigures arranged at regular intervals along the shoreline. The sea was a deep sapphire blue, and crystal clear, stretching to the horizon which had been broken by a small, but very bright, yellow orb. A thin line of grey clouds smudged in with the orange that stretched out on either side of the rising sun. The sky above was already a light azure colour, and there were no further clouds; the promise of a fine day. The scene reminded me of a painter's palette, where someone had smeared together the primary colours, experimenting with different shades and combinations.

Although it was early on a winter's day, the most dedicated surfers were already out. They sat on colourful boards, gently rising and falling, waiting for the perfect wave.

I watched a girl in a purple wetsuit paddling fast on the edge of a swell. As the wave broke, she stood up, dipping and weaving, her board a natural extension of her body. Her balance was in perfect harmony with the rhythm of the sea.

Jackson had been pacing behind me, but he stopped and placed his hand in the middle of my back. I leaned my head back against his chest and he rested his chin on my forehead. His breathing was fast and shallow, and his anxiety weighed heavily across my shoulders. It pulled my attention away from the surfer girl and I stifled a sigh. I looked up to give him what I hoped was a reassuring smile. He pushed his hair back from his face and returned the smile, but it was a weak attempt and did not reach his dark, cocoa-coloured eyes. Although we were both putting on a brave face, the churning butterflies told a different story.

No one else knew we were here. It was not a very smart move, but Cooper had been clear. It was only to be Jackson and me.

Taking a deep breath, I held it in, and then made a long, slow exhale. It was an intentional calming technique. I heard Jackson doing the same.

"Do you think Cooper has been living here?" His voice was quiet, even though we were the only people in the room. "That's his bag in the bedroom."

"I guess." I shrugged. "It's a really nice place. And a brilliant view."

The blank stare he returned suggested he had not even seen the scope of colours I had noticed.

It was a small, self-contained, one-bedroom apartment in a tall high-rise, overlooking Surfers Paradise Beach. The walls and floor tiles were white, and the carpet was a soft beige. The furnishings were also mostly white or cream, with an occasional splash of colour in the blue couch cushions and red kitchen appliances. Everything was neat and clean. Too much so. Sterile, even. It didn't have the look of someone living here.

"Yeah, but he couldn't afford this on his own. So, does Theo pay for it? And then what does that mean? It doesn't look like he's being held against his will. Is Cooper one of the *gang*?" Jackson put a sarcastic emphasis on the last word. "And he's supposed to be the good boy."

Jackson and Cooper were twin brothers. They were similar but not identical, and Jackson was not only a little darker in hair colour and eyes, but also in temperament. He was more reserved than Cooper, wary of new people, usually sarcastic, and often moody. He wore a lot of black and rode a motorbike. Cooper was friendly and popular, and yes, he was usually considered the good boy.

I could feel that Jackson's anxiety was rising again. It was no longer a dead weight. Instead, it was a painful burn in my chest. Anger at his brother was feeding off his fear and frustration. My throat tightened and shivers ran up and down my spine.

I was able to sense Jackson's feelings, and actually feel them as if they were my own.

That is what it is like being an empath.

I also had the ability to influence the emotions of those around me, and I knew I had to keep us both calm.

Taking another deep breath, I arched my back in a stretch and closed my hands into fists, then released them with my exhale and let my shoulders relax forward, feeling the tension go. I returned to watch the beach scene below, clearing my mind of other thoughts.

My quiet composure passed through to Jackson. He let out the breath he had been holding and I felt his anger ease into a controlled simmer.

"Sorry," he whispered.

I just nodded and kept my focus on the beach.

It took me a moment to find the surfer girl again. She was out the back, beyond the breaking waves, sitting on her board, waiting patiently for her next ride. Other surfers floated on their boards around her, and I imagined the easy banter between them. They rose and fell with the gentle swell. Their colours braided with the ocean blue all around them. It all seemed so effortless and peaceful.

Until it wasn't.

The door clanged as it opened, slamming back against the plastic doorstopper.

We turned to face Cooper, who stepped into the room but then stopped in the entry area, as if he were a puppet being held in place by its strings. He wore a black t-shirt, black jacket, and jeans.

Behind him was Theo, then three other men, also dressed in black t-shirts, black jackets, and jeans. Gang members.

Theo's eyes locked with mine.

His hatred roared across the room in an emotional tidal wave. It was angry, it was vengeful, and it was lethal. I felt like the skin was being seared from my bones. For a moment the air felt so hot, I couldn't inhale. Seconds later that heat had receded, but it was replaced with an ice-cold suspicion. I held back a shudder.

It was inherently clear to me that we had been very naive in coming here alone.

I knew, with every sense that I had, every cell of my body, every empathic essence, that Theo wanted to kill me. He did not intend for me to leave this room alive.

And I did not know how I was going to stop him.

2

Three Months Ago

The woman beckoned for me to follow, but the path was completely dark; impenetrable. There was fire all around us, but although I could feel the heat, it provided no light. I hung back, wanting to trust this woman, but I was not sure I could. She was tall, with long, black hair that floated about her shoulders. I could not make out her face. Taking a step forward, I was engulfed by the darkness. I could not even see my own hands in front of me. The flames licked at my heels.

I woke up sweating, scared, frustrated.

It was only a dream. The same one I'd been having every night for over a week. A recurring nightmare.

I stared up at the stars on my ceiling. Stickers that glowed in the dark, left there from when I was a child. Who was I kidding? I still loved them.

The light was barely peeking through my blinds, suggesting it was another cloudy, rainy day.

Like every other morning, when I first woke up, I would forget for a minute. I would think that I was normal, just for a second or two.

I would think that the world still had Sage in it, and I did not have that darkness inside me.

Then I remembered, and it crashed in on me.

Sage was dead. It had been two months now, and the world was moving on without her.

And I was not normal.

It was like having broken ribs. On the outside I might seem fine, but every breath I took was painful with grief.

A blackness hung in my heart and penetrated through to my core.

I gave an involuntary groan and the noise made Mia stir. She was asleep in the bed, next to me. It was a girls' weekend sleepover at my house. Yay!

I moved carefully, trying not to dislodge the kitten sleeping between my feet.

Mia's auburn brown hair was a messy frizz on her pillow. It had grown into a short bob after she had shaved off her dreadlocks last year. Her eyes stayed shut, so I quietly climbed out of bed and left her sleeping.

The kitten jumped off the bed and stepped between my legs, rubbing against me, reminding me that I needed to feed her. I had called her Ripley. She was a rescue. Someone had brought her into the local veterinarian, half-starved and dehydrated. When they tried to find her a home, Mia thought of me. That was three weeks ago. Ripley was now part of the family.

My reflection looked back at me from the full-length wall mirror. Brown hair hung limp and straggly down to my shoulders. I combed my fingers through it, which made little difference, and shrugged. Dark circles smudged below my green eyes, which glistened with unshed tears. I had not been sleeping very well.

I scrummaged for a scrunchie amidst the mess on my dressing table – my brush, bobby pins, odd earrings, deodorant. A bunch of old Polaroids were blu-tacked to the wall. Shots of my friends, crowded against each other, arms around each other's shoulders. Sage smiling and laughing, sometimes pouting. Snapshots of perfect moments in time. And me, squinting or turning away, never quite nailing the timing, but usually still laughing. Probably at something Sage had said.

"Stick together?" I asked quietly, looking at the photos, waiting for the required response – "Like glue."

But there was no response. No Sage.

The loss, the sadness, was still raw.

Sage Ferry had been my best friend since primary school, part of my life for ten years. She was the Yang to my Yin. But, just two months ago, Abraham had killed her.

Abraham was a gangster, a crime lord, an all-round bad guy. He had ruled Melbourne's south-eastern suburbs. Until I killed him. I had shot him after he murdered Sage instead of me.

I heard Jackson's voice in my head. *Nova, Abe would have either taken you or killed you. And he would have killed Luca. You had no choice. It was self-defence. Basic survival.*

The police had also considered it was self-defence, and there were no charges laid. It was all hushed-up, and my name had been removed from all the documentation. That had been done to protect me.

Self-defence, maybe. But it had still left me with a darkness deep inside. When you take someone's life, no matter the circumstances, you lose a part of your own too. That black shadow was a part of me now, and there was no Sage to help lighten that darkness.

I moved into the bathroom and splashed my face with cold water. It helped clear my thoughts and brought me back to the present.

In the lounge room, there were more sleeping bodies. Ava and Imogen were at opposite ends of the couch. Devon was sprawled out on a foam mattress and her round Harry Potter glasses were lying on the floor next to her. I knew Spencer was asleep in the spare room. She was pregnant, and so she had scored the bed. They would all soon be waking up. I had to focus on that.

Everyone here had lost family and friends in the last year. The current world climate was one of chaos and aggression. Everywhere, people were more angry, more destructive, more violent. Crime and death were the result of that. Grief was a familiar companion for all of us.

I was being morbid. *Stop it, Nova!*

With a forced smile plastered across my face I moved into the kitchen to feed the insistent kitten.

△

Breakfast had been eaten, music was blaring, and laughter was flowing.

"Nova, you smell nice." Spencer came up behind me, sniffing at my hair.

"It's my banana shampoo." I pulled gently on her long blonde ponytail.

"I'm having weird cravings all the time. Now I feel like a banana!" She patted her small pregnant belly.

"Help yourself." I pointed to the fruit bowl, which had a banana and two green apples – my favourite fruits.

"How can you eat anything else?" Imogen moaned and rubbed her stomach, which was full of pancakes but still flat and trim. She was slumped on the couch.

"I'm pretty sure this is actually a baby hippopotamus!" Spencer rubbed her belly again and gave a laugh that was a cross between a snort and bark. It set us all off.

Spencer had such a positive energy. She was easy to be around, and I was drawn to her optimism like a moth to a light.

"What other cravings have you had?" Devon was wriggling her fingers while Ripley pounced on her hand and attacked her.

"Well, passionfruit sorbet is the main one."

"I have my shift today at the ice-cream shop in town," I said. "You should come in and I'll give you a giant scoop."

Spencer's mouth gaped, and her grey-blue eyes opened wide. "Oh my god, Nova, that would be amazing."

My heart blossomed with the simple joy she felt about getting an ice-cream. It was often the little things that made us the happiest.

"I've also been craving peanut butter and butter chicken curry. But not together." Spencer gave another snort-laugh. "That Indian restaurant in the main street has the best butter chicken."

"I love their food." Ava's voice was a high-pitched squeak, and she blushed when we all turned to look at her.

"Spill! What's going on at that restaurant?" Mia leaned forward, watching Ava carefully.

Mia Taylor was the centre of our social circle. A reliable confidant, she was quick to gain people's trust and always up with the latest gossip. She was the one that organised events and managed all the group chats. Her huge, generous heart had room to care for all of us.

"Nothing … well, nothing at the restaurant. It's just that … well, it's … well, I've sort of been seeing a girl, and she works in the boutique. The one next to that restaurant." Ava held her hands in front of her mouth and the words tumbled out around her fingers. The excitement was bright and clear in her eyes and I felt it bubble in my throat. "It's Brooklyn Atkinson."

"Brooklyn, who was a year ahead of us at school?" Mia waited for Ava to nod. "She is so lovely. Her mum is a physio. Brooklyn always wears such pretty dresses; she must get a discount from the boutique."

"Yeah, well, I'm not really a dressy kind of girl, so I've been getting a lot of takeaways and then I can drop in to see her." Ava's freckled face flushed even redder as she gave an embarrassed laugh and frowned down at her ripped jeans and navy t-shirt.

Imogen, Mia, and I shared a look. Ava was raped last year, and it had changed her in so many ways, including a loss of social confidence. This was a huge step for her, to be considering a relationship with someone.

"We are so happy for you." Mia blinked away the tears in her eyes as the three of us swarmed around Ava in a group hug. I could feel the ties of friendship weaving between us like soft bindings.

Ava giggled and made feeble attempts at pushing us away. "It's early days yet. Don't jinx me." She paused and glanced sideways at me. "Cooper is often there too. Getting takeaways. Almost every time I go in."

Mia turned her appraising eyes on me. "You do eat a lot of takeaways."

"Hey! They're not for me." I shook my head. "Cooper and I are barely talking."

"They're probably for me, actually." Spencer blushed but gave a small smile.

"What?" Mia asked, looking between me and Spencer.

I shrugged, feeling as bewildered as Mia.

"Cooper has been coming to see me and he usually picks up a butter chicken on the way over. He's been so nice to me. He's easy to talk to and he doesn't judge me for being a single mum. Mum likes him too. He's a really good friend." Her words came out in a rush.

A warmth spread through my chest, and I had a sense that Spencer had feelings for Cooper beyond simple friendship.

"He is." Imogen and I spoke at the same time.

Mia raised her eyebrows and glanced between the three of us, shaking her head.

I sighed. My history with Cooper had been complicated. Actually, complicated was an understatement. He had been my first boyfriend, and still held a special place in my heart. But while we had been dating, Cooper had cheated on me. With Imogen, one of my best friends. So, the betrayal was doubled. Cooper and I had got back together for a while, until he broke it off again. He had said I was too intense and, to be fair, I was, but my heart still twisted with that pain.

Anyway, it got even more complicated when, a few months later, I started going out with Jackson, Cooper's twin brother. Jackson didn't think I was too intense. My lips twitched as I held back a cheeky smile.

I knew I should be happy for Cooper and Spencer if they liked each other, and I was. *I was.*

"It was my fault that you and Cooper didn't work out. I'm sorry." Imogen spoke quietly to me, but everyone heard her.

I felt like there was a bone caught in the back of my throat. The hurt was still there a little bit. Well, a lot. But it had all happened almost a year ago now, and I had forgiven them both.

"No, it's okay. It wasn't that simple. And it wasn't just that. I was a bit much for him. Anyway, I'm with Jack now, and that's really, really good." My heart skipped a few beats.

"Is it weird because they are twins?" Spencer had that way of asking the blunt questions no one else would voice, but she did it with such a caring innocence that you couldn't be offended.

"Super weird." I laughed and felt the heat flush through my cheeks and down my neck.

"Didn't you and Jack get together when you and Sage were living in Melbourne? Sorry, you probably don't want to talk about that." Devon was new to our friendship group and did not know much about what had happened, except that Sage had been killed.

"It's okay." But my voice shook, and I turned away. It was not okay, it was hard.

Soft clouds of sympathy stretched out from Mia and wrapped around me like a warm, protective layer of cotton wool. "That's a story for another time," she said. "We better get packed up and let you get off to work."

We moved about the house cleaning up, putting things away, and washing up the remnants of our pancake feast. Mia hummed as she moved around, and there were light giggles from Spencer and Ava as they looked at my childhood photos on the bookcase shelves.

"Nova, do you have a photo of your mum?" Ava gestured at the photos which were all of me, or me and Dad.

"I guess there must be photos somewhere, but Dad never spoke about her much. I think her death was too painful for him."

"I can imagine," Ava said, with a slight tremble in her voice.

Her fragility had returned, and it made me feel like I was hanging on to a ledge with just my fingertips. Ava's mother had been killed in a shooting at the food bank in town last year. She had still been dealing with the trauma of her own attack, her rape, when she had to suffer through the loss of her mother.

"How old were you when she died?" Devon asked me.

"Eight. I can't really remember much. She was in hospital, and we visited her, and then one day we never went into the hospital again. I think it was cancer. And then we moved here, and it was just me and Dad. It's probably easier losing a parent when you are younger." I heard the flat tone of my voice, but it wasn't truly reflective of the gaping hole that yawned inside me.

Both my parents were dead. My father had been killed last year. Shot, murdered by persons unknown. He was considered to be just another victim of the many random acts of violence that had become so commonplace over the last twelve months.

"It's hard at any age." Mia's voice faltered. Her father, a police officer, had been killed when he had tried to apprehend the shooter at the food bank. The same incident where Ava's mother had died.

Grief and loss hung in the room like heavy, dark, blockout curtains. It was something we all shared.

"God, this is depressing!" Spencer sighed.

There was an awkward silence.

"So, who's going to the Lewis's beach house for Easter?" Mia's question was a clear attempt to change the subject.

I smiled at her and let the love I felt for my friends spread around the room. Gradually the emotional climate lifted, as if the curtains were being pulled open to let in the light.

We discussed our Easter plans and were soon laughing again.

$$\triangle$$

"Are men allowed in here?" Jet called out from the door.

"Only if you're cute!" Devon called back.

"I'm allowed then," Jet replied, coming through to the lounge where we were all sitting. "I'm the cutest. Everyone okay?" His voice was light and friendly, but he raised his eyebrows at me and I knew he was genuinely checking in.

I nodded and smiled, and he nodded back, relieved.

"Nova, he actually is the cutest," Devon whispered and nudged me. She smoothed back her shoulder-length brown hair, which was already neat.

Jet gave Devon a friendly but professional smile. He towered above us, faded blue jeans hugging his hips and his white t-shirt a stark contrast to his dark skin. Muscles bulged from his sleeves and rippled across his chest when he moved. His deep brown eyes shone with a friendly welcome, but behind them there was an obvious level of steel. You knew you did not want to mess with this guy.

He was in the Australian Army, Special Air Service regiment (SAS), and he was kind of my protection detail. His unit worked with the Department of Violence Eradication (DOVE) to re-establish security and order and to stop the gang violence that had spread throughout our capital cities.

Midway through last year I'd had a chance meeting with another empath, Sawyer Young, who was a negotiation specialist with DOVE. Sawyer ran the Victorian operation, and he had offered me and my friends casual work. With all the violence and crime, the schools had already closed down and moved to online learning. It was bad timing for our final year of high school, but it did give us the freedom to move to Melbourne and become part of Sawyer's team. Sage, her boyfriend Luca, Jackson, and me. We had all gone. I had been an assistant to Sawyer in his negotiations and meetings. That was where I had met Abraham, the gang-lord of south-east Melbourne. His curiosity about my empathetic ability had eventually led to him kidnapping me. And even though I had escaped, it was not long before he found me again. That was when he killed Sage, who had been protecting me. Then I had killed him.

After Abraham was gone, DOVE moved in to break the power-hold that the street gangs had over such a large area of Melbourne. That had left disgruntled gang members without leadership, without direction. Although my role in everything was covered up, Jet was tasked with making sure I was kept safe in case of any retaliation. Hence, my protection detail.

"Nova, are you almost ready to go to work?" Jet took his role seriously and, although two months had passed without incident, he was never far away from me. This included driving me around while I was still saving up for a car. "Anyone need a ride home?"

"I do," Devon said immediately.

"I can give you a lift, Devon." Imogen laughed and dodged the elbow Devon aimed at her ribcage. "Or not!"

"I'll come too," said Spencer, but I knew she was just interested in the passionfruit sorbet I had promised her.

3

After the usual lunchtime rush, it was quiet at the ice-cream shop. I was keeping myself busy, wiping down the tables and counter tops until my shift ended.

"Nova, I can't believe you don't drink coffee." Nigel, the barista, was cleaning the coffee machine.

"I don't like the smell, and it's really bitter."

"Well, it doesn't have to be. I bet I can change your mind." He gave me a cheeky smile. "It's about finding the right blend."

I shook my head. "No, thanks anyway. I can't cope with the pretentious latte art you put on the top." I kept my voice even and bit on my bottom lip to stifle a smile, but I made sure to put a playful energy into the room.

Nigel's jaw dropped and his eyes opened wide. I knew he took pride in his latte art. That's why it was so easy to tease him.

His eyes narrowed as he moved in to place his hands on my shoulders, demanding my full attention. "My ferns are amazing, and you know it."

I shrugged but could not hide my smile any longer. Nigel grinned back and gave my shoulders a gentle squeeze.

"Hey, Nova!" The loud voice came from behind us and seemed to slice through the air like a sharp knife.

Nigel's smile disappeared in an instant. His hands were suddenly busy with the coffee machine again, wiping the already shiny surfaces.

"Hey!" I said lightly, turning around to face Jackson. "You're early."

"I came in to get an ice-cream." One side of his mouth lifted in a sarcastic smirk. "Hi, Nigel."

"Hey." Nigel nodded but kept his focus on his polishing.

"Are you sure you don't want a coffee? Nigel makes them with a fancy fern design." I sent a cheeky smile in the direction of Nigel, but he didn't respond.

"No, thanks." Jackson moved around the counter to drop a firm kiss on my lips. I knew he was deliberately giving Nigel a clear message of territory. "I want you to get me an ice-cream. Double cone. Cookies 'n cream and mint choc chip. If you're done flirting, that is." He whispered the last sentence close to my ear.

Heat flooded my cheeks, but I still glared at him and pushed him away. "Customers are not allowed back here. Go and sit down."

Moving to a booth in a few lazy strides, Jackson Lewis folded his tall frame into the bench seat and crossed his ankles under the table. He pushed his hair back from his face and his deep brown eyes were wide with a false innocence. A flicker of a smile shifted across his face, gone before it took proper form.

He was incredibly sexy.

The sense of playful mischief from Jackson danced around my heart and I hid my own smile.

Nigel was now rearranging the cups and mugs.

I moved to the ice-cream freezer and thumped the scoop against the frozen tubs. Getting the ice-cream out was like chiselling wood.

"I was not flirting." I passed Jackson his cone, resisting the temptation to squash the ice-cream into his smug face.

"Hmm. I'm not an empath but I'm sure I sensed some flirting, so it must have just been from Nigel." He took a small nibble of his ice-cream and licked his lips with an exaggerated sensuality. "Not that I blame him for trying."

I shook my head in pretend annoyance, but I could not help laughing with him.

△

Jackson rubbed his fingers over the rough stubble across his chin that hid a couple of red spots. He wrinkled up his nose. "You never get pimples."

"I do so." I had a very fair complexion; in fact, I was so pale that you could sometimes see a faint line of blue where a vein ran down one side of my face. But thankfully, my skin was usually clear.

"When? When was the last time you had a pimple?" He shook his head.

I shrugged. "I don't know. Last week."

"No, you didn't. And it's not fair. You eat so much junk food, but not one pimple."

I poked at his chest. "Why does everyone keep saying I eat a lot of junk food?"

19

He raised his eyebrows and his eyes swept from the burger in my hand to the Anzac biscuits and Coke bottle on the table. "Gee, I don't know."

"Well, it's healthy junk food. This is a veggie burger."

He shook his head again and laughed.

Jackson was staying the night with me.

Despite only being eighteen, with both my parents dead, I lived alone in my father's house. Well, it was mine now. I had Ripley, my kitten, and I enjoyed my own space, but I did not like the nights. Anger and violence were never far away, and it was hard to feel safe. Like all the surrounding houses, I had security screens on the windows and triple locks on the doors. My neighbours were kind and looked out for me, but I preferred to have someone stay over most nights. Usually it was Mia, sometimes one of the other girls, and often Jackson.

Jet rented a house in the next street. He managed a good balance of giving me some privacy and checking on me constantly.

I lived a quiet life. My university studies and work kept me busy. I had Jackson and my friends; they were my family.

And I had junk food. It was just so easy and convenient. Before my dad had died I had cooked all the time for the two of us, but I just didn't feel like it anymore.

Jackson reached for the last Anzac biscuit.

"Lewis, if you eat that last biscuit then our relationship is over, and we are never, ever, getting back together." I gave him what I hoped was a stern look.

He looked at me through narrowed eyes but still plucked the last biscuit out of the packet. Balancing it delicately between his thumb and first finger, he held it up.

"That isn't going to work on me, Taylor Swift," he said with a smirk.

I glared at him. "Tay-Tay is cool."

He turned the biscuit over in his fingers as if examining it.

"You would end our relationship over this biscuit."

"It's the last biscuit."

He bent his hand and moved the biscuit slowly towards his mouth. I watched as he took a large bite and his jaw moved in an exaggerated chew. There was half the biscuit remaining.

"It's goood," he mumbled, his mouth full of biscuit.

I poked out my tongue at him.

With a solemn face, he offered me the remaining half. "I'll share it."

I took it and stuffed the whole half into my mouth before he could change his mind.

"Thanks." My sarcastic tone lost any impact with the biscuit crumbs I spat all over him.

Jackson burst out laughing as he dusted down his shirt, then proceeded to sing the chorus of the Taylor Swift song.

I flipped my middle finger up at him, but he caught it and pulled me into his chest. He bent his head, nuzzled his stubbly chin into my shoulder, and his lips tickled my neck with soft, velvet kisses. "Wilson, I love you even more than I love Anzac biscuits."

I suppressed a giggle and wrapped my arms around him. Our love sat comfortably in my belly, which was full of junk food.

△

The next morning, we had training.

Twice a week, at the local gym, Jackson and I trained with Jet and whoever else wanted to come along. We did self-defence and fitness classes, a mix of martial arts and boxing. I was not particularly good at it, but I was improving slowly. It was important that I be able to defend myself if I needed to. The world was dangerous.

Today, Han had joined us. A black belt in Karate, he was a good match for Jackson.

Jet trained with me. He said Jackson was too soft on me when we trained together. Jackson felt his role was to protect me, and he couldn't bring himself to intentionally hurt me. As if I needed protection. Well, I mean, I had in the past. And Jet was my fulltime protection detail now. But I did not need my boyfriend protecting me as well.

Jet worked me hard. He was patient, and I knew he held back, but it was still challenging for me.

Han and I sat together after the session while Jackson and Jet had another few rounds of sparring. I was red in the face and breathing hard, still recovering.

"Did you hear about the fight in town last night?" Han spoke quietly while watching the others.

"No! Tell me." I wondered why Jet had not mentioned it.

"About ten guys arrived in town. Two carloads. Probably gang members from Melbourne." Han kept his voice low. "They were spoiling for a fight, and when there wasn't anyone around, they went on a bit of a rampage at the Grand Junction and at The Crown as well. Broke furniture, smashed glasses, beat up the security bouncers. The police came, but they took off. No arrests. It was all calculated, I reckon."

"Oh no. Did they have weapons? Was anyone seriously hurt?"

"Yeah, they had knives and baseball bats. There are two people in the hospital, but no one was killed, thank goodness."

In a world full of anger and violent crime, our regional town was usually a little safer than most. My friends often gave me the credit for that. As an empath, I had tried to foster an emotional climate of peace and a sense of community throughout the town. But it was not fail-safe. We still had vandalism, robberies, assaults, and domestic disputes. And nothing could stop the street gangs that came out from Melbourne.

"I heard they were looking for someone, asking questions. They didn't give a name, but described a young woman, a brunette, with green eyes." Han never took his eyes off Jackson and Jet fighting, but he nudged me gently. "I thought you should know."

That was why neither Jet nor Jackson had told me. Those men had been looking for me. My hands had turned cold, while hot electric shocks seared through the rest of my body.

"Thank you for telling me," I said. "I need to know these things."

I focused on my breathing. Slow, deep breaths in, and out; in, and out. We knew this could happen, and that was why Jet was here. That was why I was learning self-defence.

"How's Langford?" I asked, needing a change of topic.

"We broke up. He didn't talk about anything except motorbikes. We never had a proper conversation. It just wasn't working."

Tall, dark, and solid in build, Han Li was tough and formidable, especially when sitting astride his motorbike in his leathers. Like Jackson, he had worked hard to develop his bad-boy-bikie persona in high school but, beneath that intimidating exterior, he was a funny, intelligent, and loyal guy. I gave his back a sympathetic rub. He was wearing last year's school jersey, which, instead of his name, had *Made in China* plastered across the back.

"I think it's generally more interesting dating girls. It's better conversation. But there is something about a hot sweaty guy that is just so sexy." Han tipped his head towards Jackson and Jet. "I mean look at these two."

I followed his gaze. Jackson and Jet were fighting with fingerless padded gloves. They both wore loose tracksuit pants that hung low across their hips. Their bare chests showed off their well-toned muscles. When Jackson made a series of short, fast jabs, Jet held up his arms to defend the blows. Although bigger and broader, Jet was also faster. He twisted his body in a blur of movement, made a high kick to Jackson's chest, and Jackson fell backwards with a splat. He was flat on the mat and breathing heavily.

With his hands on his hips, Jet threw his head back, laughing.

Jackson groaned and held out his hand to be pulled to his feet.

They were hot and sweaty. And Han was right; they were both very sexy.

Jackson came over, picked up his shirt, and used it to wipe the sweat off his body. Han and I sighed in unison.

"What? Why are you two looking at me like that?" Jackson asked.

Han let out a loud snort of laughter. "We were just saying that you had your arse handed to you by Jet."

"I did not. Didn't you see me …" Jackson went on to describe all the successful moves he had made, but Han and I continued to laugh at him.

Jet joined us and gave Jackson a cuff around the head. "You did good, mate."

As we left the gym, Jet and Jackson were still analysing their fight blow-by-blow and discussing how to improve. The information Han had given me hung heavily in my thoughts. It felt like someone was wringing out my lungs every time I took a breath.

I knew it was just a matter of time before the gang members found me.

And then what?

△

I opened the News app on my phone, for the first time in a while. It never brought good news.

The stories were the same every day, in every state. Violence, crime, death. And these were the stories that made the news. There were hundreds more that did not.

Series of violent assaults in Sydney. City parks are not safe.

16-year-old Adelaide boy stabs his brother to death over burnt toast.

Armed man takes hostages and barricades himself in Geelong supermarket.

Bikie turf war in Surfers Paradise: Five police killed as gangs clash.

Protests against violence turn ugly.

Words jumped off my screen, describing devastation and wreckage. It was depressing and frightening, like a disease crawling under my skin, spreading fever and pain.

The world news was even worse than the local stories.

Ten dead, hundreds injured in Vancouver apartment building massacre.

Renewed call for gun reform as crime spikes in NY.

US-Mexican border patrol agents fear for their lives.

English football team in hiding after violent rioting. Finals in jeopardy.

150 dead after parade stampede in Italy.

Maybe the violence in our town wasn't as bad as these headlines but, a little over a year ago, it had been much safer, much more welcoming, much friendlier. Children had played in the parks, neighbours had met for coffee in the main street, people had walked their dogs in the evenings, and all without needing a weapon for protection.

Then the violence had started. It had swept around the world and our small town had not been spared. A plague of anger; a pandemic of aggression. Governments were ineffective in policing the ever-increasing crime rates – robbery, theft, assault, road rage, rape, and murder. The violence was everywhere. It was in the streets, in workplaces, on sporting fields, and even in the playgrounds. Curfews and lockdown procedures were implemented as desperate measures. Schools were closed and working from home became the norm. People carried weapons when they went out and barricaded themselves behind barbed wire and security steel when they were at home. Isolation was considered the best safety response, but the violence had continued behind closed doors and left the empty cities open for the street gangs to take over.

Conspiracy theories had exploded, blaming violence in computer games, vaccines, mobile phone towers, and food additives.

A lot of evidence pointed to the warrior gene, which is carried by about a third of the world's population. But while scientists struggled to find a cure, they also managed to create an artificial enzyme that stimulated anger and aggression. I knew from experience that gangs used this artificial warrior gene to create their warriors. Abraham had used it on his men, and he had even injected me. That was not something I wanted to remember.

Swallowing the lump in my throat, I put my phone down and used my calming technique. Deep breaths, and my exhales longer than my inhales.

While these news stories were depressing, I reminded myself that DOVE was making huge progress all the time. All the essential services were operating, students were back in schools, most people had returned to work, and while the pubs, restaurants, and cafés had limited hours and lots of security, they were open again.

In our town, after the awful spike in violence last year, the recent months had seen a return to normal. Sure, there was still crime, but not like it had been. The neighbourhood watch and concerned citizens groups had done a lot of good work in bringing people together, re-establishing community spirit, and providing support for those in need.

With my eyes shut, I conjured up the mental images of the neighbours and friends that I loved.

Someone once told me that we cannot always help everyone, but we do what we can. That was Finn. He was my protection detail before Jet. Until Abraham had brutally murdered him. I blinked away the tears that rose with that horrific memory and made myself picture Finn's kind smile. I wanted to believe that he was right. That every little bit of empathy could still make a difference in the world.

I knew what I needed to do. Stay calm, spread empathy, spread kindness.

4

It was Kenji's nineteenth birthday party. There were only twenty guests, his footy mates and their partners mostly, but Mia had also invited Imogen, Jackson, and me. People were still cautious about having and attending a party, especially at night.

The speeches had been made and the cake had been cut. In the lounge, a game of truth or dare was developing. Imogen had dared Kenji to do the latest viral TikTok dance. He performed it with a natural ease and somehow managed to look cool at the same time.

Jackson and I had moved in to sit on the couch next to Mia, and we joined in the laughter.

Kenji still held the floor. "Okay, who's next? Cooper! Truth or dare?"

"Well, you'll probably make me go naked for a dare, so I'm choosing truth."

"That's easy. Who in this room would you most like to have sex with tonight?"

Cooper hesitated and seemed as if he was deciding whether to answer or take the dare instead. He looked around the room while everyone watched him. Like Jackson, he was muscular and fit from working out. He looked good in his jeans, and a grey shirt hanging loose over his hips. His hair was a lighter, tawny blond compared to his brother's, but when he pushed back his fringe from his eyes it was exactly the same gesture that Jackson used when he was about to say something serious.

"Nova." Cooper gave his answer, looking directly at me. There was no laugh or smile, just a softening around his dark brown eyes. I had the feeling he was pleading with me and apologising at the same time.

The heat rose in my face, and my heart twisted in my chest. I sank back deeper into the soft couch cushions, wishing they would swallow me up.

Kenji let out a shout of laughter. "You Lewis twins are still just little boys fighting over your toys!"

"Fuck off," Jackson muttered under his breath. He stood up and stalked out of the room.

I went to follow, but Mia pulled me back down. "You'll make it worse." She turned to Kenji and glared at him. "That wasn't funny."

"It's just a game," he said defiantly. "I didn't know who he'd pick."

The look that Mia gave Kenji would have made a less confident guy wither into dust. She stood up. "It's my turn. I want a dare."

Cooper gave Kenji a wicked grin and turned to Mia. "I dare you to kiss someone on the mouth, properly, with tongue, but not Kenji."

Kenji just smirked, and I felt sure he expected Mia to turn it down and ask for a truth. Mia cocked her head, fiddled with her septum piercing, and then strode over to Evan. He was sitting on a stool behind the couch. She raised her eyebrows, asking for his consent.

Evan nodded with a wide smile. Mia kissed him. It was a full kiss, on the lips, open-mouthed. Her hand rested against his cheek while his arm snaked around her back, pulling her in against him.

The kiss lasted as long as it took Kenji to cross the floor. He pulled Evan away and punched him in the jaw. There was genuine anger in his eyes, and I felt it burning across my skin.

It was on.

Evan pushed Kenji away with a snarl. Cooper moved in, as if to break them apart, but then he punched Kenji. More of their footy mates joined in, siding with Kenji or Cooper or Evan. It did not seem to matter, it was just about hitting someone, anyone.

A fiery fury danced around the room, and I could almost see the sparks in the air. The anger combined with the alcohol that had been consumed made for a volatile mix. I felt like I was standing on red-hot coals.

Jackson was suddenly beside me. He had a half-full bottle of bourbon in his hand, and he raised it to his lips, sculling a long mouthful. "Let's go. I can't handle this bullshit."

I raised my eyebrows. He was really pissed off.

"Shouldn't we try to stop them?"

Jackson's eyes were stormy, and he shook his head, but then he put the bottle down and moved in, pulling people apart. A few punches were thrown his way, but he blocked them easily, just as Jet had taught him.

I spread some calming vibes, but as this hostility was alcohol-fuelled it made it much harder for me to have any influence on them.

"That is enough. Stop it, or I will call the police!" Kenji's mother stood in the doorway. She was a tiny woman, but her voice was shrill and loud. The music had been turned off.

She said something else, this time more quietly and in Japanese, and Kenji jumped back with his hands in the air. He gave his mother a sheepish look and I felt his shame burn hotter than the anger it had replaced.

"It's okay, Mum. Just the guys having fun." Kenji was breathing hard.

There was some grumbling, and a sly push or shove, as everyone moved away and sat down.

Their anger was disappearing as quickly as it had arisen.

There were scratched faces, a swollen lip or two, and a lot of red patches of skin which would no doubt form deep purple bruises come morning.

Cooper dropped into a chair, rubbing his knuckles. I could feel him staring at me, but I made a point of not meeting his eyes and instead watched Mia. She was holding a small ice pack against Kenji's cheek and he was playing with her hair. They seemed to have made up.

Jackson had returned to my side and looked between me and Cooper. "Can we go now?" His irritation was like a sharp stick poking me in the back.

"Yeah. Sure." I reached for Jackson's hand and squeezed it. He kept hold of my hand, but he did not squeeze it back.

Kenji's house was close to my place, so we walked.

My chest was tight and constricted. I knew Jackson was still annoyed. Kenji had been right. Cooper and Jackson did act like little boys. They competed over everything, including me.

Jackson and I were together, and even though I thought I had made my feelings clear to both of them, Jackson hated to be reminded that Cooper had been my first boyfriend. Cooper seemed to take every opportunity he could to mention it.

After walking a couple of blocks in silence, Jackson turned his back to me, crouched a little, and held his arms wide.

"Piggyback?" His voice was a soft apology.

"Seriously? I'm too heavy."

He snorted. "Come on."

I jumped on his back and wrapped my arms around his neck. He pulled on my legs, linking his arms through them. He was warm and solid. I giggled and a simple joy rumbled through us both.

"My god, you are heavy!"

"Let me down, then."

"I'm kidding. It's fine. You are so warm. You must have a small fire in you."

"I always think that about you."

"Maybe it's just the heat between us."

I cuddled in closer against his back. While I might be the empath, Jackson had a distinct way of making me feel safe and secure.

At the end of my street, he gestured with his head towards the vacant corner block. Four years prior, a neighbour had hung a rope swing from one of the giant trees that clustered in the middle of the empty property. It was sturdy, with a large wooden seat.

"Swing?"

I nodded. There was no one else around.

While the cool night air nipped at my ears and nose, the rest of me was toasty warm. I sat between Jackson's legs and his body was wrapped around mine. We both held onto the ropes. His longer, stronger legs pushed off from the ground to send us sailing up into the air, hovering for a second before we dropped again and swung back, building the momentum.

"So, who would you have kissed, properly, on the mouth, with tongue, if it couldn't be me?" His voice was a soft murmur against my ear, and whilst I heard the teasing curiosity in his tone, there was also his underlying resentment which made my stomach muscles clench.

"Mia," I said, without hesitation.

Jackson gave a loud, boisterous laugh. It echoed into the still night. "I wonder if Kenji would have punched you!"

His relief floated between us like a feather, rising and falling with the motion of the swing. Relief that I had not chosen Cooper.

△

The following afternoon we were at Jackson's house, studying. He was doing first-year medicine, and his dad had drawn him up a proper study plan which he was trying to stick to. It was good for me too. Although I was undecided about a career, I had started a science degree. The first-year university courses were mostly online, and I knew from my experiences with homeschooling for Year 12 last year that it was important not to leave all the lecture recordings and readings until the last minute.

It was complicated being at the Lewis house.

Ever since her oldest son had been killed, Mrs Lewis had been withdrawn and depressed. I could feel it hanging over her each time I was near. She still kept an immaculate home, but now spent long hours in her bed or just sitting in the lounge, and she rarely went out. Dr Lewis and the twins stayed with her to keep her company as often as they could manage. Today Mrs Lewis was in her bed, but she called for me to come in and say hello.

The bedroom was spotlessly tidy. A carved wooden mirror rested above an antique mahogany dressing table with drawers on each side, clawed feet, and a matching cushioned stool. There was a large desk in one corner, also mahogany, piled with papers and medical textbooks. It was the only slice of disorder in the room. The bed was high and large, covered with a beautifully patterned quilt. I suspected Mrs Lewis had made it herself. She was propped up against the crisp white pillows. A book lay beside her, face down, but the pages were stiff and the spine barely creased.

Jackson pulled across the stool for me to sit on while he perched on the edge of the bed. We made polite conversation until Mrs Lewis complained of being weary and needing to rest.

While Jackson remained with his mother, quietly chatting, I went into his bedroom and opened my laptop. Cooper appeared in the doorway.

"Hi."

"Hi, Coop." This was the other complication at the Lewis house. I had not expected him to be at home today.

"Where's Jack?"

"He's in with your mum."

My heart felt like it was held in a vice.

"Can I say something to you?" Cooper moved into the room, kicked aside some shoes, and leant up against Jackson's desk.

In contrast to his parents' room, Jackson's bedroom was a cluttered mess. His bed was a simple light pine frame, and the sheets and quilt were a tangled ball in the middle of the mattress. His chest of drawers had been painted a dark blue and it was covered in dinosaur stickers – relics of his child-hood. The top was crowded with various men's toiletries. His desk was a modern white one, recently purchased from Ikea, with his laptop charging amongst a jumble of other cords. There were dumbbells in one corner of the room, and clothes and books were scattered over the floor.

"Of course." I was sitting in the chair at the desk and pushed it back, creating more distance between us.

There had been a lot of these chats but, given what happened at Kenji's party, it still seemed unresolved. For Cooper, at least.

"I just want you to know I'm trying, but it's hard to just be friends with you." He brushed his hair back from his face, exposing large brown puppy-dog eyes. His vulnerability pulled on my heart strings, but at the same time my stomach was churning like a whirlpool. These conversations were unbearably awkward.

Although he had paused, as if waiting for me to say something, I just rammed my hands under my thighs and shuffled my legs, staying silent, wanting the conversation to be over.

"See, I still have feelings for you, and I think you do for me. I can feel it when I'm near you." Cooper's declaration felt like a hand was tightening around my throat. "I know I made mistakes, but we were great together. Really great."

I shuffled my legs again, but this time he waited for me to respond.

"Coop, we had good times together, and I will always value that. I do care for you." It was a mistake to keep going over old ground, but I did not know what else to say. "But as a friend. I'm with Jack."

35

"I'll be happy if you're happy." Cooper was certainly persistent. "But are you sure that's with him?"

Jackson must have heard our voices. He came into the room and sat on his bed. "What's going on?"

Cooper turned on him, and his eyes had frosted over with resentment. "This all started when you took her up to the beach house. You came between us."

"She needed a friend. You lost her all by yourself when you cheated on her."

They were going over old ground, old arguments. Again.

"That was your fault," said Cooper.

They were both standing now, facing off, an angry mirror image of each other.

"So, you're saying it was my fault that you hooked up with Imogen. And after Nova took you back, you walked out on her again. Because it got too *intense*. I suppose that was my fault too." Jackson's words were dripping with sarcasm.

The whirlpool inside me was gaining momentum. Getting faster, more destructive. Cooper was breathing loudly through his nose and Jackson glared back at him.

"We just needed some space. You never gave us a chance to work it out," said Cooper.

"She loves me, don't you?" Jackson turned to me for confirmation but did not wait for me to answer. "I let her go when I came back from Melbourne. I let her choose, and she picked me, not you. You need to back off." He puffed out his chest.

"Did you really give her a choice? She was grieving for Sage; she wasn't thinking straight. She loves me too, don't you?" Cooper turned to me.

Jackson looked at me. Cooper looked at me.

There was silence.

My anger felt like it was boiling beneath my skin.

That was the other part to my story with these two brothers. Jackson and I were together when we had lived in Melbourne with the DOVE team last year, after Cooper had broken up with me. We'd had three months together, and it was amazing, and chaotic, and never boring. When his older brother died, Jackson had left to come home. He had broken up with me and told me I had to choose between him and Cooper.

I had. I had chosen Jackson. Sure, it was after Sage had been killed, and I was grieving. But it had been the right choice. I was still choosing Jackson.

But I could also feel the hurt that twisted through Cooper. It was exhausting.

There was a bitter taste in my mouth.

I cleared my throat and let the anger ride through my voice. "You two seem to have already decided who I love and what I want, so why bother to ask me?"

Jackson lowered his eyes, and Cooper sucked his lips into a pout.

I closed my laptop with a dramatic snap and stood up. "I'm going home."

My heart was racing, my palms were sweaty, and my head ached.

I needed to talk to someone. I needed Sage, but she was not here.

Jackson followed me down the stairs. "I'm sorry that happened. I didn't know he'd be home. I should have punched him last night."

"That would not have helped. You would have just made it worse." My tone was sharp, and he opened his mouth as if to protest but then shut it again.

Their competitiveness was so frustrating, but I knew my reaction was intensified by the heavy mantle of guilt that had draped itself across my back. Cooper had cheated on me, and he had hurt me deeply. I knew I could never be with him again, but I also knew that I had hurt him by choosing instead to be with his twin brother.

"I'll take you home," said Jackson.

I nodded. He gave me a weak smile.

△

I rang Mia when I got home and talked it through with her.

"I feel like they are constantly trying to outdo each other, and I'm caught in the middle," I complained.

"They suck. They compete over everything. Cooper's problem is that you are with Jack. If it were anyone else, he would be okay."

"I know, right?"

"They each have their own things and they don't like losing to each other. That's probably why Jack didn't play football, because Coop was better. And Coop never really tried at school because getting good marks was Jack's thing. Coop was the one who was popular with the girls. We even wondered if Jack was gay for a while because he never seemed interested in girls and he was always with Han. Until you."

I could not help my involuntary smile at her last sentence. Mia's family was close to the Lewis family, and she had grown up with the twins. She was like a sister to them, so she would have been privy to all the gossip. However, I was still left with an unsettled stomach, as if things were not quite right and it was all my fault. "So, what do I do?"

"It's not your problem. You need to do what's right for you. And that's being with Jack. It's pretty clear to everyone except Cooper. I know you adored Cooper, and he loved you, but he was always the main act and you were the support. You were downplaying your potential, and he let you. Maybe not intentionally, but he just likes being the centre of things and you don't. But with Jack, you guys match. Together you're the best versions of yourselves. You both shine. He's happier, nicer, more relaxed. And you're stronger and braver. You're more you. And he's more him."

"Wow, thanks Mia. That's … so sweet." Her insights made me feel warm and fuzzy.

I loved Jackson with all my heart, and every time I saw him I just wanted to walk into the safety of his arms and stay there. But she was right. At the same time, he challenged me to be bolder, more confident about who I was. Because he loved that about me.

I sighed.

"Look, Nova, Coop will just have to get over it. He had his chance and he left you. He should not have said that at the party. And Kenji was a dick about it. Maybe even Spencer and Cooper …" Mia left the sentence unfinished.

"Yeah, that would be good, I guess." My heart skipped a beat.

"Are you okay? Do you want me to come over tonight?"

"No, I think I just need some space. Thanks, though."

Mia was a wonderful friend, and she had so much compassion to share, but she was not Sage.

I stood on my back patio and leaned against the corner post for support. The sun was setting above the trees, and the sky looked as if it had been painted with broad, clumsy, brush strokes of red and pink. They culminated in a small orange sun which was sliding down into the horizon.

Despite the beauty, my chest felt heavy and sore. I missed Sage with every sunset, every sunrise, and all the time in between. Her advice, her warm hugs, our long talks about nothing much.

I closed my eyes and took a deep breath, then I opened them again.

The loss was still there. It stuck to me. Like glue.

5

I woke with a start.

It was not my nightmare this time. There were noises outside the back door. I heard voices and the door rattled as if someone was trying to get in.

Ripley hissed from the end of my bed. Her fur was standing on end, and she looked like a fluffy ball. Not particularly frightening.

I glanced at my phone. It was 11:08 pm. After curfew.

Although it was dark, my home was so familiar that I navigated my way easily amongst the furniture. A faint light filtered through from the streetlights at the front, but at the rear it was pitch black. The back door was off the laundry. I could hear murmurings. It sounded like there were two people, at least.

My feet were cold, and my legs were shaky. I had my panic alarm clutched tightly in one hand. It was the size of a tiny remote control. Once I pressed the button it sent a message straight to Jet, and I knew he would be here just minutes later. But I did not want to wake him for a false alarm.

"Nova!" Cooper's voice was loud. It was followed by thumping on the door.

A swirl of confused emotions twisted through my body. I felt nauseous and slightly off balance, which made me suspect that Cooper was drunk.

I unlocked the door and opened it just enough to peer through a small gap. Cooper saw me and he leaned against the door so that it swung wide, with a crack, into the wall. He fell into the house and onto me while I struggled to keep us both upright.

Behind Cooper was a stranger.

"Coop, what's going on?" I asked.

"Nova-you're-home." His voice was garbled, and the words all ran together.

"Is this her?" asked the other guy.

"She's her." Cooper giggled. "Nova, Griffin. Griffin, Nova."

It was too dark to see clearly, but I gave an automatic nod of acknowledgement. Although there was just silence from Griffin, waves of aggression rolled off him like peals of thunder and it sent shivers up and down my spine. There were alarm bells ringing through my head, but I had not yet pushed my panic button. I let my thumb hover over it.

"Coop, what are you doing here?" My voice was polite but firm.

I reached for the light switch, and it momentarily blinded us as the brightness flooded the room.

Cooper was swaying on his feet and gripped my shoulder for stability, but Griffin stood with his feet apart, solid and steady. He was shorter than Cooper, but bigger in build. Long blond hair was pulled back and tied into a messy knot at the nape of his neck. His grey-blue eyes were narrow, and one side of his mouth was turned up in a sneer. The hair rose on the back of my neck as I sensed a cruel streak in Griffin. When I took a step back, I left Cooper without his support. He reached for Griffin, who pushed him aside. That was when I saw the weapon clutched in Griffin's fist. It had a wooden handle and a long, skinny, needle-like blade. It took me a moment to realise that it was an ice pick.

A lot of people carried weapons these days, guns and knives mostly. An ice pick was unusual. It looked deadly.

Instinctively, I pushed down on my panic alarm, squeezing my hand around the control.

"He's been telling me all about you." Griffin's voice was low and rough.

I looked from his face back down to that ice pick and felt the muscles in my legs tense up, as if ready for flight. My lungs seemed to struggle to get enough air.

Griffin was dangerous. There was a crushing weight pressing down on me and I was sure it was the artificial warrior gene. It was racing through his body.

The handle of the ice pick rolled back and forth between his fingers and across his palm while he watched me. A predator watching its prey.

"Nova, Nova, Nova. I am ... you know ..." Cooper's words were just background noise.

My attention was solely on Griffin. I knew I needed to keep him calm, but my empathic abilities were going to struggle against the influence of the warrior gene injection. And the alcohol.

"We've been looking for you for a while now." Griffin moved forward quickly, and I found myself backed up against the wall.

The ice pick was pressed against my collarbone, above the neckline of my pyjama shirt.

I felt a short, sharp pain as he pushed the tip into my flesh. It barely broke the skin, but a spot of blood swelled around it. The familiar rusty smell was not welcome. My heart was pounding so hard I half expected it to leap out of my body.

Griffin shifted to press his body firmly against mine and thrust his hips at me. It was not a seductive gesture, but a controlling one. I could not move.

"I fucking hate bitches like you." Small droplets of saliva hit my face as he spat the words out. His breath was hot and reeked of bourbon.

Despite my self-defence training, I could not think of a single action that would help. Griffin was strong, and his legs had trapped mine so I could not even lift my knee into his groin. But that did not mean I was defenceless. I was better at the emotional stuff anyway.

Closing my eyes, I counted in my head and concentrated on breathing through my nose. Slow and deep, making my exhales longer than my inhales. Just like Sawyer had taught me. I clenched my teeth tightly together, trying to hold in the fear that had formed itself into a huge lump in the back of my throat.

Cooper was saying something, and his tone was a clear objection, but I blocked out the sounds.

When I felt like I had a little more control over myself, I focused on Griffin's emotions. I could sense pockets of darkness in him, and they made my skin crawl. As if aware of my emotional probing, his body pressed against mine with another forceful thrust. I knew I had to turn down that warrior gene, dial back that aggression.

Those dark parts of him were likely a result of trauma in his life that I could only guess at. I let sympathy draw out my compassion.

When I opened my eyes, Griffin stepped away from me. He lowered the ice pick and looked at me in confusion. From the throb behind my eyes, I knew his hostility still ran just below the surface. But I was also aware of the loosening in the muscles of my neck. He was a little less angry, a little less tense.

My chest was stinging, and I raised my hand to the wound. There was not much blood. It was more of a scratch.

"You're bleeding." Cooper's concern was having a sobering effect on him.

Griffin let out a sudden grunt and dropped to the ground. I looked past his unconscious body and into Jet's steely brown eyes. He had arrived.

Jackson stood behind him, and his eyes were like a storm cloud, dark and foreboding. I knew he must have broken the speed limit on his bike to get here so quickly.

△

When Cooper had sobered up, he was full of remorse and apologies. Griffin was new in town, and he was working at the paint store with Cooper. They had met at the pub for a drink, which had turned into six or seven, or more.

Jet had taken Griffin to the police station and dropped Cooper home.

The police were holding Griffin overnight, but it was mostly as a favour to Jet. They would let him go in the morning with a severe warning. No one had been hurt. Violence had become the new normal.

Jackson was staying with me for the rest of the night.

He and Jet had been gaming online when Jet's alarm went off. Jackson had jumped on his bike and come over, despite the curfew. His fury at his brother still simmered in his eyes and I could feel the tension that ran through his body. I rolled my shoulders, looking for some release.

Noticing my movements, but not realising the tension was his, Jackson put his hands on my shoulders, giving them a gentle massage with his fingers. "How are you feeling?"

He had already cleaned and dressed the small cut on my chest with a tiny bandaid.

I gave a small smile. "Fine. It's just a scratch."

"Hmm. Another one." Jackson ran his fingers lightly over my other scars.

I had a mark from a bullet graze on one arm and a knife puncture on the other. On my left side there was a thin pink line just above my waist that ran from below my ribs at the front around to the middle of my back. It was also from a knife wound.

"I actually meant emotionally." Anxiety rattled through his voice.

I sighed. He raised his eyebrows but stayed silent, waiting.

I had been quiet since Jet had left, mostly because I had not yet worked out what I was feeling. My empathic abilities gave me a keen awareness of the secrets and violence that people hid deep. They left a black scar. Whenever I touched the darkness in people, it filled me with fear. And despair. And I knew I had the same darkness inside me. Ever since I had taken Abraham's life.

Then there was the anger created by the artificial warrior gene. It felt like a toxic oil spill.

But I did not want Jackson to worry, nor did I want to add to the friction between him and Cooper.

"I feel safe now." And I did.

"You're always safe with me." Jackson's smile was smug, but it did not last long. "But that's not all, is it? Are you going to tell me what's wrong, Wilson, or are you going to continue moping around?"

I sighed again. He would keep pestering me if I did not try to explain. Jackson had become extremely sensitive to my emotions, even when I tried to hide them from him.

"It's like some people carry light and some carry darkness. I could feel a patch of dark in Griffin. Maybe that's from something that happened to him, or maybe it's from something he has done. I don't know." I paused and searched for the right words. "But what if when you do something that creates that darkness, it then corrupts you. What if it makes you bad from then on?"

Jackson shook his head. "I don't know about him, but I do know about you. Are you worried that what happened with Abe has corrupted you?" I knew he had purposely avoided saying the words – that I had killed Abraham. Nevertheless, he had narrowed in on the issue like one of those homing torpedoes.

"Well, yeah."

"The fact that you are even asking that question shows that you are not corrupted. Besides, I will keep an eye on you. If you are turning to the dark side, I'll bring you back to the light, young Jedi apprentice."

I knew Jackson was using humour to try and lighten the mood. "Funny." I gave a weak smile.

He smirked.

"But what if you can't bring me back?" I could not let it go.

"Then I'll follow you into the darkness." Jackson grinned, but then he turned serious. "But I won't have to. You won't turn to the dark side; it is not in you."

"Maybe it is now."

He shook his head at me again. "You're not dark, Nova." His love folded around me like a favourite jacket.

I pulled him down onto the bed. "Hold me tight." His arms wrapped around me. "Tighter." I was in a close lock against his body, and it felt like the safest place I could ever be.

Jackson carried pure light. It swept around me, over me, through me. It helped bury that dark stain I carried.

When he yawned, I let his sleepy contentment spread over me.

His steady breathing set a peaceful rhythm, until I knew he was well and truly asleep. The arm he had draped around my middle had loosened but was still a warm, solid weight. Comforting and protective. I wondered if Ripley felt it too. She was curled up against his legs.

I yawned and gave myself over to sleep.

△

"How's my favourite empath this morning?" Jet asked, with a cheery nod.

I raised my eyebrows at him. "Are you saying you like me better than Sawyer?"

"Today I do." He gave me a cheeky grin, which disappeared when Sawyer came into the room.

I had more training today, but it was not at the gym.

Sawyer Young was the first person to tell me that I was an empath, and ever since then he had been helping me to develop a greater awareness of my empathic skills. He still had me down as a casual employee with DOVE, but I had not been involved in any of his mediation or negotiation activities since Sage had been killed. Nevertheless, he had set up the protection around me and visited weekly to check in and do our practice sessions.

It was not really training; it was more talking and comparing notes on what we could feel or sense. I had learned a lot from Sawyer about recognising emotions and reading the sensations in my own body to better understand other people. Through this, we were able to imagine what someone else might be thinking. Sawyer called it cognitive empathy, and it allowed a better understanding of another person's perspective. We also worked on influencing others' emotions, especially calming people. That was his specialty. It was what made him an excellent mediator.

Normally, when Sawyer entered a room, an air of peaceful cooperation followed him. Today, it was like the floor was covered in eggshells. His blue eyes, which usually glistened with compassion and humour, were hooded. I could sense his frustration by the dryness in my mouth. He could probably feel the fear that I was hiding from everyone else.

Sawyer ran his fingers through his already tousled blond hair and got straight to the point. "I heard about last night. Are you okay?" I barely had time to nod before he continued. "It might have something to do with Abe's followers. Griffin is not a local, he's from Melbourne. We're still checking him out. I don't want you sleeping in this house on your own. Jet will stay in your spare room for the next little while. We need to tighten up your security. I don't want you going out anywhere on your own, and it needs to be made clear that your friends cannot just bring over new people we haven't vetted."

Sawyer was well-known for his diplomacy, so giving orders in this sharp tone was another clear indication of his concern. The tension coming off him felt like a layer of thick syrup.

I glanced at Jet, behind Sawyer, who was standing at military attention even though we were in my kitchen. His face was expressionless and professional, but I could sense his remorse and knew he had already been reprimanded. That explained why I was the favourite today. I smothered a giggle.

"Okay, that's fine," I conceded. "But we are going to Woodside Beach this weekend. It's all arranged. Ten of us. All school friends. And I'm sure they have already been vetted." I kept my voice soft and even, but I knew Sawyer would feel my determination, firm and strong like his own.

He shook his head and pursed his lips.

Sawyer was much more than my mentor, much more than my boss at DOVE. He was a close friend. He was like a cool uncle. I knew he cared deeply about me, and he felt responsible for my safety. Especially after everything that had happened with Abraham and Sage.

The restrictions he wanted to impose were for my own good.

I took a breath and straightened my back.

"Jet has already made plans to come with us. There is no more room at the house, but he is staying at a house nearby." I glanced at Jet, but his eyes were still fixed forward.

Sawyer sighed and watched me, as if assessing how determined I was. I felt my jaw go tight and then loosen again. He really had no grounds to demand anything, but we both knew that if Sawyer spoke to Jackson he had the skills to persuade Jackson to cancel the whole weekend, using my safety as a reason.

I looked back at him with what I hoped was a soft, but firm, expression.

He finally nodded. We had reached a suitable compromise without needing any further words.

Although we could not actually read each other's thoughts, our emotions provided a lot of insight into what we were thinking. Just by sensing the other person's emotions, Sawyer and I managed to do a lot of this nonverbal communication.

I felt Jet relax, and he even gave me a sly wink when Sawyer was not looking.

A niggly feeling sent a small shiver through my body that I smothered quickly, hoping Sawyer would not notice it. I still had not told anyone what Griffin had said, and I was not going to tell Sawyer now. He would never let us go if I told him.

That Griffin had been looking for me.

And that I had been found.

△

Jackson was perfectly still, staring ahead as if frozen with fear. I could feel it. My heart pounded, my body was cold, my stomach was clenched.

At the same time, I was creating it. I was making him feel it, and in turn it was bouncing back onto me.

I released it gradually and replaced it with contentment.

"Christ, Nova. That felt awful. It was like something horrible was coming for me in the dark." His voice was shaky, and his eyes were wide.

"That is pretty much what I was picturing."

He shuddered and then pulled me in close, drawing deep, restorative breaths. "Ok, do it again."

"Are you sure?"

"Yeah. There's a part of me that knows it's not real and it's just you. It's ok."

After my lessons with Sawyer, it had become a routine for me to practice my skills with Jackson. Usually, I set myself into a comfortable headspace which allowed me to spread a cooperative, calming energy. It was useful, not only in the negotiations that Sawyer ran, but also when diffusing conflict or potential violence. But the altercation with Griffin had left us all feeling anxious, and Sawyer wanted me to try being more offensive, rather than defensive.

I was working on creating fear. Drawing on the feelings I had in those dreams of the tall woman in the fire and the darkness. Those nightmares which gave me a sense of dread. The darkness was bleak and desolate, while the fire was painful and raw.

After a few more times, I was tiring. I had to feel the emotion to be able to pass it through to Jackson, and then I received it back from him. It was double dipping, and it drained my energy.

"That's enough." I could hear the weariness in my voice.

"Okay." He ran a finger across my jawline and then down to my collar bone. I could sense the sparks of desire that skipped across his skin. "You could make me feel something else now, something that's more fun."

I smirked at his pretence of innocence. "I don't need to make you feel that. It's simmering in you almost all the time."

Jackson gave me his cheeky grin. "Only when I'm with you."

I gave him a light shove away, but he rocked back and gently nudged arms with me. We leaned our heads back against the couch. A comfortable drowsiness spread through my body.

Jackson turned his face toward mine. His brown eyes were soft and warm. "You know, your empathy is growing stronger each day."

I raised my eyebrows. "What makes you say that?"

He sat quietly, watching me, until I poked at his chest. "Well, there has always been an energy about you. But now it's in every touch. I can't really explain it, but I can feel it."

I didn't say anything, but I could feel it too. A force within myself.

Sawyer was convinced that I was the reason that our town, our whole region, had less crime, less violence. My friends said the same. I did influence people's emotions, especially people I knew. But if I was feeling good, feeling happy, it was easy. I was just sending out ripples in a pond. On specific occasions, like at Kenji's party, when people were under the influence of alcohol, it was harder. That was more like wading through thick mud. And with the artificial warrior gene, like with Griffin, it was like pushing against stone. But it was not completely impossible. Not anymore.

What was most difficult was controlling my own emotions. When I was feeling sad or angry it was much harder to spread kindness and compassion.

And I was very aware of the darkness I carried deep inside.

While it had been tiring, it had almost been too easy to make Jackson feel afraid.

That shadow was a part of my energy too.

And it frightened me.

I might be getting stronger, but I did not know what that darker part of me was capable of.

6

I lay back, leaning against Jackson's chest, which was hard and muscular but warm and comfortable at the same time. We sat on the high tide line.

The sand was wet and firm beneath us, but the incoming waves did not reach our feet. Our bodies were still damp from our swim. Stray water droplets on my skin sparkled like glass and tingled as they dried.

Jackson's legs stretched out on the sand on either side of mine. His body surrounded me, keeping me safe.

"You smell good. It's like salt and sunscreen and the beach, all mixed together."

"You do too." I giggled.

He nuzzled my neck, purposely tickling me with the stubble on his chin. His teeth lightly tugged on my earlobe and his hands were rubbing my shoulders in a soft, sensuous massage. My stomach muscles tightened. His desire was inviting, welcoming, familiar.

"We probably should get back," I said evenly, giving no hint of the matching passion he awoke in me.

We had left our phones behind when we came for a swim, just to have some peace for a short while, but he knew I needed to check in regularly with Jet to let him know I was okay.

I pushed Jackson back onto the sand and made to stand up, but he tugged on my arms and pulled me down. My body stretched out on top of his.

Deep, cocoa-brown eyes twinkled at me, both loving and mischievous. His arms hugged around me, protective and strong. My hands were tangled in his damp hair. Soft lips pressed against mine and our tongues teased and tangled. Shifting his knees between mine, Jackson nudged my thighs apart so they wrapped around his. His board shorts and my bikini were a thin layer between us.

I let myself get lost in his embrace and I took him with me. What had started out gentle became more sensual, until the fireworks exploded, and it was like we were soaring in the heavens. I felt a shift when Jackson took back the control.

He groaned and broke away, rolling me over onto the sand.

"We better get back before ..." He did not complete the sentence, just shook his head at me.

Although his breathing was loud and fast, his face wore a masculine smugness. He stood up and adjusted his board shorts.

I gave him a wicked grin, and he shook his head again. He had not expected such a passionate response from me, not in public. I was not usually a PDA sort of person.

"You started it," I said. "And I like kissing you."

"Clearly!" His voice was sarcastic but affectionate. "Is kissing me better than kissing anyone else?" He was pretending it was a general question, but I knew he wanted to know how he compared to Cooper.

"Well ..." His face hardened when I paused. "In my limited experience ..." I paused again, letting him simmer, and his eyes narrowed. "You can be a little intense." I giggled at his frown but drew him back into an embrace. "You are the best by far," I whispered against his mouth.

Our lips met with a crash. No longer two, but one. My delight echoed his. We were riding a wave.

He was the one to break us apart again, with that same self-satisfied smile across his face. My heart blossomed with a joyful simplicity.

△

Mia and Kenji arrived at the beach house later that afternoon. Everyone else was arriving the next day. Tonight, it was just the four of us.

It was dusk and we sat on the back deck looking out at the darkening sand dunes. The sound of the waves beyond were a lulling soundtrack. A light breeze carried a salty but fresh smell of the ocean. It was peaceful. Except that Jackson kept looking sideways at me and smiling. I could sense the excitement fizzing in him.

"Okay, what's up?" I asked at last. "You're weirdly happy; you're up to something."

"Maybe I'm happy because I'm with you."

I studied his face. Jackson could be very romantic at times, but the tingling over my skin and the increase in my heart rate suggested it was more. "That is very sweet, but there is something else going on."

He laughed. "Well ... I once promised you that we would do lots of stupid teenager things." Jackson paused, watching me. Sage had been there with us when he had made that promise, and the pain twisted through my heart with the memory. He reached for my hand, and I knew he was remembering it too. "And that we would do them when this violence pandemic was over. But we can't keep putting it off. I'm nineteen, and I don't have much longer as a teenager. So, we are going to have a stupid teenage things weekend, starting tonight."

"Umm, like what?" The anticipation that bubbled through Jackson turned my stomach into knots.

"Like, tonight, we are going skinny-dipping." Jackson rubbed his thumb lightly across my knuckles. I knew it was supposed to be in reassurance, but it did not stop my blood freezing.

"In the ocean? We can't." I knew my face must reflect the self-conscious horror I was feeling.

Kenji grinned wickedly at Jackson, and I could tell that it was no surprise to him. "I'm in, mate." He turned to Mia and wiggled his eyebrows suggestively.

Mia giggled and then looked at me. "I'm game if you are." With the rush of delight that bounced through me, I knew she had also been in on the idea.

"What if there are other people on the beach?" This was first on my long list of protests.

"There is barely anyone around and no one comes out this late." Jackson shrugged out of his shirt and looked at me.

"There might be sharks."

"We won't go in that deep. I'll be right beside you all the time."

"If there is a shark, I'll punch it on the nose," said Kenji. Mia scoffed at him. "As if."

"You wanted to do stupid teenage stuff." Jackson's tone was gentle but firm.

"Yeah, but I thought, I dunno, getting drunk or something."

Mia took pity on me. "Let's have some shots first. For courage."

While downing our shots and trying to find the promised courage, I examined my friends. The night had closed in, but the moon was full and high. I knew there would be enough light on the beach to be able to see each other.

Jackson and Kenji were both broad-shouldered and well-built. There was not a centimetre of fat on either of them. They had the self-assurance that made them naturally attractive. Mia was equally as confident about her curvy body.

I sucked in my junk-food belly and squeezed my thighs together as if that would make me look skinnier. It didn't work. Goosebumps had formed all over my arms and legs. No way. I could not do this.

Jack sidled up to me. "You're beautiful."

I snorted softly. He was my boyfriend, he had to say that, but it was still nice to hear.

"Come on! Kenji and Mia can go in first and punch any sharks. You can stand behind me. I promise it'll be okay." He raised his eyebrows and his eyes were soft and pleading.

It was hard to say no to that face. And their enthusiasm was contagious.

We were going skinny-dipping. Stupid teenage fun.

△

"You're quiet. What's going on in that head?" Jackson came up behind me as we were getting ready for bed and nuzzled into my neck. He was still on a high after the fun we'd had skinny-dipping and his contentment danced through me like the tune of a favourite song.

I knew he was expecting me to say something flirtatious, but I was about to bring down the mood. And I couldn't seem to help it. "I was thinking about Sage. I guess because of the whole stupid teenage fun thing."

"Yeah. I'm sorry." His voice had lost the playful tone.

"You know what I hate. That there's all this stuff she doesn't know about."

"Like what?" He turned me to face him and dropped his forehead to rest against mine.

"That we're together again. That we went skinny-dipping. The shows we're watching on Netflix."

He was quiet for a minute as if thinking about what to say. "You're upset because she doesn't know we're watching *Stranger Things* again."

"Yes, exactly."

He looked at the floor and I thought he was stifling a laugh, but when he looked up his eyes were rimmed with silver. "Yeah, I hate that too."

Jackson put his arms around me, and just held me. He was warm and solid. I stretched my arms around his neck and clasped my hands behind his head. We stood together for a few moments, but then he pulled away. I raised my eyebrows, wondering what he was doing.

He reached into his jeans pocket and brought out a tiny, polished green crystal. He pressed it into my palm. "It's not until tomorrow and maybe this is bad timing, but maybe it's good timing. Happy five-month anniversary. For tomorrow. It's jade, for serenity and harmony."

My fingers clutched the smooth stone. It was cool to touch and comforting somehow.

Five-month anniversary. Jackson was counting the three months we had been together in Melbourne and adding it on to these two months since I had returned. He was ignoring the three months in between when we were apart. I think he wanted to emphasise that we were together longer than I had been with Cooper, which had been four and a half months. I wasn't sure if it was for my sake or for his, or for Cooper's. But it didn't matter. Every day was precious. And I just wanted to spend them all with Jackson.

This was the second crystal Jackson had given me. The first had been a small amethyst stone on our four-month anniversary. It sat on my bedside table at home. Amethyst was calming. To me, it was infused with Jackson's love, as was this one.

I held the crystal against my heart. "It's perfect timing. Thank you."

△

The room swelled with friendship and excitement.

Imogen had arrived with Devon, and Han had come on his motorbike.

Awkward hugs were exchanged, amidst giggles and good-natured taunts.

The Lewis beach house was perfect for a small party. The combined lounge, kitchen, and dining area was a large, open space, with wooden floors and colourful retro rugs. Four double bedrooms, a comfortable couch, and a couple of camp beds meant we could all stay the night.

A party was always potentially dangerous because it could attract unwanted attention, but Woodside Beach was a small community and safer than the larger towns or big cities. Most of the surrounding holiday houses were empty, despite it being the Easter weekend.

We also had Jet staying only four houses away, and Rayna was with him on Sawyer's orders. Rayna was also SAS protection detail, and she was usually posted with Sawyer. Her presence was another indication of his concern about me.

"So, you said you guys are just staying in." Jet glanced out at the grey skies. "But if you do go to the beach, go in a group and stay together." He had come by to see who had arrived, but I knew he would not stay long.

I also knew that he and Rayna would show up at regular intervals throughout the day, and the night too. They were not like parents, though, and their presence was more reassurance than an imposition.

"Yeah, yeah." Jackson spoke in an off-hand manner, but he gave Jet a nod to show he was taking the advice seriously.

"Yell if you need us." Rayna gave my shoulder a squeeze as they turned to go.

Although she was dressed in casual activewear, Rayna still gave off a military vibe. She was tall and slim, and held herself with a straight stance that made me think of soldiers marching in a parade. This was tempered by the humour that danced in her eyes, and her quick smile.

I sensed a strong bond between her and Jet, and there was a cheekiness to the look they exchanged as they turned to leave. It made me suspect they were more than just friends or work colleagues. They were both such professionals, though, that they did not give much away, so it was difficult to be sure.

Mia and Kenji were sorting out the playlist and turned up the volume as soon as Jet and Rayna left. They were still laughing together about our skinny-dipping fun from the night before.

Jackson had laid out bowls of chips on the kitchen bench and there was frozen pizza in the oven for lunch.

Imogen passed out drinks, moving with a graceful poise. Her hair was recently styled and flowed in caramel-coloured waves to her shoulders. Her golden Gucci handbag matched her shoes and jewellery, and her beige woollen dress was simple yet elegant.

As I took the offered drink, I lurched forward, managing a clumsy save but still spilling it down my leg. Even basic coordination was often a challenge for me. I looked down at the damp patches on my ripped black jeans and sighed. At least black did not stain. My gaze dropped to my favourite khaki combat boots, and while I was relieved to see they had escaped the spill, I reflected for the millionth time that there was nothing elegant about me.

"Did Ava text you? She'll be a little late, but she is coming up with Brooklyn." Imogen had a conspiratorial smile on her face.

"Oh, bless them," said Mia with a broad smile.

"Is Spencer coming?" asked Devon.

"Cooper is bringing her once he finishes work," I said loudly, and then I lowered my voice so only the girls would hear the next part. "After he was so drunk the other night, he has been really good about Jack and me. They are back to their annoyingly competitive twin stuff, but not about me."

"About time." Mia gave me a broad smile.

Ava arrived a while later, and as Brooklyn walked through the door I was reminded of an angel. She had generous curves, with very fair skin and long blonde hair. Her maxi-length, white dress floated over her body in a soft, silky flow. With a warm smile, she radiated kindness. No wonder Ava was drawn to her.

The party had begun.

△

There was a comfortable afternoon lull. People were talking, laughing and eating. The music played softly in the background.

Jackson had planned some drinking games and had set up for beer pong on the plastic table outside. More stupid teenage fun.

Beside me on the couch, Ava was laughing while she told Brooklyn stories about the last time we had all stayed at the beach house. There was a looseness to my limbs and a cosy feeling deep in my body. I knew it meant that Ava felt comfortable and relaxed. The beach house held some pleasant memories. Along with Jackson, Cooper, Mia, Sage, and Luca, we had lived here during the worst stages of the violence last year. And whilst there had been some tragedy and some heart break, I was glad that Ava was remembering the good times we'd had.

The beach house was also where my feelings for Jackson had developed into more than a friendship. I looked around until my gaze rested on him, playing Nintendo Switch with Han. There is a wonderful feeling of excitement that you have at the beginning of a relationship, where it is all before you. The stolen kisses, the sideways glances, the subtext in casual conversations. Every time I looked at Jackson, I still had that hitch in my breath. That giddiness had not faded for me.

Feeling my gaze, he looked up. He placed his hand on his chest, over his heart, and gave me a wink. It was a quick, affectionate gesture. The corners of his mouth were raised in a light smile. I felt the heat flood my cheeks and flush down my neck. I knew he was telling me that he loved me. My own heart pounded out a steady response. I placed my hand on my chest, my heart, and I winked back, hiding a secret smile. Jackson's face split in a wider grin. It was like a secret code we had.

I ran my fingers over the crystal that I still had in my pocket. My heart was warm and full.

There was just one small prickle of discomfort in the very pit of my stomach.

Cooper had not yet arrived. He was coming after work and should have been here by now.

As if on cue, there was the sound of a car arriving and door slamming.

Spencer walked in. Alone.

"Hey!" She was greeted by the others, but I stayed quiet.

Her anxiety twisted through my body like a pit of writhing snakes.

There was no answering smile from Spencer, and she walked straight over to Jackson.

"Cooper's gone," she said.

The room was suddenly silent except for the gentle melody of a love song playing through the speaker. It was as if the grey clouds had clustered over us.

"Gone where?" asked Jackson.

"He's in Melbourne. He went with Griffin." Spencer's voice was shrill, and her fists were clenched at her sides. "I waited and waited and eventually I went to the store thinking he might be held up at work. But they said he had quit. He told them he was going to live in Melbourne. His boss is not happy. Griffin was fired yesterday because of that trouble with the police. And Cooper went to Melbourne with him."

Spencer looked at me, despair darkening her eyes. "He hasn't answered any of my texts or calls. I didn't know what else to do, so I just came up here."

She sank into a chair, as if suddenly deflated. The energy seemed to drain from the room.

"But why would he go with Griffin? After what he did." Mia knew what had happened with Griffin, that he had threatened me. They all did.

Spencer shrugged.

Mia moved to sit with her and wrapped a comforting arm around her. Her compassion was like the shade of a leafy tree on a scorching hot day.

On the other hand, Jackson's face was thunderous. He knew what the others did not. That Sawyer was checking on Griffin to see if he was associated with the street gangs in Melbourne.

Those same gang members that had a vendetta against me. And I still had not told Jackson what Griffin had said to me. That they had been looking for me.

"There has got to be a logical explanation," I said evenly, swallowing the panic that was building. It left a taste so bad that I wanted to spit it out.

"Okay, Spock. So, what is it?" Jackson's voice was laced with sarcasm, but I felt the layers of concern underneath his tone.

Cooper might be in real danger.

Han put a hand on Jackson's shoulder as if to calm him. "What if you and Kenji both text Cooper and just ask if he's still coming up? Tell him we're waiting on him. See if you get a response, before we start jumping to any conclusions." It was the voice of reason.

They sent off messages to Cooper. Jackson also called his dad, who did not know anything at all. They had assumed he was with us. Cooper would now be getting a message from his father as well.

Cooper was nineteen. He could go to Melbourne if he wanted to, but he should have let his parents know what he was doing so they would not worry. And none of us liked the idea that he had quit his job and gone with Griffin.

I texted Sawyer and Jet. Sawyer had connections throughout the various street gangs in Melbourne and promised to see what they could find out.

We waited.

I uncrossed my legs and stretched them out on the floor in front of me. Then crossed them again. Then uncrossed them.

The atmosphere in the house had turned flat, and it felt as if those grey clouds above us were getting darker and thicker.

Eventually, as night was falling, Kenji and Jackson received the same text from Cooper.

I've gone to Melbourne. Everything is good but I won't make it to Woodside.

A moment later, Jackson heard from his parents. They had received a similar text.

"I'm going into Melbourne tomorrow to find him and see what's going on," Jackson announced.

I felt like I was breathing in fire, and I knew that Jackson was both angry with Cooper and afraid for him.

"I'll come with you," Han and I said together.

Jackson looked from Han to me with a grim expression. "No, I'd rather go on my own." He was only looking at me when he said it. I knew he would probably appreciate Han's help, but not mine. He didn't want to put me in any danger.

My neck was stiff, and I stretched it from side to side. Although it didn't make a sound, it felt like it was cracking.

Suddenly Kenji stood up. "Well, there's nothing more anyone can do tonight. Coop said he's good. He stood us up, but that's his loss. Let's do what we came here to do and have some fun."

He and Mia worked hard to lift the party vibe. They poured drinks, heated up more sausage rolls, and turned up the music.

Spencer was still on edge, but she relaxed within the inclusive circle of love that Mia had created for all of us.

Ava had her head resting on Brooklyn's shoulder. Her mood had plunged with the concern about Cooper, and I knew the talk of Griffin's violence would have triggered memories of her own trauma. As Brooklyn gently patted Ava's soft red curls, I heard her quiet, reassuring words and felt the compassion she was sharing with her new girlfriend. It was soothing for me as well.

Imogen, ever the school captain, got us all organised to play games, including beer pong and then limbo. It gradually led to shared laughter and a lightening of the mood. Ava, who had done gymnastics for years, was the most flexible, and she won limbo easily. Kenji was the beer pong champion.

Afterwards, Han and Devon sat huddled at one end of the couch, and I sensed a mutual attraction swinging between them. More than anything else, that left a sweeter taste in my mouth.

I realised I should have been making more of an effort to lift the mood. Pushing away the emotional storm clouds, I drew on the friendship in the room. It made it easy to disperse the love.

Jackson stood at the kitchen bench, mechanically washing glasses, clearly distracted. I had felt his earlier shift into cold calculation and knew he was making plans for tomorrow. There was no way I was letting him go alone, but I would leave that argument for later.

Jabbing him in the ribs, I was rewarded with his disarming grin. His eyes held a tiny sparkle, and I could tell by the flutter in my heart that the efforts I had made to spread around good vibes had sifted through to him.

I shoved my misgivings even deeper inside myself and smiled back, aiming for reassurance.

An invisible cloud of contentment wafted through the room.

7

The highway through to Melbourne was open, and there were no longer roadblocks or detours. It was, however, heavily patrolled by the police and, as we were on the motorbikes, we were stopped several times.

I rode with Jackson. Sawyer had said he wanted to see me in Melbourne, so that became an easy excuse for me to come along. Han came on his own bike. Jet and Rayna followed behind in a DOVE jeep and got us through all the police checks.

It was not a pleasant ride. A damp wind bit at my face. An occasional rain shower soaked our clothes. My arms were wrapped tightly around Jackson, but he was stiff and aloof. It was like I could feel the heat of sunburn through his jacket, but it wasn't sunburn. It was anger burning through his skin. At me for coming. At Cooper for making us go. And I knew by the nausea that swam in my stomach that this anger was hiding his worry and uncertainty.

Jackson had wanted to take the bike, and I knew it was often a way for him to blow off steam, release the tension, but it wasn't working this time.

The violence pandemic had left tragic changes in the regional Victorian towns that we passed through. Burnt-out cars littered the highway exits and streets. Many of the buildings and homes we could see from the road were derelict, left deserted by tragedy. People were hidden in the houses that were still occupied, behind security fences.

It got worse the closer we came to the big city.

When we had arrived in Melbourne nine months prior, Abraham and his gang had ruled the south-eastern suburbs. There had been a border checkpoint staffed by armed militia who allowed entry, or not. Since Abraham's death three months ago, DOVE had removed the border and the militia had been disbanded. The police and legal systems were back in place, and the military had provided additional security and support. There was still a lot of violence and crime, but the street gangs no longer held the balance of power.

Today, although there were no checkpoints, and no militia, there were the after-effects of those long months of gangland control.

The highway traffic rapidly dispersed into deserted suburban streets. Everyone was intent on getting to their destination, to safety, as quickly as possible. The grey urban landscape was decorated with crime-scene tape and colourful graffiti which splashed across buildings and walls. We passed schools and parks where the playground equipment had been vandalised and set on fire, leaving large sculptures of melted plastic in giant fields of ash. The surrounding houses looked old and tired. A nostalgic pulse of the freedom that had been enjoyed in bygone years was buried beneath the fear and anger that now hung heavily in the air.

It felt like there was a huge weight pressing on my chest and across my shoulders.

Although we had been up early that morning, it was late afternoon by the time we got to the city. There had been the cleaning and packing up to do, and we had dropped in at home for more supplies. Then there were delays from all the police checks on the road. When we finally arrived at the apartment Sawyer had arranged for us, he was waiting.

The apartment was on the second floor of an old white-brick building, close to Camberwell Junction. The grey carpet had been recently cleaned and when I shuffled my feet they made smudges in the pile. We unloaded our bags and then gathered in the lounge.

Han sat in one of the green reclining armchairs, playing with the electric controls which lifted the footrest and lowered the back. Jackson sat in another, sullen and silent.

Sawyer gave Jackson a sympathetic look and sat down on the couch, next to me. "Okay, the bad news is that we are sure that Griffin is one of Abe's followers. Or, I guess I should say one of Theo's followers, as he is now in charge. The good news, well, is that Theo is doing a decent job of staying out of trouble. It mostly fell apart after Abe. Theo took over the legitimate gambling activities, and while we know they are still dealing drugs and managing escort services, it's small stuff. The word is, he is not as cruel as Abe, nor as ambitious. There are rumours, however, that Theo is moving his business to the Gold Coast, and he is currently out of town checking that out. They still use the gym where you were kept, Nova." Sawyer gave my shoulder a soft pat. "But it is used as a proper training gym, nothing illegal. Griffin was seen going into the gym yesterday, but there have been no sightings of Cooper."

"They might be keeping him on the second floor, where they kept me," I said quietly.

"Maybe, but we have no evidence of that, and we have had it under surveillance." Sawyer gave my shoulder another pat. "They may also have another space somewhere. But if they do, we don't know about it. Don't forget, if Cooper is here it would seem to be voluntary, so we have no grounds to go in and search their premises."

"We don't know that for sure." Jackson was rubbing his chin with the back of his hand, and I couldn't help wriggling my own jaw, which was stiff and rigid.

"It would seem that way from his text." Sawyer's voice was soft and compassionate. "Nova, have you been able to sense anything?"

I shook my head. Once before, I had managed to find one of my friends who had gone missing by sensing her emotions and then tracing those feelings to where she was. But with Cooper I had drawn a blank. She had just been down the road. Melbourne was a big city.

"There is something, though, that I probably should have mentioned before." I took a deep breath and looked at my feet, avoiding eye contact with any of them. "That night with Griffin. He told me that he had been specifically looking for me."

Jackson's anger surged across to me, accompanied by several swear words.

Sawyer shook his head and gave me a glare that implied I should have told him, but his voice remained calm. "Well, okay. That is not good, but we knew it was only a matter of time. I just wish Cooper had not gotten involved. Theo is out of town, so that's in our favour. I can't see anyone making a move on you without him."

Jackson swore again, this time directing his wrath at Cooper.

Sawyer turned to him. "What do you want to do? And how can I help?"

Jackson shrugged. "I guess I'll just keep texting Cooper. I don't know how else you can help." There was a dull pain behind my eyes, and I knew he was really at a loss.

"Well, I've also reached out to Luca. He's doing some splendid work and has good connections with the kids on the streets. They may know more than we do. Luca's excited to see you all, so Jet will take you there tomorrow." Sawyer was trying to lift our emotional energy, and he gave me a meaningful look which clearly implied that I should be helping him.

I added my own efforts, fidgeting with the jade crystal I had kept in my pocket. It was smooth, cold, and soothing. I focused on the friendship I felt for Cooper, rather than my fears.

The room shifted, and it felt a little brighter. Sawyer gave me a nod.

"I have something on tomorrow, so I'm not available, but Jet will stay with you. Be careful, stay together, don't go out on your own, and don't take any risks." Sawyer was looking back and forth between Jackson and me, and there was a level of steel in his words.

We all knew this was serious. There was a collective nodding.

"Nova, can I talk to you for a minute?" Sawyer gestured to the hallway, and we walked out together. "I have someone arriving tomorrow that I want you to meet. We can organise it for the day after, depending on what you find out tomorrow."

"Who is it?"

"They're an empath too."

"Whoa. Okay. Sure." My curiosity had been piqued, but he would not tell me anything else.

Sawyer was the only other empath I had ever met.

△

When I came into the bedroom, Jackson was sitting on the bed, his head in his hands. It made me feel like the world was a little off kilter. Jackson always had a funny retort and a reckless bravado, but there had been a moody silence from him all day.

"How are you feeling?" I asked gently.

"Why don't you just tell me?"

His anger felt like fingernails scraping down a blackboard and it made me shiver, but I tried again anyway. "Jackson ..."

"I don't know what I'm feeling!" he snapped.

There was no point in pushing him, so I just sat quietly.

"I'm sorry," he said at last. "I'm worried. Cooper might be a bit of a dick. But he's in way over his head. I don't know if he can handle it. And now you are in danger. You should have told me about Griffin. You shouldn't be here. I feel like we are going down the rabbit hole again."

I had nothing to say that would reassure him. It felt like that to me too.

△

Jackson had finally fallen into a restless sleep.

I lay still and silent beside him in the darkness, while tears pricked in my eyes.

As well as the concern for Cooper, and an uneasy feeling about Griffin's connection with Theo, being back in Melbourne brought up memories of Sage.

I had lived here for six months up until last January, and Jackson was with me for the first three, but Sage and her boyfriend Luca were with me the whole time. We had all worked with DOVE – me with Sawyer, Sage and Jackson in the hospital, and Luca with a youth agency. We had felt like we were helping people, doing something useful, making a difference in this angry world. It had been scary, but it had been fun too. At least until the end. Until Sage had been killed.

"Stick together?" I asked quietly, of no one. Well, of Sage, but she couldn't answer. So, I answered myself. "Like glue." That would be her response. It had always given me courage. And I needed that now.

She did not live nearly long enough. For the rest of my life, I would remember why she died. It was for me; it was why I was alive. And where she died, which was only a few kilometres away. And how she died. It was a ruthless, cold-blooded murder.

Death through violence had become so familiar, and we barely had time to mourn one person before we lost another. My father had been killed just a year ago. Sage, three months ago. There was also Jackson's brother, Sage's parents ... and the list went on.

I blinked away the tears and clenched my teeth.

There was no time for this.

I mentally shut the drawer on my grief, and I locked it. Tight.

Sawyer said I was compartmentalising. Well, it worked for me.

One compartment was for my dad. It had two drawers. One was filled with sadness and regret, and I usually kept this shut. The other held sweet memories, and I let these seep out. They gave me strength and confidence.

Sage had a large compartment of her own. This was still too raw to open, even though the emotions and thoughts were straining to get out. It also held my guilt over her death.

I even had a compartment for Cooper. He had been my first love, and there were good memories amongst the angst. Today, this drawer kept rattling in my head. There was guilt there too.

It was hard. Apparently you were supposed to process things, not bottle them up. But processing was an emotional rollercoaster for an empath.

There was a time and a place for processing. And it was not now.

I rolled onto my side and shut my eyes. I needed to sleep.

My compartments would have to stay locked for now.

8

Luca Harrison worked for a youth agency. Amongst the other services they provided, the agency ran a drop-in centre for teenagers who lived in supported accommodation or on the streets. Many had been removed from violent homes or had been orphaned. Luca was organising some of the activities the agency provided, including fitness and self-defence programs.

Classes were held in a big open hall. Large, cushioned mats were scattered across the wooden floor, forming four separate training areas.

There was a karate demonstration on the front mats, which Han and Jet stayed to watch while Jackson and I moved down to the back of the room where we had seen Luca. He was instructing a teenage boy and a girl in a variety of self-defence techniques. We sat quietly on the plastic seats that ran along the wall.

The boy initially had his back to me until the girl made an elbow strike that clipped him across the face. As the boy stepped to the side, he saw us. It was Bellamy.

His face lit up with a small, crooked smile – the best you could expect from Bellamy. "Nova, hi!"

"Hey, Bellamy!" With these simple words came an audible release of the tension I had been holding in. Seeing him brightened up my day.

We moved in for a hug but, as he was even more awkward than I was, it merged into a feeble pat of each other's backs with stiff arms. It made me giggle, and his eyes gleamed with a quiet joy that matched the soft flutter in my chest.

Bellamy was taller than when I had last seen him, less scrawny, and he no longer had the clumsiness of early adolescence. His longish blond hair was clean and shiny, and tied back into a skinny ponytail. His clothes looked new and freshly washed, and I wondered if he was still stealing them off clotheslines. When he had found me last year, after I had escaped from Abraham, he had taught me those tricks of survival – where to get food, how to find shelter, how to stay hidden and safe. The skills of the homeless, which most people, thankfully, never have to learn.

"Bellamy, we haven't finished here," Luca reprimanded, but with a smile on his face.

The girl was standing still, looking at the ground.

I moved off the mats to let them continue, but it was not long before a large blond man came to relieve Luca and took over the self-defence training with Bellamy and the girl.

Jackson and Luca exchanged a back-slapping hug, but I held Luca in a tight grip that let him know how much I had missed him. Friendship flowed between us – warm and familiar, yet also rippling with sadness. Like my own, his grief was still raw, and his pain sent small shocks running through my body. Luca had also seen Sage die.

He was the same, but different. Leaner than he had been, but more muscular. His dark hair hung to his shoulders, longer than Sage would have liked, but it suited him. There were dark smudges under his eyes, but those hazel brown eyes still sparkled with his quick humour and sense of fun. Frown lines across his forehead made him look older and more confident, but I knew from the weakness in my legs that Luca was also feeling a little lost.

The three of us chatted quietly while we watched Bellamy and the girl training.

Bellamy made several successful moves that I recognised from my own classes. He broke free from a head lock and wrestled the girl to the floor. As his chest puffed out, I felt his swell of pride. He was showing off. The girl kept her gaze on the floor and moved intuitively, with a thoughtful deliberation.

I was getting an unusual vibe from her. While my back was firm with her determination, there was a gnawing feeling in my stomach of uncertainty or instability. When they moved to opposite sides of the mat I noticed she walked with a rocky limp, but when she was fighting there was no indication of any imbalance.

Poised in a crouch to the side of Bellamy, she stayed very still, as if listening for Bellamy to make his move.

"She's blind!" I exclaimed in a whisper.

Luca nodded. "It takes a while to realise, doesn't it? That's Maize. She also has a leg injury from a few years ago. Not that you can tell when she fights."

"Was she born blind?"

"No. Apparently she went blind at the same time as her leg injury."

"Do you know what happened?"

"I don't like to ask. She'll tell me in her own time."

"She's amazing."

"She is. She's seventeen, a couple of years older than Bellamy, but they're tight. He's her eyes, though she hardly needs him, and she tends to speak for him. You'll remember how quiet he is."

I nodded. "Is he still living on the streets?"

Luca chuckled. "On and off. They both are. I think they prefer it. At least until the weather turns really cold."

The tall blond instructor was demonstrating a technique, and he guided Maize's hands to the correct positions. He reminded me of Jet. While solid and muscular, he was also fast and light on his feet. He was clearly an experienced fighter.

"And that's Mike." Luca gestured with his head. "We call him Magic. Magic Mike because of his other skills."

"Is he a stripper?" I was imagining Magic Mike with less clothes on, and it was an alluring image.

Luca's laughter exploded around me. It echoed off the wall behind and through me, lifting my heart. It was like the sun had suddenly appeared from behind the clouds.

"Nova, he does magic tricks," said Luca.

"Oh, umm, right." The heat flared in my face. "That makes more sense."

Jackson joined in with the laughter and nudged me. "We know where your mind went."

A renewed flush of heat swept over my face and travelled through my whole body.

Luca elbowed me on my other side. "It's so good to see you guys."

His affection was like a comfortable blanket that draped over us, and I felt Jackson's mood lighten with it.

"Magic is SAS." Luca nudged me again. "Organised by Sawyer. Here to protect me. Not that we've had any trouble. He's great with the kids. They love his magic tricks." He barked out another laugh and shook his head at me.

When their class had finished, Bellamy and Maize joined us. They had news of Cooper. I called out to Jet and Han.

Maize had heard that Luca was looking for someone and she had asked around. She knew everyone on the streets. "Yesterday morning, he was with Griffin Watt at Reggie's café in Camberwell," she said. "I was there. They came out and got into a car together."

"But how do you know what he looks like? How can you be sure it was him?" Jackson looked directly at Maize as he challenged her, but then he dropped his gaze and blushed.

"I saw him. And he looks just like you." Bellamy pointed a finger at Jackson.

Jackson's blush deepened and he tipped his head towards Bellamy in a silent apology. "Yeah, we're twins."

"Do you know where we can find them?" Han asked.

"Griffin likes to pretend he is important, but he's not." Maize turned her head towards Han when she spoke but kept her gaze on the floor as if looking at his feet. "You'll find him at the gym behind Reggie's. Theo's guys hang out there most afternoons. Griffin is trying to be one of the gang. That's where your twin will be too."

Jackson frowned. "But someone has been watching the gym and Cooper hasn't been seen there. Do you know where Griffin lives?"

"He has a fancy apartment in Richmond. I can show you if you want. But you're better off going to the gym. He'll be there this afternoon, for sure. They all will. Theo is out of town, so they slack off and play cards. That's where you'll find him." A fearless confidence born of street-smarts oozed from Maize. "Be careful. They'll know you've been watching, and they don't like the military." She inclined her head towards where Jet was standing, even though he had not said a word.

"Maize, Bellamy, thank you so much. This is all really helpful." I let my gratitude flow into them.

"Yeah, thanks," said Jackson, with an emphatic nod. I knew he was feeling embarrassed by his initial doubt of Maize.

Bellamy gave a small shrug.

Maize turned her head towards me and looked up for the first time. Her eyes were a dazzling blue colour. "It's okay. We owe you. It's so much better now that Abe is gone. Bellamy told me what you did. Thank you." She spoke with a simple sincerity.

I shook my head, but then remembered that she could not see me. "I don't want any thanks." My tone was flat and hollow. I was not proud of what I had done.

"Well, I'm glad he's dead." Maize spoke of death in that matter-of-fact way I had noticed before with young people who were homeless or had been through trauma.

Death was just another part of their daily lives.

9

We were not waiting for Jet. He had asked us to, and I knew we should, but he was looking for a car park and that might take him a while.

"We can check out the gym and just see if Coop is there. Because if he's not, there's no point in parking the car anyway, and we'll just message Jet to come and collect us." I was deliberately feeding Jackson's impatience to find Cooper so he would not focus on his worry over my safety.

Along the main road, quite a few of the stores and cafés were open and there were several people about. Despite the undercurrent of inner-city tension, there was a casual, long-weekend vibe about the area. The gym was situated in a grungy, one-way street that ran behind the shops.

Han strolled off to check out the cafés in case Cooper was in one of them, while Jackson and I took the back street.

It was a narrow lane allowing for deliveries to the back entrances of the shops. Illegally parked cars straddled the skinny pavements, competing for space with the overflowing wheelie bins. The gym was about halfway along. It was a small, dingy, grey building that was easily overlooked.

Two guys were having a cigarette out the back of the small grocery shop on the corner, amidst the empty boxes and cartons. Their eyes were narrow with suspicion, and one man shifted his jacket to show the gun he had tucked into his pants. It was a warning for us to keep on walking.

Jackson responded by moving his hand to his back, to the waistband of his jeans, where I knew he had a gun tucked into his pants. Thanks to lessons with Jet, he knew how to use it, and, like many people, he had become accustomed to carrying it with him. He claimed it was for his own protection. And mine. But I didn't like it at all.

Moving with a lethal grace, he scanned the street as if it were a battlefield. We stopped behind some industrial bins, past the grocery shop and a short distance from the gym entrance. Pins and needles ran through my hands, and there was a tightness around my chest.

A big man, with wide shoulders and a shaved head, came out of the gym and crossed the street to the back door of the café opposite. He glanced in our direction.

"Kiss me," I said quietly.

"What?"

I slid my arms around Jackson's neck and his lips instantly met mine. My fingers caressed the bare skin at the nape of his neck and curled around the strands of his hair. The kiss had left me breathless and energised at the same time. It sent an explosion of need through my body, and from the glazed look in his eyes, I knew that Jackson felt the same. For a few moments, nothing existed but the two of us.

It was the adrenaline, the anxiety that rode through us, fuelling our passion.

Pulling away with a small moan, I checked the street. The guy had gone.

"Umm, I was just trying to avoid being seen by that guy."
I still had one hand wrapped around his neck, and our faces
were only centimetres apart.

"Oh. Good excuse." Jackson was breathing hard.

"He was looking in this direction. I figured he wouldn't
really look at us if we were kissing." For some reason, I felt
the need to keep explaining.

Jackson raised his eyebrows as if considering my state-
ment, then nodded.

"Kiss me," he demanded.

"What, why?"

I was about to turn and look behind me, but Jackson
pulled me back in, up against his body. His mouth was soft
against mine, and his arms were firm and strong. I could feel
the gallop of his heart, matching my own.

"Was there another guy?" My voice was a little shaky.

"No." He gave a throaty chuckle. "I just wanted to kiss
you again. And now I'm finding it really hard to remember
what we were supposed to be doing."

"Umm … We're supposed to be looking for Cooper." I
giggled. "We should probably stop being awkward in public."

"I don't feel awkward." He gave me a wry smile.

"You wouldn't." I pushed him away with a reluctant sigh,
and he let me.

Jackson's phone vibrated. It was Han. He had found
Griffin in a café and was watching him. No Cooper. Han
would keep an eye out for Jet.

We had to find Cooper. *Focus, Nova!*

Jackson grabbed my hand and kept me close at his side,
but I felt the change in him as he made a wary assessment of
our surroundings once again. "Okay, now what?"

△

We climbed the fire escape stairs, reversing the way I escaped from this building last year. It was a rickety, old metal staircase that shifted and groaned with our weight and should have been replaced long ago. The fire door was unlocked, and we slid inside. A lucky break.

The hallway was short, with two rooms to one side and one room and a bathroom to the other side. The doors were open wide. The stairs to the ground-floor gym were at the end.

I held my finger against my lips. Jackson nodded at me.

We crept carefully past the rooms, which were all empty. White walls, no windows, spotlessly clean. Goosebumps shivered over my body as memories flooded my brain. I had been held captive in one of these rooms. My hands were sweaty, and I rubbed them against my jeans. I couldn't think about that now.

At the top of the internal staircase, we could hear talking and laughter from below. The steps led into a small alcove, and the gym extended around to the right. We could not see into the room, and they could not see up the stairs.

"I fold." A voice from below.

"Give me two."

They were playing cards, as Maize had predicted.

Jackson leaned in close and whispered in my ear. "I can't hear Cooper. Do you recognise any of the voices?"

I shook my head.

He wriggled his fingers in a walking motion and gestured to the stairs. I shook my head; I was not going down into the gym.

"Finn," I said quietly, by way of explanation.

Finn had been murdered in the gym. By Abraham.

Saying his name sent my head spinning, and I grabbed Jackson's arm for support. A warm wave of sympathy echoed across me as he moved into a crouch and pulled me down with him. He was pushing on my head, and I resisted until I realised that he wanted me to put my head between my knees. He had thought I was going to faint.

I took three deep, slow, breaths, then stood up and pressed my feet hard into the floor, grounding myself. "I'm okay," I mouthed.

Jackson nodded and gave a weak smile. Although his face was lined with worry, I could feel his courage pulsing through me like the steady beats of a clock.

He pointed to me and held up his hand in a stop signal, then pointed to himself and gave the wriggling motion with his fingers again. He was going down the stairs.

I watched as Jackson took one step at a time, listening each time he paused. We heard more voices, suggesting at least five people. It was all about the card game. Still no Cooper.

On the last step, Jackson stopped. He leaned forward, craning his neck to look around the edge of the wall and into the gym.

Almost immediately there was a yell. "Hey!" Followed by several exclamations. "Dude, who's that?" Chairs scraped on the floor. "What the hell?"

We did not wait. Jackson was already back at the top of the stairs and pulling me behind him in a stumbling run to the fire escape. We exploded through the fire door and onto the outside steps. As I turned to see if anyone was following, I lost my footing and we fell.

It was not an elegant fall, but more of a scrambling tumble down the wobbly staircase. There was a mix of elbow and head bumps, with knees and legs thudding against the metal. Jackson curled his body around mine, trying to take the brunt of the impact. At the bottom, I heard his back crack onto the pavement as I crashed onto his solid chest. The breath was knocked from my lungs.

Everything hurt.

I felt like a piece of meat that had been pounded by a mallet.

Jackson sucked in a breath, and I could feel the pain that it caused him.

I twisted off him with a sob. His eyes were closed in a tight squeeze, but they snapped open at my cry.

"I'm okay. Nothing broken." His voice was raspy, but steady. "Are you okay?"

I nodded and reached out a hand to help him up. My heart was singing with relief.

Jackson rubbed his head and stretched his back, groaning. "God, you're heavy." He pulled the gun out of his waistband and checked it over. "I landed on this. Lucky the safety was on."

I shook my head at his cheeky grin and wiped at the tears blurring my eyes. "Can you walk?"

"I think every one of my bones has been shaken loose, but yeah, everything still works. You?"

"I'm fine, though you are not exactly soft to land on."

He giggled, but then I saw his face change, just as I felt the grip of fear around my throat. At the top of the stairs were two men, silhouetted by the sunlight behind them.

"Run." Jackson grabbed my hand and we staggered down the lane, pulling each other along.

"Wait." I came to an abrupt stop, panting, and Jackson froze beside me. "It's Cooper." I could sense him.

We had reached the end of the lane, and Jackson pulled me around the corner and up against some shopfront windows. He was twisting his hands together. "Are you sure it's Coop?"

I nodded.

Jackson stepped out, back around the corner, holding me behind him. He rocked on his toes as if ready for a fight and flexed his fingers. I took a deep breath to keep myself centred and lifted my chin, drawing on Jackson's courage.

Cooper was jogging towards us but slowed when he saw that Jackson had stopped. There was another guy behind him, but he was not in any hurry. He hung back when he saw the three of us had stopped.

It was Neo. He wore dark sunglasses, so I could not see his eyes. His mouth was set in a thin line, and his fists were clenched at his sides. But a flutter of my heart told me he was pleased to see me, and I knew we were in no danger from him.

Cooper, on the other hand, was pissed off. His nostrils flared as he pushed the hair from his eyes, and he glared at us. "What the hell are you two doing here?"

"We came for you, to take you home." Jackson's voice was laced with a matching fury.

"Why? I don't want to go home."

"We were worried, Coop." I spoke evenly, sending out appeasing vibes. "You left home all of a sudden, you quit your job, you didn't come up to the beach house, and we just wanted to make sure everything was okay."

"Yeah, okay, sorry about that. But I'm fine." Cooper's tone was already more relaxed.

"But why are you here, in Melbourne?" Jackson's voice was still abrupt, but I could feel that his anger was dissipating too.

"I needed to get away for a while. From everyone." Cooper looked from Jackson to me, and back again. My heart twisted. "It's no big deal. You lived here for a few months last year. That's all I'm doing. I'll be fine. I've already got a new job. Painting. Commercial premises. I'm staying with … a mate."

We knew he meant Griffin. I felt like my insides were quivering.

"Yeah, well these mates you are running with are criminals." Jackson gestured back towards the gym and his voice was loaded with sarcasm.

"That's quite an accusation." Cooper frowned, but then his face relaxed, and he reached out a hand to grip Jackson's shoulder. "Jack, I'm not stupid. Go back home. I can look after myself. I need to do this. It's time for me to be on my own for a bit. I'll ring Dad and explain everything. I'll stay in touch with Mum."

There was really nothing more we could say. My back was firm with Cooper's resolve and there were even some bubbles of excitement that I could sense in him. I felt sure that he was making this decision himself, and not being pressured by anyone. It seemed like he wanted to prove himself. I just wasn't sure who it was for.

"Coop, what about Spencer?" I had to make one last try.

"Spencer? We're just friends. What do you mean?" His tone was puzzled and a little defensive.

"I just meant that you have been a good friend to her, and she'll miss you coming around." It sounded lame, even to me.

The crinkles in his forehead relaxed. "Oh, okay. I'll talk to her too. Look, I gotta go."

I felt the resignation in Jackson, a sudden easing of the tightness across my chest.

"You better call Mum and Dad." Jackson gave Cooper a gentle shove.

"I will. I'll be fine," Cooper said again. He left us standing in the street and walked back towards the gym.

Cooper nodded at Neo as he passed him, but no words were exchanged.

Neo took two steps closer. "Hi, Nova. You look good." His face lit up with a shy smile, although I still could not see his eyes behind his dark sunglasses.

"Thanks, Neo. You do too."

His hair was dark and straight, longer than I remembered, and he had a short, cropped beard that looked good on him. There was an ugly, red burn mark on the side of his neck, where his tattoo had been. It had been the symbol of his gang membership with Abraham. I guessed that he had grown his hair and beard to try and cover the scar.

I moved my hand up and tapped my own neck. "What happened?"

"Abe. One of my punishments." His voice was layered with the shared memory. He had helped me escape from Abraham.

I grimaced. "I'm sorry."

He gave a dismissive shrug. "I survived. It's good to see you again." He lifted his sunglasses and rested them on his head. His dark blue eyes twinkled at me.

"This is Jack." I put my hand on Jackson's arm.

Neo looked Jackson up and down. "Cooper's twin brother. Griffin told me all about the love triangle."

"There is no love triangle." Resentment burned in Jackson's eyes. "Just Nova and me."

The air felt thick with tension, but Neo just raised his eyebrows and gave a little smirk.

He turned back to me, and his face relaxed into a friendly smile. "How did you know Cooper was here? Was it Maize? I thought I saw her hanging around."

"You know Maize?" I smiled back and nodded.

"Everyone knows Maize. She's fierce." Neo was still grinning at me, and intentionally ignoring Jackson. "A lot like you."

"Neo, are things okay with you?"

"Things are good. It's quieter now." Neo glanced at Jackson, and I felt his reluctance to talk in front of him. "We're all working. Real jobs. I'm doing an IT course at TAFE. Theo is fair. He won't be happy that you were spying on us, though."

"Does he have to know?"

"He probably knows already. It would've been posted in our gangster group chat by now."

"Really?" My question was met with a snort of laughter from Neo, while Jackson remained stony-faced. "Oh. Ha-ha. Seriously though, will Cooper be okay?"

Neo shrugged. "He can look after himself. He's staying with Griffin, who is harmless. He just gets stupid when he drinks too much. I heard about his meeting with you."

"Griffin said he had been looking for me. What's that supposed to mean?"

Jackson dug his elbow into my ribs, hard. It especially hurt because I was bruised from the fall down the stairs. I knew he thought I was sharing too much with Neo, but I ignored the warning. I trusted Neo. He had once risked his life for me.

Neo shrugged. "He speaks a lot of shit. Don't worry about it. Theo is talking about moving to the Gold Coast, anyway. It's getting too hard around here. Your people have moved in." He was talking about DOVE.

"Neo, don't let them give Cooper the artificial warrior gene."

"You mean the injection we get before a fight? I know it did weird things to you, but it's just an energy supplement. It makes us strong. And anyway, supply is short. Theo won't give it to him if he doesn't want it. He doesn't force it on us. Theo is good like that. He looks after us."

Jackson sucked in a loud breath. He was clenching and unclenching his fists, and his distrust of Neo was as cold as a winter night.

"We'd better go," I said. "Thanks, Neo. It's good to see you. Please look after Cooper for me."

"Nova, he's not a baby. But I'll do what I can." Neo winked at me, then lowered his sunglasses back over his eyes.

We watched him walk away. He did not look back. He was too cool for that.

I hoped both Neo and Cooper stayed safe. Theo might be better than Abraham, but he was still a criminal, and that made him dangerous.

When Neo was out of hearing range, Jackson turned to me. "What? Does he actually think he's from *The Matrix*?" His voice dripped with loathing.

10

We stayed another night in Melbourne to meet Sawyer's special guest.

I was extremely curious to meet another empath. Sawyer had taught me a lot, and the opportunity to find out about another person's experiences and abilities was beyond exciting.

As we climbed the stairs to the apartment, I moved my shoulder blades back and forth and around in circles. I was stiff and sore, both from falling down the fire-escape staircase the previous day and being dropped to the floor several times that morning by Maize. She was brutal.

We had all gone to the drop-in centre for the morning training session with Luca and the young people. Maize and I had paired up, but she was far better than I was, much to her delight. I had spent most of the session flat on my back and, after the first time she flipped me, I learned to take my time getting back up.

Jackson and Jet had returned with me to the apartment, but Han was remaining with Luca to teach some karate to the kids.

Low voices drifted down the stairwell, and I knew Sawyer was already there waiting for us. I sniffed under my arms and grimaced. I had hoped for a shower first.

Jackson gave a laugh and pushed me lightly in the back. "Don't worry about it. He'll be too busy probing your feelings to notice what you smell like."

In anticipation, I put out my own sensors. I could feel Sawyer. His kindness and compassion swirled through my heart, both comforting and familiar. There was nothing else, though. I could not sense another person at all. It was blank. He must have put up walls to block us out. That was strange.

From the top of the stairs we could see that the door to our apartment was open, and I heard Sawyer's polite laughter. Jet kept moving but I stopped, with Jackson behind me.

An eerie coldness had crept up my back. I shivered.

"Are you okay?" Jackson asked.

"Just nervous, I guess. What if he doesn't like me?"

"Don't worry. He'll be in awe of you, just like everyone else." Jackson put his hand on my arm, gently guiding me forward.

As we came through the door, Sawyer greeted us with a smile. The other empath was standing at the window and had their back to us. They had long, shiny, black hair that floated past their shoulders.

I don't know why but, like Jackson, I had assumed that the empath we were meeting would be a man. There was no reason for this assumption. I guess it was just because Sawyer was the only other empath I knew. But this was a woman.

For a second, I felt like I was back in my dream, my nightmare, with the woman whose face I could not see. The woman who wanted me to follow her, into the darkness, into the fire. I pinched myself on the arm. It hurt.

"Nova, this is Corben Moreau," said Sawyer.

She turned around and smiled. "Hello, Nova, it's so good to see you again." Her voice was soft and musical.

I was in my nightmare. How could it be *her*?

It felt like I had jumped into another reality. I closed my gaping mouth with a snap that hurt my jaw. Unsure of what I was looking at, who I was looking at, I rubbed my eyes and blinked four times in quick succession. She was still there. I was still here.

Her simple black dress looked new and expensive. It drew my attention to a tiny gold star pedant that hung from a thin chain around her neck. When I lifted my gaze to her face, light brown eyes probed mine. Wrinkles around her eyes and mouth betrayed her age, late forties. Forty-nine, to be exact. Her eyebrows were raised as if asking a question.

Emotions pelted me from within.

My stomach pitched and rolled, while my heart was twisted with an aching, painful disbelief. Betrayal, resentment, suspicion. It swirled around me and through me like a sandstorm in a desert, stripping off layers of skin, leaving me bare, just bones and blood. Then a fiery rage boiled through my blood and scorched my bones. It was like there was nothing left of me. Just a raw husk. I was hurting, and angrier than I had ever been before.

Jackson must have felt the turmoil, and he put his hand on my back. I was surprised it did not go up in flames.

"Corben, this is Jet. He's SAS. And this is Jackson, Nova's friend." Sawyer continued with the introductions when I did not say anything. He would have felt my explosion as well. The waves of calm reassurance he sent turned to ash as soon as they touched me.

Jet and Jackson made small sounds of acknowledgement.

Corben barely looked at the others. Her eyes studied mine, wide at first, but then they narrowed, probably when she felt my anger. The smile faded as her mouth pressed into a thin line. I could not sense her emotions, but her reaction left a sour taste in my mouth.

The room was deadly quiet, as if waiting for me to breathe. I couldn't. White walls closed in on me; the space felt too small to contain my fury.

"How ... what are you doing here, *Corben Moreau*?" I virtually spat out the words because her name twisted my tongue and clogged my throat.

Jackson reached down to grab my hand and he linked his fingers through mine. His eyebrows were drawn in a frown of confusion, but his deep brown eyes shone with a trust I did not deserve. I let his strength soak into me.

"Nova, Corben wants to get to know you." Sawyer's voice was a soft plea.

He knew.

It felt like the fire I had burning inside was abruptly doused with freezing cold water.

I shivered.

Everything that had made sense in this crazy world abruptly ceased to make sense.

"So, after ten years of being dead, now she wants to get to know me." This time I deliberately coated my words with a cold venom.

"Nova ..." Sawyer hesitated and looked back and forth between Corben and me, like a polite spectator at the tennis.

Corben stayed silent, avoiding all of us by staring at her shiny, black ankle boots. She was still a blank slate. I had no idea what she was feeling or thinking. It was so frustrating.

Jackson's gaze also moved from me, to Corben, to Sawyer, and back again. It felt like he was trying to connect the dots without knowing the pattern. When his eyes opened wide, fixed on Corben, and his mouth dropped, I knew he had worked out the connections.

My body jumped as if I had just received a small electric shock.

He had remembered that Corben was my middle name.

"Well, it's too late. I don't need a mother." I swung on my heels, marching for the door, pulling Jackson with me, relying on him to keep me upright.

△

My dramatic exit had been from our apartment, so we had nowhere else to go. Jackson guided me to a café nearby.

It was the sort of place where normally you were crowded in, no space between the tables, the waiters jostling your chair as they moved about behind you. Today there was us and one other couple. It was quiet and it was private.

We sat in silence for a few minutes after we had given our order. I was alternating between hot anger and cold shock, and it left me feeling numb and sick. Jackson reached for my hand. Our fingers entwined and his thumb rubbed back and forth across my wrist. His palm was warm, and his skin was a little rough beneath my fingers.

"That was mind-blowing!" He gave a loud exhalation. "I thought your mum was dead."

"Yeah. So did I." My voice sounded strange to my ears.

Jackson looked at me with large sympathetic eyes and squeezed my hand. "Well, she doesn't look dead." He shook his head slowly, and I knew from the dizziness I felt that he, like me, was still coming to terms with what had just happened. "I don't really know what to say. It's weird. She does look a bit like you." He tilted his head to the side. "I'm sorry. You must be in shock."

I paused for a moment, considering. A tightness in my chest. A sinking feeling in my stomach. An itchiness all over my skin. Heat flushing through my body. "I guess. I don't know. I'm angry and I'm confused, mostly."

He nodded. "So, where has she been? And why has she suddenly turned up?" I could feel the suspicion that circled through him.

"I don't know, and I don't know. She was completely closed off to me."

Our drinks and cookies arrived. I had ordered a raspberry-Coke slushie. It was cool and refreshing. Hopefully I could keep it down.

Jackson sipped on his coffee. He offered me one of the biscuits. Large, homemade cookies with macadamia nuts and white chocolate chunks. They would not look so delicious when I vomited them on the floor. I pushed his hand away and groaned.

"You know if you want any answers, you're going to have to see her again."

I shook my head, but then I nodded.

"And she is your mum." With a mouthful of cookie, he sprayed crumbs over the table.

"So? What does that mean?"

He shrugged. "Just that you probably should hear her out, give her a chance to explain."

"Dad was lying to me this whole time."

I shut my eyes and took a deep breath. There was no memory of her funeral. But he had told me that she had died.

Big fat lies. But why? I could not believe my dad had done that to me.

I shivered. The slushie was cold.

Jackson was right. If I wanted explanations, I would need to see her again.

Corben. My mother.

Jackson had been texting on his phone, but he put it down as Jet came through the door. I knew they would have been messaging about me.

Jet pulled up a chair. "Are you okay?"

I nodded and saw Jackson also nodding, reassuring Jet.

"Sawyer is worried about you," said Jet.

"Yeah, well he shouldn't have sprung that on me." I heard the accusation in my voice and felt the anger take hold again. It burned like a fire deep within my body.

"Sawyer and … they have gone." Jet kept his voice smooth and even. "Can you please come back to the apartment? It's safer. We can get some lunch to take back." He picked up the second cookie and raised his eyebrows at me.

"You can have it." I gave Jet what I hoped was a small smile. He did not deserve my anger.

△

At the apartment, I lay on the couch while Jackson and Jet demolished a couple of pizzas. Han returned a while later, bringing his own pizzas, and Jackson filled him in. They peppered Jet with questions, but he didn't know anything more than we did. Corben had only just arrived yesterday, and he had never heard of her before.

I didn't contribute much to the conversation, but listening to their deep voices was soothing, like white noise.

It was like I was on a roller-coaster. Both anger and hurt burned hot in my body. Confusion and curiosity clouded my head. I felt strange. It was like my clothes didn't fit me properly and my thoughts belonged to someone else. I didn't feel like the person I had always been. Instead, I was suddenly someone else.

Someone that had a mum. A mother. I didn't feel like I could call her a mum; it sounded too informal, too familiar. And she was not familiar at all.

"But you recognised her?" Han turned to me and spoke gently.

"I knew as soon as she turned around. But I couldn't believe it. I thought it was a dream. She looks the same as I remember her. But older. Definitely older." I huffed. "What does this mean? Did she just run off and leave us and start a new life? Did she pretend we didn't exist? She might have a whole new family for all I know. She is still using her own name. And she was looking, I don't know, normal, as if she hadn't done anything wrong. That really pissed me off." I paused and turned to Jackson and Jet. "I guess I was pretty rude, wasn't I?"

"Well, you were kind of blunt. Not that she didn't deserve it," Jackson qualified when I glared at him.

"Are you going to see her again?" asked Han.

"I don't know if I want to. What would you do?"

"I'd see her. Hear her out. You don't have to have a relationship with her, but you need to let her explain where she has been all these years. Otherwise, you'll always wonder. It's your mother." I felt the swell of compassion Han sent me. There was also a circle of tender affection that floated around my heart, and I knew it was the love he felt when he thought of his own mother.

I let my eyes rest on Jackson. "It's up to you," he said gently. "But it would be good to find out more about her."

There was a tightness around my eyes, as if I were holding back tears, and I knew it was because Jackson was thinking of his mother and the depression she had struggled with since his older brother had died.

They wanted me to see Corben again, simply because she was my mother. But I wasn't sure I could agree with that. My brain was still struggling with the idea of even having a mother. I didn't owe her anything.

I turned to Jet.

"I think it's important for your own sake, not hers, that you take the time to sort it out." Jet spoke softly but firmly, and the twists through my body gave me the sense that he was relating to his own childhood trauma.

I blew out my breath in a huff. Boys and their mothers. It was a Freudian field day. "So, it's unanimous. You think I should meet with her again."

They all just looked at me. Waiting. My heart rapped a strange new beat. "But it would mean staying on in Melbourne for a bit longer."

Jet shrugged. "I'm here with you, for as long as it takes."

"I'm here for you too," added Jackson. "Always. You know that."

"I'm good. It's uni holidays and I told Dad I wasn't working this week." Han was studying mechanical engineering and he worked part time as a mechanic in his father's workshop.

I snorted. "Well, I'll think about it."

△

My heart was still drumming to its strange new rhythm and my skin felt tight and itchy, but when Han mentioned a night out, I jumped at it. I needed a distraction from the turmoil in my head.

Luca had recommended a new cocktail bar. He was meeting us there.

The hairs of the back of my neck were raised and goosebumps crawled up my arms. There were higher levels of fear and anxiety that drifted through the streets of Melbourne, much more than what I sensed at home, but I could also feel a strong longing for reconnection with others. My body felt like it was being pulled in different directions. People were tired of staying at home and were venturing out again, but the bravado was tempered by a dread of being out in public and the very real possibility of danger.

The police, with the help of DOVE and the Army, had restored order, and certainly put an end to the street gang dominance. But they could not predict, nor prevent, the random acts of violence that still threatened people's safety. There were still no big events, no big crowds. Football games were played in front of an empty stadium, and there were no concerts or shows anymore. But the cafés, restaurants, and clubs were mostly open. They had doubled their security and they adhered to a lock-out curfew, but at least it meant there was somewhere to go.

We arrived at the bar and entered through a small black door at the end of an old arcade. Without Luca, I would have walked straight past it. Han and Jet had to duck their heads to get through the doorway, and inside they only barely had the headroom to stand up properly.

A security bouncer asked for a password, and when Luca mumbled something he moved aside to let us in.

"What did you say?" I asked.

Luca moved his fingers across his lips, as if zipping up his mouth. "If I told you, I'd have to kill you."

I smothered a giggle. "Do we have to press one of the bricks to open a secret entrance?"

Luca chuckled. "That's only on Wednesdays."

It was a small, dark room, dimly lit with red lightbulbs that hung from the ceiling on long, black cords. Floor-to-ceiling mirrored shelves behind the bar were stocked with dozens of bottles that reflected the red light. The walls were black, the floor was a dark mahogany, and a long, black, shiny bar ran the length of the room. Black cushioned stools, most of which were occupied, lined the bar. There were booths along the opposite wall, and Luca led us to one of these.

Jet sat at a small table near the door with Mike, and I knew they would assess everyone that came in as well as keeping a check on us.

We crowded into the corner booth and grinned at each other. This was cool.

"Is there a menu or a cocktail list or something?" asked Han.

"Just wait a minute." Luca's hazel eyes gave off a mysterious sparkle.

As if on cue, out of the shadows, a tall, slim man appeared.

"Guys, this is Raziel. This is his place." Although Luca held out a hand to shake, the man pulled him into a hug, kissing him on both cheeks.

"Welcome to Potions. Call me Raz."

Raziel looked about thirty. He wore a long, red coat that flowed to his knees, with a black shirt and black jeans. His short hair was bleached white and gelled into spikes. Around his neck, he wore a gold chain with a half-moon medallion and a thin leather band threaded with a couple of beads. One ear had multiple studs, and from the other dangled a large gold cross. His eyes were a dark cobalt blue and danced with a lively sense of fun. He was gorgeous.

"So, what can I get you, handsome?" His voice was silky and seductive as he leaned forward to look directly into Jackson's eyes.

Jackson blushed. "Umm ... have you got a list?"

"No lists here. You just have to tell me what you dream about, and I'll make it for you."

Jackson blushed an even deeper shade of red. He opened and shut his mouth without making a sound. Raziel wriggled his eyebrows at me, and I stifled a giggle.

Han's jaw had also dropped open, and he was looking up like an adoring puppy. A giant puppy.

"Luca, where do you find all these silent, sexy men?" Raziel gave us all another brilliant smile and let his gaze wander over to Mike and Jet as well.

"How about a round of the daily special?" Luca shook his head at Raziel, with a huge smile.

"What's in them?" Han had found his voice at last.

"Doesn't matter. Raz is a wizard."

"You know it." Raziel gave us a salute with two fingers and left to make our drinks.

"This place is awesome," I said. It was just what I needed.

"Are you going to tell Luca about Corben?" Jackson bent his head close to my ear and spoke quietly.

"You can." I was tired of thinking about it.

Jackson related the story, and I could sense a very different vibe from Luca than I had from the others. There was a chill around my heart. His mother had been an alcoholic, and his childhood had been far less stable.

"What are you going to do?" Luca asked.

I shrugged. "I'm not sure. What would you do?"

"I always ask myself WWSS – What would Sage say?" Luca gave a sad smile.

"Well," I paused and felt myself bite on my bottom lip. "She would probably say I need to see her again, hear her out. Oh. Shit."

Jackson squeezed my hand and Luca gave me another sad smile.

I was still feeling numb and a little nauseous, but a warmth had spread through me. It was as if Sage was sending me strength. Damn her.

Once I'd made the decision, I felt better. I would meet with Corben again, just to hear what she had to say. No further commitment.

Our drinks came and they were amazing. They were both sweet and sour, sharp and refreshing. Raz called them 'Back from the Dead'.

Just like my mother.

It was like the universe was trying to tell me something. Or laughing at me. Or both.

11

"Has anyone got a tie?" Jackson walked into the lounge wearing a light-blue collared shirt, freshly washed jeans, and his white Nike sneakers. With his clean-shaven face, neatly combed hair, and the light-coloured clothes, he looked fresh and bright and ... not normal.

I did an exaggerated double-take. "Who are you, and what have you done with Jackson?"

"What?" His tone carried a hurt embarrassment.

"She's right." Han wore his usual black biker jacket and grubby black jeans. "Anyone would think you were going to meet the mother-in-law." He sniggered as Jackson turned a bright shade of beetroot red.

We were going to meet Corben at Sawyer's apartment this time. At least if I walked out again, I could return to our place.

"Don't listen to them, mate." Jet gave him a nod of approval. "And you don't need a tie."

Jet had exchanged his usual white t-shirt and faded jeans for a cream jumper, which hugged his muscular body, and smart black pants. His black shoes were so shiny they were blinding me.

"Who said this was formal?" Even though I made the snappy retort, I then felt self-conscious as everyone's eyes were now on my old green hoodie and ripped jeans.

"It doesn't hurt to make a good first impression." Jet tilted his head and raised his eyebrows.

"She is not a queen." A stubborn rod was hard against my back. "And I have already made my first impression. She probably thinks I'm a bitch. But, then again, she has been dead, so ..." I stuck my hands on my hips, daring anyone to make a comment about my clothes.

No one did.

I went and changed anyway.

My reflection in the mirror grimaced. The best outfit I had with me was a short, red, floral dress, and I did not want to look like I was trying too hard. She was not that important. I added the black leather jacket I wore on the bike. It was Jackson's originally, but I had claimed it ever since the first time he had let me wear it. With my black combat boots as well, I felt better. Not too formal.

Jackson winked at me when I returned to the lounge. "You look hot."

I shrugged in a pretence of nonchalance, but I was secretly pleased.

△

Corben answered the door when I knocked, and stepped back to let us in.

"Hi," I said hesitantly.

"Hi." Her eyes swept over my outfit, and she smiled. "You look great." She sounded genuine.

The heat rose in my face, but I was glad I had changed into a dress.

"Umm, you too." I gave her one of those awkward smiles where the corners of your mouth turn up but you don't show any teeth.

She did look good, in dark blue jeans and a burgundy silk shirt that hung loosely over her hips. My throat tightened with the thought that she had much better fashion sense than me. But, then again, she had left me to be raised by a single father who only ever wore jeans and jumpers, or a lab coat. I bit on my bottom lip, holding back my smart retort, keeping my cool.

Jackson nudged me.

"Sorry. Umm, Corben, this is Jackson. He is my boyfriend." I stumbled over the last sentence as if I were a teenager introducing my boyfriend to my mother for the first time. Which I was.

This was so weird.

"Hello." Jackson shook the hand she offered in greeting.

"It's good to see you again. Do I call you Jackson, or Jack?" She was so polite. It was making my skin crawl.

"Jack is fine." He gave her a warm smile.

Everyone was being nice. The atmosphere was calm and friendly. I knew it was Sawyer's influence. It definitely wasn't from me.

"Thanks for coming, Nova." He gave me a grateful smile. "I am sure you two have a lot of catching up to do. What if Jack and I go for a walk and let the two of you talk alone?"

"No. I'd like Jack to stay." I reached for Jackson's hand and gripped it, hard. If they wanted me to stay agreeable, I might need back up.

Jackson started to shake his head, but then shrugged when I squeezed his hand again. He wriggled his fingers within mine, letting me know I was cutting off his circulation.

"I don't mind," said Corben evenly. "Sawyer, you should stay too."

We sat around the dining room table. It was a heavy, wooden setting, but the chairs had soft, bright-yellow seat cushions. I swung my legs back and forth, fidgeting with the cushion fringe. Sawyer put the kettle on to make coffee for Jackson and himself, and tea for Corben. He passed me a glass of water and placed a huge plate of biscuits in the centre of the table. I wondered if that meant he was expecting a long session.

The apartment was clean and open. It smelled faintly of bacon. A light breeze wafted through the small kitchen window, carrying the low buzz of street sounds from outside. Jet had moved through to one of the bedrooms, and I could hear him talking quietly with Rayna, trying to be inconspicuous but close enough if we needed them.

I still sensed nothing at all from Corben. She had been pleasant, friendly, and respectful. Yet, there was an impenetrable wall up around her emotions. A twitch in the back of my neck suggested she was probing my feelings, and probably Jackson's too.

"So, you're an empath." With my sharp tone it sounded like an accusation, or a dirty word.

Sawyer shot me a disapproving glance as he passed out the mugs.

Jackson gave a small sigh.

Okay, it was not the most gracious way to start, but I had waited ten whole years.

Corben patted Sawyer's hand in a conciliatory way, then turned to me with a sweet smile. "I am. As are you."

"Then, how come I can't feel your emotions? You've closed them off to us."

I looked to Sawyer for confirmation, knowing he would be just as interested in the answer, but he would not make eye contact with me. His face was set in the neutral expression he used for mediation sessions.

"Can I come back to that one later?" Corben took a sip of her tea and closed her eyes for a moment. She could have just been enjoying the taste, or she could have been mentally preparing herself for the conversation about to follow. "I am sure you have lots of questions. What if I start at the beginning?"

"When you died," I said sarcastically.

Jackson gave my leg a squeeze, and I knew he wanted me to stay calm and let her explain. Corben sent him an appreciative nod, so she was clearly sensing his feelings too.

I let out a huff of breath.

"Well, I'm not sure how much you remember, and how much your father told you. So, I'll start before that, before you were born." Corben paused and bit her lower lip. She looked up towards the ceiling. "I didn't realise I was an empath until I was in my mid-twenties. It was when I met your father and fell in love with him. I think that is what brings it on, the empathic ability. Not just a schoolgirl crush, but truly, deeply, falling in love. That is what I felt for Harley. That was when we both noticed my abilities developing far beyond the normal sensitivity I had always shown."

A wave of warmth had surged through my heart when she mentioned my dad, but it would take more than that to thaw the icy suspicion I held. I knew that my dad had loved her. It had been clear on his face and in his voice the few times he had talked about her. I had always assumed he did not talk about her much because it hurt him to do so.

So, she had loved him too. But, then again, she had also left him. Left me. Left us.

Corben gave me a small smile. "Your ability is strong for someone your age." She made a point of looking from me to Jackson and back again. "You are very young to be truly in love."

Jackson turned to me, his deep brown eyes large and soft. He put his hand over his heart and gave that grin that would always melt my heart.

I turned back to see Sawyer smiling at us indulgently, like a proud parent.

Corben, my real parent, still wore her polite, pleasant expression. The smile you give for a photograph, which does not necessarily mean you are happy. I had no way of knowing what she thought of me, or of Jackson. It was infuriating, and it was unnerving.

I bit down on my bottom lip, holding back the words that would tell Corben that my relationships were none of her business. Which they were not. She had not been around for the last ten years, so we were not going to have a deep and meaningful about my personal life any time soon.

If she was as strong an empath as she made out, she must have realised I was not going to share anything. And, after a few seconds of silence, she gave a small shrug and continued.

"Harley and I were both teaching at Monash and working on projects in genetic research." She spoke as if giving a lecture – clear and precise, but impersonal. "We were not looking at the genes that carried diseases, though, like everyone else; we were looking for the genes that carried empathy. It was our own personal passion. And, at the same time, we were searching for other people with the same abilities I had. People that can sense what someone is feeling, even thinking, and is able to influence them as well. Like me, like you. Like Sawyer." She nodded at him, but it seemed like an afterthought. Her words, this story, it was all for me.

"We lived in our own bubble of happiness, and when we had you our life was perfect. Harley loved being a father, he doted on you. We used to take you to work with us. Our students adored you too. It was too good to be true. We were content. But we were also naive." Corben gave a small cough and took a mouthful of her water.

My heart rate jumped a little. Beneath the attentive curiosity in the room, there was an ominous feeling that the unpleasant twist was coming.

"You were a toddler when my research took me off on a tangent. It was so hard to define and isolate what created empathy. So, I had started exploring the opposite. Aggression, anger, apathy. The warrior gene. Word gets around in the research community. Eventually, I was approached by the Australian Department of Defence. They wanted me to investigate the genetic make-up of the perfect soldier. They were offering full funding, and I would not even have to keep teaching. I was looking for the genes that carried strength and resilience. Detachment, rather than empathy. They wanted to reduce the likelihood of post-traumatic stress disorder. It all kept coming back to the warrior gene."

I saw Sawyer's forehead crease in a small frown, but then smooth out again just as quickly.

"Because of my abilities, I was able to sense the warrior gene in people." Corben kept talking, with an unfocused stare at the ceiling. "I could tell which soldiers had it and whether they could control it. I became a recruitment specialist for the defence forces. It did not take long for word to spread further, and the United States Secretary of Defense contacted me. It was huge. I felt so important. Harley stayed with you, and I was flown to Washington for meetings. I also met with the NSA, the CIA, and a bunch of other departments with acronyms for names. I was so excited; it seemed like such an opportunity. As I said, I was naive."

Corben dropped her gaze. She looked at her feet for a moment, crossing and uncrossing her legs.

Jackson bit into a biscuit, and it made an audible crunch in the silent room. Dipping his head with a self-conscious wince, I knew he was trying to chew without making a noise. His curiosity tingled through my body with a restless energy, while Sawyer sat quietly attentive and non-judgemental. He was still exerting his usual gentle, calming influence over all of us.

"They had been experimenting with biohackers, synthetic biology, and artificial enzymes to create the perfect solider. I offered them another option." Corben's voice had a slight hoarseness, the only indication that this was difficult for her to talk about. "Harley was still teaching and doing his research into empathy, so they left him alone. But I had found a way to not only sense but activate the warrior gene in their soldiers. Without the synthetics. They wanted me to move to the United States permanently. I could tell them who to recruit and who to promote. And I could activate the gene in the soldiers being deployed."

She took a deep breath and held it for a second before letting it out. The next words came out in a rush, as if Corben wanted to get them over with quickly. "Over the next couple of years, I was away a lot. Harley and I grew apart. He was here with you. Which he loved. I was completely caught up in my work. When I came home, we argued. He was angry; I was angry. It wasn't a good environment for you." She looked at me through lowered lids. "I was selfish. I wasn't a good wife, and I wasn't a good mother."

I could feel the resentment smouldering within me, just waiting for more fuel to set it ablaze.

"Then, I got sick," she continued. "It was emotional fatigue. Harley could see it long before I could, and he got me admitted to hospital when I came home. Long-term exposure to an overly aggressive military environment is extremely hard on an empath. I think he hoped it would be a wake-up call for me, but it wasn't. He wanted me to get out, and he wasn't quiet about it. They didn't like the stir he was creating. They wanted their super soldiers."

Corben paused and slowly shook her head. "They tried to shut him up by threatening to take you from him and bring you to the States with me. Harley was furious. And he had every right to be. I realise now I was probably feeding his anger with the emotions I was carrying even then. But at that time, I just resented him. Because I didn't want out. I still thought, then, that I could make a difference. Do something amazing." She grimaced.

"I knew it was the end of our relationship, and I knew you were better with him. You had such a strong connection with your father. I was not going to let them take you from him. So ... I left. I disappeared. I didn't tell him that I was going. The last time I saw you was at the hospital. You knew I was sick. Harley brought you in. You were crying. I could see what it was doing to you. What I was doing to you. And to him."

Corben stopped again. She had been gazing above our heads while relating her story, looking into space, remembering. Now, she looked straight at me. Her eyes were light brown with tiny green flecks. She did not blink.

My mouth was dry.

"Harley called me, emailed, texted. He tried everything to contact me. I didn't answer anything. He even went through official channels, but, on my request, they wouldn't tell him anything. They hid me from him. I had asked them to. It's possible someone even told him I was dead. It certainly must have seemed to him like I was."

I tried unsuccessfully to swallow the lump that blocked my throat.

"I understand what he did. Harley needed a clean break, and he thought that would be best for you too. Somewhere safe, where no one knew about me or my work. Harley didn't want you to feel abandoned, and he didn't want you to try and find me. So, he told you I was dead."

Memories swarmed at me like bees, giving nasty stings.

I blinked away the tears that were forming. "But it was still a lie."

Corben nodded and cleared her throat. She placed her hands on the table, and I noticed she was twisting her wedding ring around and around on her finger. I wondered if she always wore it or had just put it on for today.

"I think he regretted it later, but at the time he thought it would be better for you. And then he couldn't take it back." She looked off into the distance above my right shoulder. "I had made sure that you and Harley would be left alone. There was a provision to fund his research so he would not have to teach and he could look after you." Her voice dropped to a quiet, almost pleading tone, as if she were trying to convince herself as well as me. "When I heard that you believed I was dead, I told myself it was the best thing, the safest thing, for him, for you. And so, I stayed away."

My heart was thumping, and I was fighting a losing battle against my tears. It felt like a cyclone raged through my head, tearing up my memories, the familiar things I knew about myself, and twisting them around, reshaping them and putting them down in new places where they did not quite fit. There was a path of devastation left behind. What was once orderly was now a mess. It was all wrong.

I blamed my dad for the lie, but I blamed her for leaving me. It was a contest for who was worse, but there were no winners.

The tabletop was smooth and hard beneath my fingers. I traced around the wooden swirls, making circular motions. There was a damp mark from my glass of water, now empty. The biscuits had a sweet smell, but I had lost my appetite.

Corben had stopped talking, and the street noise intruded into the silence. A car started with a roar of the engine and a blare of the radio. Goodbyes were called from the window of the neighbouring apartment. A melody of beeps dwindled away as the car moved off down the street.

Until it was quiet again.

Corben was watching me, waiting.

"But I didn't have a mother. I didn't have you." My voice was barely above a whisper.

There was a collective intake of breath.

Corben's expression changed. Her eyes went wide, her mouth gaped.

Then I caught a flash of emotions. The wall she had erected around herself dropped, just for a few seconds.

It was a glimpse into total chaos.

Rage roared through my body. From my gut, my core, tearing up through blood and bone to break free. It was dark, it was hungry, and it was vengeful.

All hell broke loose.

12

Several things happened at once.

There was a furious shout from Jet as he and Rayna ran into the kitchen.

His hands gripped the edge of the kitchen bench as he worked to maintain his self-control.

Rayna kicked out at a stool, knocking it to the floor. Her fists were clenched tightly at her sides, her chest was heaving, her eyes were wild.

I knew I was sensing the warrior gene activated and storming through them both.

There were shouts from next door where an argument had started. Doors slammed, followed by a thumping on the wall. From the street outside, horns blared as abuse was hurled from cars and exchanged between pedestrians. There was even the sound of gunshots in the distance.

Beside me, I felt the heat rise in Jackson. It was as much confusion as anger. He had no warrior gene to activate, but he could not help responding to the tempest that raged around him.

Sawyer was the calm in the middle of the chaos and sent waves of comfort around the room, but they were about as effective as an umbrella in a tornado.

It had taken about twenty seconds for the world around us to descend into madness.

Then Corben dropped her shield back into place.

And just as suddenly as it appeared, that darkness disappeared. The solid barrier was back. I could not sense anything from her at all. She was blocking us again.

Jet and Rayna were relatively quick to regain their control, but I knew that it was a substantial effort. It felt like steel cables were winding around my body as they reined themselves in. Rayna picked up the stool and placed it upright. Jet looked at Sawyer, with his eyebrows raised and his forehead knotted in confusion, waiting for instructions.

Sawyer stood up slowly, his palms splayed flat on the tabletop. I could feel him grounding himself. He nodded at Jet, and then at each of us, checking in, sending reassurance, without saying a word.

I pressed my feet hard against the floor and folded my arms, hugging myself tightly. When Jackson put his arm around me, I leaned into him. Confusion and fear rode through him and made my stomach clench, but when he buried his head into my neck the tension in my muscles gradually loosened, until his body was a firm, solid warmth against mine. I could smell the familiar sweetness of the strawberry shampoo he had used that morning.

Corben rose and gripped the back of her chair, as if steadying herself. She looked directly at me and her eyes were lined with silver, but there was only emptiness when I probed for feelings.

"I know I wasn't there for you, Nova, and I can't tell you how sorry I am for that." She turned to Sawyer. "I have to go."

△

We were left with the aftermath of the storm.

Screams of abuse indicated that the argument from next door had escalated.

There was also the sound of someone thumping on metal and shouting from the street outside.

"Nova, I need your help." Sawyer's eyes locked on mine, and I felt him evaluating how stable I was. He gave me a reassuring smile, apparently satisfied. "Jack, stay close to her. Let her draw on your energy."

Jackson gripped my hand tightly as we both stood up.

"Jet?" Sawyer did not have to ask the question. Jet gave him a firm nod. "Take them outside, check what is happening on the street. Nova, Jet needs you to calm things down, pacify people. Rayna, you're with me. We'd better go next door."

Sawyer's authority was comforting. Jet tucked a gun into the back of his pants and pulled his shirt out over the top. Rayna adjusted her shoulder holster, where a gun was tucked under one arm.

Jet led us outside. It was an inner-city suburb, gentrified and modernised. New low-rise apartment blocks, like the one Sawyer was staying in, were intermingled with old brown-brick houses on tiny blocks of land. Trees lined the wide nature strip on both sides of the street, which was crowded with parked cars. Behind the buildings opposite, I could see an expanse of green grass and leafy trees. It was a parkland area.

The air throbbed with a hungry aggression.

An old man on the corner was yelling abuse at a young cyclist who had sped past him.

People who had been outside hurried indoors.

Some of the curtains were pulled closed, while in other houses terrified neighbours peered from their windows, not game to make a sound or draw attention to themselves.

A group of angry young people surrounded a car. It looked like an attempted carjacking. There was a short, thin boy, about eighteen, leaning through the open car door. He was trying to pull the driver out of his seat by his neck, but the man was held in place by his seatbelt.

The driver was a middle-aged man, going bald in a neat, round dome on the top of his skull. He was pushing at his attacker with one hand, while trying to close the car door with his other hand.

The other young people, four boys and a girl, were jeering at the driver while they rocked the car from side to side. Their movements were making the car scrape against the parked car beside it. There was a jarring sound of metal on metal.

The teenagers were heavily tattooed and wore mostly black. They looked a little out of place in the middle-class suburban street, and I wondered where they had come from.

Jet placed his hand on my arm and pulled me up. "You two stay back here."

At his touch, I could feel the tight lid he had clamped over the fury that still seethed through his body. It was like he was wearing a muzzle.

I knew my role. With deep, slow breaths, I focused on pushing through the haze of aggression and replacing it with a peaceful tranquillity. Jackson pulled me back against his chest. His arms encircled me in a protective fold.

Jet towered above the short, thin boy like a formidable giant. He pried the boy's hands off the throat of the driver and bent one of his arms behind his back, so the young man had no choice but to back away from the car.

"Take it easy, mate. Let's just walk away from this." Jet's voice was smooth but commanding at the same time.

The teenager's frightened rage leapt out at me. It felt like there were flames travelling down my arms, burning my skin. Although he struggled against Jet, he was in a secure head-lock and I knew from experience that the boy was no match for Jet's strength.

Two of the boy's friends switched their focus from the car to Jet. With some vicious cursing, one jumped onto Jet's back and the other pulled at the hold Jet had on his friend. They were about as effective as kittens wrestling with a tiger. Even with the two of them hanging off him, Jet maintained the hold on the short boy, squeezing until the boy's eyes rolled up and he slumped to the ground, unconscious. Jet pulled the other two off him and pushed them aside.

The driver had remained in his car and pulled the door shut. Jet stood between him and the teenagers like a solid, human shield.

While the girl hovered over the unconscious boy on the ground, the remaining four boys fanned out from Jet in a semi-circle.

There were verbal threats and false bravado, but not one of them moved within reach of Jet's muscular arms. They had seen the display of his strength.

"Are you okay if I help Jet?" Jackson whispered against my ear.

Nodding, I supressed a shiver when his arms withdrew from their safety lock around me. The anger from the young people was still sizzling across my skin.

I watched as Jackson, largely ignored by the teenagers, joined Jet beside the car. He rolled his shoulders, and I could see the powerful lines of his body and the determination in his eyes. It was those subtle movements, and the courage that stiffened through my back, that indicated he was ready for a fight.

The boys were skinny, and they looked inexperienced at any kind of fighting, but they were still dangerous. Resentment at the driver, at Jet, at any adult, any authority, pumped hot and fast through their veins. Through my veins.

I pressed my feet flat against the cement footpath. It was stable, it was grounding, and it was reassuring. My gentle probing brushed against the darkness inside the teenagers. I sensed the fear in three of them. They were reluctant to engage. But one of them was harder to shift. Pride was at stake, and his reputation within the group. I knew he was the leader.

The girl had managed to help up the shorter boy who sagged against her, barely conscious.

"Guys, how about you help your friend and take him home. He'll likely have quite a headache after this." Jet's voice held a natural authority. He held his hands out, palms up, in a non-threating manner, but his body was still on full alert.

"Why don't you fuck off." The leader was the tallest of the group, and wore a backwards baseball cap. He put his hand on his friend's forearm and gave a smirk, as if he knew a secret that the rest of us did not.

His friend was a pale boy with a face marked by teenage acne scars. He also gave a smirk; he was in on the secret.

Their smug confidence spread across my calming vibes like a slime on a pond.

The leader held up his fist. It gripped a large kitchen knife, and it was the signal for the rest of them to pull out their weapons. There was a hammer, a screwdriver, and the pale boy with the acne scars had a knife with finger holes. Even the girl was holding a small steak knife.

It changed the whole dynamic.

I knew Jet would have been holding back, trying not to hurt them, but these weapons were potentially lethal.

The leader was carving into the air with his kitchen knife, as if writing invisible sentences. He was breathing in loud, fast gasps. The boy with the acne scars held his knife above his head, like a spear, but remained quiet and still.

The boy with the hammer was shifting it from hand to hand, as if unsure what to do with it, while his friend with the screwdriver was slowly shaking his head. The anger in their eyes had been replaced by fear. It was like being doused with icy water compared with the hot fury radiating from their two friends with the knives. But I also knew that they were equally as afraid of the wrath of their friends if they did not back them up.

I wondered if Jet would pull out his gun, but he didn't. He and Jackson exchanged a couple of glances, as if silently communicating their strategy. They had trained together often enough to know each other's moves.

Each side was reluctant to take the first step, and each second seemed like an eternity.

"I really don't think you want to do this," said Jet.

"Fuck off," said the leader. He wiped his hand across his face with a huge sniff, the large knife still clutched in his fingers. It crossed my mind that he was lucky he did not slice off his nose. "You don't want to do this."

"No, that's right, I don't. And I don't want to hurt anyone." Jet's voice was calm and even, but a layer of steel ran beneath his words. I straightened my back, feeling his courage.

"Blade, let's just go," said the boy with the screwdriver. He had taken a step back from his friends.

I sent out more pacifying vibes and felt them settling around the boys, but they seemed to bounce off Blade, the leader of the group, who gave his friend a scathing look. Jet's words were a challenge to him, and there was no backing down now.

Blade turned back to Jet and lunged forward, continuing to make random swipes through the air with his kitchen knife. It made me think of a small boy playing at sword fighting. His lack of skill made him unpredictable. That made him more dangerous.

Jet moved towards him with a defensive arm raised. There was a scramble of hands as Jet and Blade locked together in what looked like an awkward bear hug.

The boy with the finger-hole knife moved in with a more lethal grace. He had clearly judged Jackson as an easier target, especially while Jackson had made the rookie mistake of being distracted by Blade and Jet.

Two seconds was all it took for the boy to cover the distance to Jackson.

Two seconds for Jet to react. While still gripping the hand coming at him with the kitchen knife, he was able to reach out with his other arm to deflect the blow aimed at Jackson. The finger-hole knife stabbed through the soft skin between Jackson's arm and shoulder.

Jet's action meant the knife went into Jackson's shoulder, rather than his chest.

A warning had caught in my throat, too late to help, but then my panic burst forth with a desperation that was like a hungry, wild tiger leaping at its prey.

Everyone froze. Suddenly. As if they were children playing at being statues. As if they were face to face with that wild tiger and couldn't move, couldn't breathe.

Paralysed by my fear. My concern for Jackson.

I flooded them with it. And with my fury. I had no compassion.

The breath I had been holding came out in a hiss. I bit hard on my bottom lip to help focus myself, and then I released Jet and Jackson.

Jet gave a shake of his head, as if clearing it, but his forehead remained creased in a frown. One arm was still gripped around Blade's hand and the kitchen knife. He twisted slowly and the knife clattered to the tarmac. Jet pushed Blade away.

Jackson's hand moved up to the hilt of the knife, where the finger holes gaped like empty rings. The thin blade was buried in his shoulder. The boy had let it go once he had struck. Blood was soaking through Jackson's new shirt. He turned to me, raised his eyebrows, and gave a weak smile.

Nausea rose in my throat, and I took a few wobbly steps towards him.

Hot anger surged through my body and I could not hold the freezing bind any longer.

Blade put his hands in the air and was backing away. The boy who had stabbed Jackson was doubled over, and he vomited on the road. The other two were already running down the street. The short, skinny boy was limping awkwardly, with his arm around the girl for support. Blade gave his vomiting friend a rough shove and they took off after their friends.

They wanted to be as far away from us as possible.

Their fear and confusion clouded my head and sent shivers down my spine, but at the pit of my stomach a terrified fury still bucked and rolled.

"Jack, you've been stabbed." Jet spoke calmly.

"No kidding." Jackson gave a snort. His fingers were holding the knife in place, the hilt still sticking out from his shoulder.

Hysterical laughter bubbled out of me but really, I wanted to scream.

13

"Take Jack inside. Rayna will have a first-aid kit." Jet waved us away.

The driver of the car had finally untangled himself from his seatbelt and climbed out of his vehicle. He came towards Jet with his arms wide open, as if to hug him, but I saw Jet extend a hand to shake instead.

Dark red blood had soaked through Jackson's shirt, and he was holding his hand around the hilt of the knife, applying pressure to the wound. He looked deathly pale, but he still gave me a small smile and a wink.

I held a hand up to my mouth, as my breakfast threatened to come back up. My nostrils flared with the metallic odour of his wound. I was not good with blood.

Police sirens wailed in the distance. Anger and aggression still reverberated around the streets. It felt as if the sky had turned dark with heavy clouds and yet, when I looked up, it was fine and clear.

We climbed the stairs slowly. With every step, there was a dull throb in my own shoulder and painful twinges down my arm. Jackson's face betrayed nothing.

The door of the neighbour's apartment was wide open and I could see straight into the lounge, where Sawyer was standing above a young man sitting on the floor. The man had his head between his knees, and his regret and shame settled heavily around my own body. Sawyer was talking quietly, maintaining a calmness that ricocheted around the room and out into the corridor.

"Rayna?" I spoke softly but could not help the tremor in my voice.

Sawyer looked from me to Jackson, and I saw his eyes widen at the knife and the blood-stained shirt. He gestured towards a closed door.

I moved into the apartment and knocked quietly at the door Sawyer had indicated. There was a muffled sobbing from the room, but no acknowledgement of my knocking. The guy looked up as I opened the door, and Sawyer bent down to place a hand on his shoulder. I got the sense that it was as much to restrain him as to calm him.

Rayna was sitting on the bed next to a woman, a box of tissues in her lap, with her hand resting on the woman's arm. I slid inside and closed the door firmly behind me. The woman looked up and blinked repeatedly. Dull blue eyes were red and swollen, and I knew it was not just from the tears. There were angry red welts around her neck.

"Sorry," I said quietly. "But I need the first-aid kit. Jack has been stabbed."

Rayna raised her eyebrows but continued to gently pat the woman's arm. "Where was he stabbed? How bad is it?"

I shrugged. "It's his shoulder. He's bleeding a lot. I don't know."

"My medical bag is on the floor in my room. Do what you can. I'll be there shortly." Rayna spoke with the same quiet authority that Jet used. It was reassuring, and I wondered if it was something they learned in the Army.

When I came out of the room, Jack was leaning up against the door jamb as if it were holding him up. My heart flipped over and my knees wobbled.

"Nova, he's fine." Sawyer shot me a look that meant I needed to pull myself together. "Take him next door. Lay him down. Clean around the wound as best as you can. I will send Rayna through in a few minutes."

I found the medical bag and pulled out anything that looked like it would be helpful. Gloves, swabs, pads, bandages, antiseptic cream. Jackson had ripped a wide hole in his shirt, and it hung from one shoulder in bloody shreds. So much for his nice, clean shirt. He stood in front of the mirror, probing at his wound with his fingers. Blood was seeping around the hilt of the knife, refusing to crust over.

I clenched my teeth to stop myself from gagging.

"It's deep, but not very wide. It's just in flesh. I think I'll need a couple of stitches." He gave a wry grin as our reflections looked back at us.

His face was pale. Mine was green.

I swallowed, twice. "I'll clean it up. You need to lie down, Sawyer said."

"I think you probably need to lie down." He gave a small laugh. "Help me out of this shirt first, then I can clean it."

With my help, he shrugged out of his torn shirt and dropped it onto the floor. While I made gentle, ineffectual dabs at his shoulder with sterilized swabs, Jackson moved with a professional precision until the wound was cleaner. He held up two small, sealed packets.

"Needle and surgical thread. I can't do it myself. Do you think you can?"

I shook my head and backed away. "No way. I don't know what to do. You've still got a fricking knife in your shoulder!"

"I can guide you."

"No, Jack. I'll stuff it up. Can't you just wait for Rayna?"

He nodded and led me through to the bedroom, where we both lay on the bed to wait.

△

Rayna gave Jackson a local anaesthetic before removing the knife.

"Put this in your mouth and bite down. This isn't going to tickle." Rayna spoke with a calm authority as she passed him a rolled-up cloth.

Jackson nodded and bit down firmly on the fabric, as Rayna placed her hand around the hilt of the knife. With the experience of someone who had done this before, swiftly and smoothly she pulled the knife from his shoulder. Blood filled the void that the blade had left behind and spilled down his arm. Placing the knife to the side, she quickly applied pressure with one hand while reaching for the needle and thread with the other.

The tears welling in Jackson's eyes betrayed his otherwise stoic expression. I could feel his fear and his pain, and it felt like I was being tortured on a stretching rack.

Rayna stitched his wound carefully as Jackson blinked away a few more tears. She dressed it with a tight bandage that wound around under his arm and over his shoulder.

Although he had full movement, it was quickly stiffening up.

The room had finally calmed and I watched the two of them sitting on the bed, heads bent together, as Rayna fastened the bandage. Tiny jealous twinges twisted through my heart, even though I knew better. Rayna was an Army medic and Jackson loved to hear about her field experiences. When they had worked together in the hospital last year, they had bonded over long discussions of gory stories which just turned my stomach.

To avoid this personal torture, I moved into the lounge.

Sawyer and Jet were talking in low voices. I slumped into a chair, and Sawyer glanced my way but kept talking. He was listing a range of crimes that had been reported to the police in the last hour. There had been a surge of violence with robberies, assaults, and domestic disputes. A riot had broken out in Bourke Street Mall, with damage to shops and offices, as well as dozens of injuries and two deaths. I could still hear police sirens wailing in the distance.

"It seems worse than ever," said Jet, massaging his forehead. I sensed the start of his headache.

"What does it all mean?" I asked Sawyer. "And what was that ... that storm that seemed to come from Corben?"

"I don't know."

I could feel Sawyer was holding something back. "What are you not saying?"

"Nova, I honestly don't know what it all means." He sighed. "I guess we need to talk to your mother again."

I cringed at the word *mother*. It did not seem right somehow. My mother had been dead for ten years. That was how I was used to thinking of her, and it was weird to have it otherwise. I was too old to start calling someone 'Mum'.

Sawyer noticed my discomfort. "I'll give Corben a call and we'll see if we can meet her again."

△

Han had comparable stories of violence to share when we all had dinner that evening.

He had been with Luca, Bellamy, and Maize, getting a tattoo.

"It was nuts. People were screaming at each other in the café next door. They were knocking over tables and smashing things. And there were gunshots down the street. Luca wanted to get the kids out of there, and the tattoo shop wanted to shut anyway, so we left. I was glad we had Luca's car. The streets were crazy. People were blocking the traffic and shouting abuse at the drivers. One guy had a baseball bat, and he was thrashing into the windscreen of this other car." Han paused and shook his head, looking from me to Jackson and back again.

I sighed. My head was aching, and I rubbed my fingers around in circles beside my eyes.

Jackson winced as he shifted his arm, and a shot of pain ran through me as it ran through him. Nevertheless, he grabbed hold of my hand and threaded his fingers through mine. I knew he was trying to offer me comfort.

"Anyway, I'll need to go back to get it finished." Han smiled. "Maize, too. And they'd not even started with Luca."

"Well, come on then. Show us," said Jackson.

Han stripped off his shirt and turned to show his back. The tattoo was shiny, and his skin was red as if sunburnt, but it was impressive. A huge Chinese dragon wound up his spine. It was both beautiful and ferocious, even in its current outlined, unfinished state.

"Very cool."

"Yeah. This girl is amazing. Maize knows her. Dragons are her specialty. Maize has a winged dragon across her back, and she is getting little extra bits around it."

"I want to get one," I said suddenly.

"You want to get a dragon tattoo?" Jackson looked at me with wide eyes.

"Actually, I want something else." I looked up at the ceiling as I felt the tears well in my eyes. "I want to get sage leaves."

"Oh, right." Jackson squeezed my fingers gently. "Good idea."

"We could go back tomorrow," Han suggested. "If they're open and if they can fit us in."

Jackson looked at me and raised his eyebrows. I nodded and his face split in a grin.

"I might get one too." Excitement bubbled up in Jackson. "I have to say this. Maize is possibly the coolest person I know, but she's blind. She can't even see her tattoos. What's the point?"

Han laughed. "I said the same to her. She said she can feel that it's there."

Jackson gave a chuckle. "Fair enough."

△

"Nova, can I talk to you for a minute before we turn in?" Jet shuffled his feet and pulled at the collar of his shirt. A light perspiration broke out on the back of my neck as I sensed his discomfort.

I nodded, giving what I hoped was a reassuring smile and followed him into the kitchen. Taking a clean glass from the dish drainer, he filled it with water from the sink. I shook my head when he offered it to me, so he took a sip himself and then put the glass on the bench. He ran his tongue over his lips and picked up the glass again, took another small sip, and placed it back on the bench. I stood quietly, waiting, while he fidgeted. Jet was rarely ill-at-ease, and my heart galloped a few beats as I wondered what he wanted.

"I know I'm lucky to have this gig. We've had a quiet spell after Finn's death, but I'm serious about keeping you safe. Sawyer thinks you have a vital role in helping the world recover from this violence pandemic, and I agree with him. I can feel what you do." He had been staring at the floor, but now he looked straight at me. "I don't know what you sensed in me today. But I know I was as close to losing control as I ever have been. I learned self-discipline long before I joined the Army, and I like to think of myself as generally pretty cool, even under pressure." I nodded when he paused. "I will fight if I must, if I need to and if it's for a good reason, but it's rare that my anger, my temper, gets the best of me. I'm sorry if it seemed that way today. I didn't mean to frighten you or disappoint you." Sincerity radiated from wide, earnest eyes.

The implicit trust I had in Jet was like an armour I wore every day, fitting snug and comfortably around me. I took a deep breath, hoping I could find the right words.

"Jet, I'm lucky to have you in my life. You always make me feel safe. I know it's your job, but you're my friend as well. You haven't ever disappointed or frightened me."

"Thank you, Nova. That means a lot." Jet gave a nod, and I felt a veil of worry float away.

"Can I ask you something?"

"Yeah. Of course." He gave me a small smile.

"I never really stop thinking about Finn, about Sage ... and about Abe. I took someone's life. Even though I know all the reasons why it can be justified, it's still a fact. I took his life. How do I stop thinking about that?"

Jet paused and chewed on his bottom lip. "I don't think you ever forget the people you've killed. But don't let that get in the way of you thinking about the people you love. Dead and alive. They deserve more of your thoughts, more of your time."

I moved in to hug Jet, and although he stood awkwardly, he wrapped a strong arm around me too. Love and care radiated from me, washing through him. Through both of us.

△

Jackson and I lay next to each other in the dark. Both of us were wide awake. His shoulder was painful and uncomfortable despite the pain killers Rayna had given him. I could feel it too.

Sleep would not come for me because my brain would not stop.

Short movies played through my mind – images of Sage and Finn, everything Corben had said, the violence on the street. They were like horror movies. But they were also our normal. Constant aggression, carjackings, people getting beaten up or killed.

I could still taste the anger in the air. It was like a layer of smoke that clogged my nostrils and caught in my throat.

From Jackson, I could sense a sadness, a grief, which was heavy on my chest. I knew he was replaying recent and past events in his head too.

When he sighed, I reached for him, running my fingers lightly over his bicep. It was not his injured side, but I was gentle nonetheless. Although I could not see clearly in the darkness, I traced a line around where Jackson had his tattoo. He and Cooper had got the same one after Alexander's death. It was three intersecting triangles, for three brothers.

"You must miss him," I whispered.

"Every day."

"We have lost so many people. Is this our life now? There is always someone trying to kill one of us, or someone we love."

"Maybe for now, but not forever." Jackson's voice was low but firm with conviction.

"You really think it will get better?"

"I do." Jackson tried to rise to his elbows, but the pain from his shoulder forced him to drop back against his pillows. I heard his quiet groan. "I have hope. Being with you gives me that. You make things seem brighter, better."

"That's just because I'm an empath." I could not help the cynicism in my voice.

"Maybe, but that's just part of it. I think it's because you are you."

"I don't know, Jack. The violence is like a bushfire. It spreads and it burns everything in its path. I feel like all I'm doing is throwing a few buckets of water on something that's already out of control. One day it will consume me, too."

"Nova, you can't burn if you were born to walk through fire."

I moved in slowly, carefully, until our noses bumped, and my lips brushed against his. When his good arm locked around me in a tight clasp, I knew he didn't want me to be gentle. His mouth was hungry, his tongue explored mine, and his breath came in fast pants. Desire leapt through me, his matching my own.

"Mmm. My favourite thing in the entire world is kissing you," Jackson murmured against my ear.

I giggled and snuggled up under his good arm. "Oh, that's like my third favourite thing about you."

"Really? What are your first and second favourite things?" A lively curiosity bubbled in his voice as the mood between us became considerably more playful.

"Your bike is definitely number one."

Jackson laughed aloud. "That's fair enough. It is the best thing about me. And number two?"

"Your leather jacket."

Jackson groaned, but not out of pain. "So, you are saying you love me for my bike and my jacket."

"Yep!" I giggled again.

"Nothing else?" I could not see his face, but I knew he was putting on a pretence of pouting.

"I like kissing you too." I paused, tapping gently on his chest. "And I suppose I could come up with a couple of other things."

"Don't stretch yourself," he said sarcastically.

"Well, you are warm and cuddly." I paused again as his arm tightened around me. "You make me laugh, even when I don't want to. You make me feel safe and strong at the same time. And you stay up half the night with me, talking shit and somehow solving all the world's problems."

There was a moment of silence as if he were unsure of a reply, then a small sound rose from deep in his throat. Despite his sore shoulder, he used both arms to pull me on top of him.

"Jack, you'll hurt yourself," I warned, but I let him hug me into a closer embrace.

He mumbled against my mouth. "Wilson, just shut up and kiss me."

Our mouths crashed together once again, and our hearts sang in harmony.

We shared kisses that soothed our fears, kisses that cradled our joy, kisses that gave us hope for a safer future.

14

The tattoo shop was small and dimly lit, except for the bright lamps attached to each bed. Creative illustrations, both in black and white and in colour, jumped off the walls. Lions roared, snakes slithered, dragons breathed fire, and wolves howled amidst the winged angels, blooming flowers, and tribal symbols. With her glasses perched precariously on the end of her nose and the tip of her tongue gripped between her teeth in concentration, Adele, a slim, long-haired girl, was adding the final details to Maize's magnificent dragon tattoo.

Jackson was sitting in a chair nearby, waiting for his turn. He was getting a creature. Not a dragon, but he had refused to tell me what it was. He had told Maize, who had decided Adele was still the best person for the job.

I lay stretched out on my back on an adjoining bed, holding out my wrist. My tattoo artist was Dash, a tall, lanky guy with a cheeky smile. Tattoos covered his muscular arms, continued up into his shirt sleeves and peeped out at his neck. A live advertisement for his trade. He kept up a light banter, which I knew was to keep me calm while the tattoo needles jabbed at my skin. I had my head firmly turned away, concentrating on Maize. She looked relaxed, as if she were enjoying the pain.

"Nova, I can hear your wheezing from over here," Maize said with a laugh. "Get into the zone."

I heard an answering chortle from Bellamy, sitting in the reception area, and I bit my bottom lip to prevent myself from giving Maize an abusive response.

"Ignore them. You're doing great," Jackson said quietly.

He gave me a reassuring wink and held his hand over his heart. I nodded but could not bring myself to smile.

There was a strong odour of disinfectant in the shop but I could still smell the distinctive scent of blood. Nausea fizzled through my stomach. Shutting my eyes, I focused on inhaling and exhaling through my mouth, slowly and quietly. The zone eluded me, but at least I was no longer wheezing.

When Maize was finished, Jackson took her place on that bed, and Adele fixed the paper transfer to his chest to check it was what he wanted. He was turned away from me, so I still couldn't see what the tattoo was.

Eventually, I felt Dash gently wiping at my arm, the clean paper towel rough against my freshly-tattooed skin. "We're almost done. Can you take a look now to make sure you're happy?"

I turned to see a pattern of sage leaves trailing elegantly up my wrist. It was perfect. Tears filled my eyes, and I blinked them away.

"Is it okay? Does it still hurt?" Dash's voice was filled with his concern.

I shook my head. "It's exactly what I wanted. Thank you."

Gladwrap circled my arm over the tattoo, but I ran my fingers lightly over the inked leaves.

It was as if I could hear Sage's voice. "Stick together?" And I answered her silently. "Like glue."

△

It was a couple of hours before Jackson's tattoo was finished. Han, Jet, Bellamy, Maize, and I had moved into the café next door. Jackson came through the door with his shirt unbuttoned and jacket open. He slumped into a chair next to mine. A clean, white dressing still covered the knife wound on his shoulder, emphasising the blue-black ink of the tattoo across his chest.

It was a phoenix, rising from the flames. The wings were spread wide as if about to take flight, and a long, feathered tail trailed into the fire below it.

Han gave a bark of laughter. "Perfect and very cool, mate."

Jet snorted and shook his head. He looked up at the ceiling as if he were avoiding eye contact with me, but his expression was neutral. Han, on the other hand, was grinning at me as if in on a private joke, but I didn't know what that was. Bellamy had finished describing the tattoo to Maize and she nodded as if she could picture it in her mind, but they did not seem to be privy to what was going on between the boys.

"Why a phoenix?" I asked, knowing it was not a random choice.

Jackson just shrugged and then grimaced with the movement. "I'll tell you later."

I didn't push him about the tattoo. He'd tell me when he was ready, but it was still annoying.

"Are you okay? Do you want to go back to the apartment?" I moved forward to rest my forehead against his and placed my hands on his knees. His pain and weariness sat heavily across my own shoulders.

He moved in for a kiss. It was not just a light peck.

We broke apart when Han interrupted with a loud snort. "Don't mind me. I'll just sit over here and try not to throw up."

Jackson gave him a friendly shove, but I felt my face flush with heat.

△

We left Melbourne to return home that afternoon.

Sawyer had been in contact with Corben, but she had gone away somewhere and wasn't sure when she'd return. There was no point hanging around Melbourne waiting for her.

Cooper was busy working and didn't really want to see us anyway. He seemed to be enjoying his new independence. I knew Sawyer and Luca would both keep checking on him.

I leaned up against the car window and looked at the sky. Grey clouds hung low and ominous. It felt like they were clogged with the hostility that had been flaring around the city for the past two days. The police were over-worked, and the Army were helping re-impose the safety restrictions and curfews that had slackened in the previous few months. Sawyer and Rayna were staying in Melbourne to assist them.

We were in the DOVE jeep with Jet, and Jackson's motorbike was loaded onto the back tray. Rayna would not let him ride with his shoulder. I turned to check on Han and was reassured to see the familiar black bike following close behind.

Jackson's playlist pumped through the speakers, a heavy metal grunge that matched the weather. I wrinkled up my nose and got out my AirPods. We really had vastly different taste in music, and I needed something that allowed me to think without being blasted by distorted electric guitar riffs.

I didn't know how to feel about Corben's sudden departure. Maybe it was my fault. I had been awful to her. On the other hand, leaving was her usual thing.

There was also that flash of darkness. It had been like standing on the edge of a huge black hole that pulled me in and pushed me away at the same time. I was starting to think I had imagined it.

My head hurt, my stomach churned, and my throat was dry. I reached for my water bottle, but I knew a drink was not really going to solve anything. Nor was Taylor Swift's latest album. Not when there was a choir of dissonant voices in my head, constantly replaying the meetings with Corben.

Reaching into my pocket, I brought out the jade crystal. I held it in my hand, enjoying the smooth, cool surface. Then I turned my wrist to look at my newly-tattooed sage leaves. I rubbed my fingers lightly over the pattern. That was comforting too.

15

I felt like I was sinking in quicksand.

Online classes at university had resumed the week after we had returned from Melbourne, and assessment due dates were looming.

I was stressing over assignments and exams.

There was an increase in crime around our town, and Jet had moved into my spare room as a precaution. He was an easy person to live with because he was military-style neat and orderly, but I could sense the aggression that lurked just beneath his skin. The tight control he maintained over it was like a steel cage holding in a wild animal. It also reminded me that I was supposed to be calming the anger in him, in others, in the town around me, and I was clearly useless at it. The violence seemed just as bad as it ever had been.

I felt like a failure.

With Cooper in Melbourne, Jackson was spending more time at home, helping with his mother. Mia was on university placement at a childcare centre and was exhausted at the end of the day, so she had not been staying over. Spencer was doing extra shifts at work to earn as much money as she could before the baby came. Ava was spending all her spare time with Brooklyn. Imogen was busy with her studies. Devon and Han had started dating. Everyone was busy.

I was lonely.

There had been no word from Corben. My mother. She had left me again.

I was angry at her.

My tattoo had healed well, and I found myself rubbing my thumb over the leaves so often I was worried I would rub them out.

I missed Sage.

Three weeks passed and I let myself wallow. Even the simplest task was all-engulfing.

Finally, Mia held out a lifeline, a rope to pull me out of that quicksand. She was celebrating the completion of her first placement with a small gathering at her place.

△

Mia clinked her champagne flute against mine. "Cheers to me!"

"Cheers to you!" I agreed, as her warmth swept through me. "Did you enjoy it?"

"I loved it. The children are adorable. There were not many there, mostly just those whose parents can't work at home, so it was pretty easy. I tell you what, though, it's amazing how exhausting it is to play games all day."

"You would be wonderful with them." I clinked her glass again.

"How are you doing?" She lowered her voice and lent in closer. "I still can't believe your mum is alive after all these years. That's wild."

I shrugged. "Yeah, I know. I can't really believe it either. She has disappeared again, though. So, there's that." I heard the bitterness in my voice, but I couldn't help it.

"Don't worry. She'll be back. She must be so proud of you." Mia was an eternal optimist. "What did she think of Jackson?"

I looked across the room. Jackson was slouched against the wall. His long, slim legs were crossed at the ankles, and his arms were folded against his broad, muscular chest. There was the glint of brooding brown eyes from behind his shaggy fringe, and he wore a lazy smile as he watched Han and Kenji comparing tattoos. He looked relaxed and very sexy.

"I couldn't really work out what she thought or felt."

"Yeah, that is weird. But don't worry. She'll love him." Mia patted my arm and moved off to look after her guests.

As if he had sensed we were discussing him, Jackson looked over at me.

He had a multitude of winks. There was a slow, sultry one, where just one side of his mouth lifted in a half smile and his eyes shone with mischief. I knew that meant he was thinking about kissing me. He had a quick wink accompanied by a broad grin, which meant he was happy. There was a deliberate one, when his eyes were solemn, and his mouth was set in a firm line. It was the wink he gave when we had something serious to do, to let me know we were thinking the same thing. He also had an enquiring wink, where he raised his eyebrows and tucked his tongue into the corner of his mouth. This is what I got now. He was checking if I was okay. I winked back at him, trying to do the slow, sultry one to let him know I wanted to kiss him. His answering grin was a smirk, so he got the message.

I felt the corners of my mouth lift as I let the friendship and joy in the room soak through my bones. It was a salve to my stressed-out body.

The excitement of a new relationship radiated from Han and Devon like a colourful aura. They slow-danced to the soft music and giggled quietly over shared intimacies.

Ava and Brooklyn sat on the couch with Spencer between them. All three had their hands resting on her pregnant belly, waiting to feel a kick. The baby was not cooperating.

Mia, Kenji, Imogen, and Jackson had started a game of cards.

Kenji's laughter bellowed around the room as Mia accused him of cheating. He had won both of the hands they had played. Imogen was supporting Mia because she hated to lose.

Jackson called me over. "Nova, tell us what you can feel. Is Kenji cheating?"

Everyone was laughing. I perched on the edge of Jackson's chair and frowned, pretending to concentrate.

"Hey, come on, Nova. I'm not cheating." Kenji eyed me warily.

I held my breath for a moment, tasting the nervous excitement that radiated from Kenji, but his natural confidence and charm was like a comforting arm around me and I did not think there was any obvious deception.

"No, he's not," I announced to both cheers and groans.

"Jack, how do you cope with that?" Kenji was looking at me with a renewed curiosity. "Being with someone that can read your mind and know if you are lying."

"I can't read minds," I protested.

Jackson laughed. "I love it. I have nothing to hide from Nova." He bumped against me, but the movement caused me to lose my balance so I fell off the side of the chair and onto the floor.

My face flushed with heat, and I laughed awkwardly as I picked myself up.

Kenji laughed too, but he looked at me with a new level of caution and I knew he would be more guarded around me, for a little while at least.

Friendship sparkled through the room like the sun breaking through the clouds. Friends teased each other, laughed at each other, cared about each other.

I was no longer falling into the quicksand; I was back in the sunshine, amongst my friends.

A comfortable warmth circulated through my body, and my heart returned to beat in its regular rhythm.

I felt safe and happy.

16

I pushed the curtain aside and peered out again for the fifteenth time in as many minutes.

Corben was coming to visit me. At home. My mother. At my house.

"They're not even five minutes late," said Jackson gently, as he placed his hands on my arms and pulled me away from the window.

I nodded and took a deep breath, drawing on his strength.

Jet had helped me clean the house, and he was now sitting calmly on a kitchen stool in our immaculate kitchen. The anger from the last few weeks had finally left him, and I could only sense a cool composure. He looked over and smiled in reassurance, and it was like a light breeze settling over me.

There was the dull throb of an engine as a car pulled into the driveway, and I waited for the knock on the door.

Sawyer's usual kind compassion swept through me as a familiar warmth when they entered the house and exchanged greetings. I gave him a nervous smile. Corben opened her arms and I moved into an awkward hug where we barely made contact. The wrinkles across her forehead and around her eyes seemed a little more prominent than last time, and there was a slight stoop to her back. Although I could not sense her emotions, she looked exhausted.

"This is a lovely home, Nova," Corben said. "It looks comfortable and cosy. Can you show me around?"

There was a prickling at the back of my neck as I looked around at the mismatched furniture and worn carpet. Without being able to read her, I wondered if she was politely saying it looked small and shabby. Thank goodness we had cleaned it.

Jackson nudged me and I realised I had not replied. "Umm, I guess so. There's not much else to see."

Leading Corben on a tour through the house, which took all of two minutes, I managed to trip over my feet, bump against the beds and chairs, and shut my hand in a door. When she tried to linger in my bedroom and pat Ripley, who was asleep on my bed, I made the excuse of needing to get drinks for everyone and ushered her back to the lounge. I didn't want her in my personal space.

We settled around the coffee table. Sawyer and Jackson sat on the couch, and I sat on the floor. Corben had sunk into my father's old armchair, and she nursed her cup of coffee. I knew she would struggle to get up when the time came, because the springs had gone in the seat.

Jet had made himself scarce, probably playing video games in the spare room. He had brought in his own monitor because he stayed there so often lately.

After several minutes of small talk, an air of expectancy hung in the lounge.

We wanted Corben to finish her story. And there were the questions about what had happened in Melbourne, that glimpse of darkness she had revealed. She knew what she was here for.

"Thanks for having me, Nova. I'm sorry I had to leave so suddenly in Melbourne. I'm easily tired these days and I've been away for a while, resting. It is hard being an empath sometimes, as I am sure you can relate." Corben looked from Sawyer to me, and then gave Jackson an inclusive smile. "I expect you must have loads of questions."

Sawyer looked at me, but I just shrugged. I had resolved to leave the talking to him. He was the professional negotiator. When I spoke to her I seemed to swing from being rude to being needy, and I didn't like either version of myself.

"I think we'd like to hear more about what you did in America, if that's okay," he said.

The room seemed to give a silent sigh, and it was like a soft comforting cloak settled over us. I knew it was Sawyer making it a safe space for Corben.

"Okay, sure. Where was I up to?" Corben swallowed and looked up at the ceiling, not expecting an answer. "I went to Washington as a consultant to the U.S. Department of Defense. As well as helping with their recruitment, I was part of a large research team of people based all around the world. We were exploring epigenetic modifications to DNA, associated with both aggressive behaviour and post-traumatic stress disorder. My focus was on the warrior gene. It was exciting and it was ground-breaking. Or so we thought at the time. I travelled a lot, visiting most of the US Army bases overseas and various research sites. But, as the years passed, I realised the military was not really interested in our work. Modifying genes to develop greater resilience and the prevention of PTSD were words they used to make it sound like a worthy cause. They really just wanted super soldiers. The

strongest, most fearless individuals, who would follow orders
and act with a perfectly controlled level of aggression. They
wanted to control the warrior gene."

Corben looked at me. "I didn't contact Harley. And,
after a while, he stopped trying to contact me. I told myself
that it was the best thing for you both. That you were better
off without me. It was like the life I had left behind was not
real to me anymore."

She stopped talking to take a sip of coffee, and ran her
fingers through her long, dark hair.

My father had told me that Corben meant raven in
French, as in raven-haired. Her hair was a glossy black colour
and hung in immaculate soft waves. It was my middle name,
but I had not lived up to it. My hair was lighter, a dull brown
colour, and always a little frizzy as if I had been caught in the
wind. Feeling suddenly self-conscious, I pulled the scrunchie
from my wrist and twisted my hair up into a messy bun.

I shifted on the floor, uncrossing my legs and stretching
them out in front of me. A sense of dread sat stiff and heavy
down my spine.

When I looked up, Corben was watching me. She raised
her eyebrows as if checking that I was ready for her to continue. It was like the others were not even there. Although
her emotions were closed to me, I knew she could sense mine.
I gave a nod.

"I kept going for eight years, but by then I knew I'd
reached breaking point. That was just over two years ago. I
could activate the warrior gene in people just by being close
by. It was easy. A lot easier than pacifying them. But there
was a cost. Being submerged in that overly aggressive environment, being around the warrior gene, the constant anger, the
constant trauma, was making me physically and emotionally

sick. I didn't believe in what I was doing anymore. I had so many regrets, and I wanted my family back. Of course, they didn't want to let me go. Even with gene testing and artificial enzymes, I was still the easiest, most reliable way they had of sensing, activating, and controlling the warrior gene. It got to be too much. I knew I had to get away. So, I made excuses that I needed to re-visit all the Army bases, but really I just started running."

It felt like the temperature dropped in the room by a few degrees, as a chilling tone rattled through Corben's voice. "I realised that I had given up everything for nothing. It was my own fault. My own blind ambition. My own stupid decisions. I knew that. I know that. But I didn't want to be in that world anymore." Her mouth was pinched in a tight smile, which was not a smile at all. "It was a big step, but eventually I reached out to Harley. He was so forgiving. So much more than I deserved. We met a few times, in secret. I asked to see you as well, but Harley was understandably wary of me and of what I might bring down on you both. He also needed to prepare you first. The truth was going to be confusing for you. We knew that, and I was prepared to wait until he thought you were ready. Meeting with him helped me a lot. He always had a way of calming and comforting me. He was really the only one that could."

I looked at my feet. My father had been like that for me too. Always calm, always accepting, and always caring. I hugged my knees as the cold slivers of loss shivered through me. "The last time, before ... Dad was coming home, he said he wanted to tell me something. I thought it was about the violence. But now I think it was probably about you." I knew tears had formed in my eyes and I blinked three times, hard and quick, trying to get rid of them.

Corben was squinting up into the corner of the room. She might have been hiding tears too, but I couldn't be sure. "I think they found out that I was meeting with Harley. I can't prove it, but I believe they had him killed." She paused but only for a moment and then the words tumbled out with barely a pause for her to breathe. "I had already realised that I was activating the warrior gene everywhere I went. Not just in the soldiers but in everyday, normal people. And from that came the anger, the aggression, and eventually this pandemic of violence. Over two years I had visited hundreds of towns and cities. And not just in the US. I had travelled all around the world. There are over eight hundred US Army bases. I didn't get to them all; I just kept running. And running."

Corben sighed and dropped her head.

"I felt like Typhoid Mary, but I was setting off the warrior gene instead of spreading infection." Her voice shook, but the strong control she clung to remained firm. "I'm not sure if they made the link and blamed me, but I didn't want to stop long enough to find out. Eventually the violence had become so prevalent, everywhere, that they had their hands full anyway, and they left me alone."

Thoughts rolled through my head like thunder. She was saying that she was responsible for all this anger. My mother had caused all this violence, all this death. She was responsible for my father being killed.

"They have left me alone for months now. That's why I finally decided it was safe to see you." Corben's voice had taken on a pleading tone in these last two sentences.

But I felt like I had been slapped.

There was a harsh, cold silence.

I pressed my fingernails into my palms and knew I was leaving deep indentations in my skin, but there was a pressure building in my body that threatened to explode. This was helping me hold it in.

"So, all this violence is your fault," I said at last. "And dad's death too."

Sawyer gasped. "Nova, that's not fair. It's not that simple."

While he looked at me with his usual kindness, the tightness in my stomach betrayed the horror I knew he must be feeling too.

"Yes, and no." Corben's eyes bored into mine. "I may have flicked a switch, but I am not responsible for people's behaviour. Not everyone with the warrior gene turns aggressive and hostile. And people without the warrior gene can be just as angry, just as violent. It is still a choice."

"But you made them more vulnerable to losing control."

"I don't know. Maybe." She dropped her gaze back to the floor. "Our world has been generating this for a long while. Gang violence, road rage, bullying, racism, domestic violence, sexual assaults, school shootings. It's not new. It was getting worse before anything I did. I think that's what made it so easy, why it spread so quickly, even in the places I have never been to."

Sawyer was watching Corben, and I could feel the compassion he was sending across to her.

"Did you know all this?" I turned to him and heard the accusation in my tone.

He cleared his throat and took a moment before answering. "No, Nova, I didn't. I knew about the artificial enzymes. The same ones that Abe used on you. They are being reproduced all around the world. And they have spread like any other drug, as has the aggression and violence they create. But I knew it had to be more than that." Sawyer was now exuding a calm acceptance, and I felt him trying to wrap me up in it. "It sounds like Corben was forced into a corner and there were some unfortunate side effects. She is a powerful empath. Her anger would have spread to the people around her. And, like yours, her range is probably quite far reaching. But I don't think it's as simple as that either. I don't think we can blame her for every bit of violence in the world." He gave another small cough and a weak smile. "Corben is right. This has been brewing for a long time. We can't take away people's responsibility for their own choices, their own behaviour."

Corben returned his smile, lifting the corners of her mouth, but her lips were still pressed together. "Sawyer, you are being kinder than I deserve. I take responsibility for what I did. Even though I didn't mean to do it, I still carry that blame. That's why I have shielded my emotions now. That's why you can't read my feelings. I will not let myself spread any more anger."

"That's what we felt in Melbourne. You lifted the shield," I said.

Corben nodded. She rubbed her forehead, and her nostrils flared. "I can't trust myself anymore."

It was all too much. My brain felt like water swirling down a drain. I wished I were a turtle so I could pull my head into my shell and hide for a while.

"Nova, there's one more thing you need to hear." Corben's voice was soft, and the words seemed to hang in the air between us. "I believe you can deactivate the warrior gene, the anger that I activated. You're stronger than me. I can sense that. You can undo what I've done, and more. You can stop the anger, prevent more violence. You can make the world better again."

It felt like there were sparks flying off my skin, sending electrical shocks out into the air. But they were inside me too. Jolting through me. I was wired and I was freaking out.

Jackson was looking back and forth between Corben and me, as if struggling to keep up with things. His mouth hung slightly open, and his eyes were wide. A horrified dread in him added to the churning rage in me.

And yet, those kind, cocoa-brown eyes also shone with awe. I knew that he was wondering what I was capable of.

Because I was wondering the same thing.

Doing something good? Maybe.

Or possibly doing terrible things, just like my mother.

17

I needed to get away. My body wanted to shut down. I needed to process what I had heard.

It was super annoying that we were at my house.

I stood up in one swift move. My yoga instructor would have been proud. "I need some air. I'm going for a walk."

"I'll come," said Jackson, also rising to his feet.

"No, I want to be alone." I met his eyes and mouthed a "please" at him. He was pulling on his fingers to crack his knuckles, a sign of the tension I could feel in him, but he nodded.

"Nova, it's okay, don't go. I'll leave." Corben was struggling to get up from the armchair. I knew that would happen. Serves her right.

"Do whatever you want." I walked out.

Jackson's concern tugged at me, but I shrugged it off. I knew it was killing him not to follow me.

Sawyer called to Jet. There was no point in telling Jet not to come; he would not listen to me, not once Sawyer had given the order. Jet was supposed to protect me.

Even though now it seemed the only protection we needed was from my mother and the violence she was spreading. Like an evil witch. Or Satan. Or Voldemort.

At least Jet didn't talk, and he didn't expect me to either. He just walked beside me as if we were going for a walk. A fast, breathless, half-running walk. Then a really slow one.

Oh my god.

I did not know what else to say about it all.

△

When we got back to the house, Corben and Sawyer had gone. Jackson was waiting for me. I got the sense that he had been pacing the room.

"Are you okay?" he asked.

"Not really."

Jackson and Jet exchanged looks, and Jet mumbled something about needing to make a phone call. He would probably report in to Sawyer.

"Can we talk about this?" Jackson's voice was gentle, and his love felt like a soft blanket that draped itself around me, keeping me warm.

"I don't deserve that."

"Deserve what?"

"The way you feel about me." My tone was impatient. "There is something inside me that's dark and wrong."

"That's your takeaway from this? That there is something wrong with you?"

"She did all this. Triggered the warrior gene everywhere. She's like a tsunami of violence sweeping around the planet."

"Is that all?"

I could not tell if he was being sarcastic or trying to be kind. "Isn't that enough? My mother is evil. So, logically, scientifically, genetically, I am evil too."

"No, she was being used. She was sick and angry, and then her feelings triggered the warrior gene in some people, quite a few people, maybe a lot of people, in various places, all over the place, while she travelled around the world." He paused, probably realising he was making it sound worse. "But she didn't mean to. She's not evil. She just messed up, made some mistakes, and they took advantage of her. And she didn't create the artificial gene stuff. Sawyer says there is a dark web social media group for gangsters, and they share all their recipes." He was trying to add some humour, but I couldn't see the funny side. "You're not evil; it's more like you're the daughter of Darth Vader."

I glared at him. That was exactly my point.

"All our friends and family that have been hurt or killed – my dad, your brother, Ava, Alice, Mia's father, Sage's parents – she caused all that." My anger coated the words with fire. "And as for me, well, it was my fault that Sage and Finn were killed. I killed Abraham. And I have come between you and your twin brother. How much more wrong can you get?" My voice trembled as my anger shifted into pain and sorrow. I was a boat adrift, with no wind for my sails. My energy drained away, and I sighed. "I need to be alone. You should go."

"Stop it, Nova. I've seen that look on your face before. You're overthinking, overreacting." Jackson's eyes held concern, but a stubborn determination ran through his voice and I could sense that he was ready to argue with me. "You can't push me away. I'm staying."

He leaned in to kiss me.

It was a light kiss, just a gentle touch, his lips to mine. I could feel his love and his passion, but they were no match for the darkness that was slowly strangling me.

"You're as bad as Cooper." My voice was harsh. "Why do you think that a kiss makes everything better?"

Jackson flinched as if I'd slapped him. "Shit! I don't think that. And do you have to keep bringing up Cooper?" His own anger sparked and jumped, and I knew that I was feeding it.

"Okay, you're as bad as my previous boyfriend who thought that kissing me would make everything better and that I would fall at his feet in appreciation."

"I know you still mean Cooper."

I started laughing. It was that hysterical laughter that you can't control and can't stop, that makes you lose your breath and almost wet your pants.

Jackson looked at me with irritation, and it made me laugh harder. Tears leaked from my eyes. I snorted. He watched me and the frustration he was feeling spread over my skin like a rash. I snorted again.

"What was that all about?" he asked when I had finally run out of breath.

"I have no idea. I told you, there is something seriously wrong with me. It is not safe to be around me."

"I don't believe that. And I am not going anywhere."

We sat in silence while I worked on controlling myself, putting up some emotional walls. I knew it was the only way I would be able to get him to leave. And I needed him to go.

"Jack, I'm okay. I've calmed down now. I just want to be alone. Please." I kept my tone even, trying to sound convincing. "I just need to sort all this out in my head. Please."

Although he was reluctant, I ushered him to the door. His concern pulsed through my body, and I gave him what I hoped was a reassuring smile. It was a false one because I was not feeling reassured at all.

In my room, alone, I stood for a moment, letting a heavy fog settle over me. Then I fell onto my bed and buried my face into my pillow. So that I could scream without anyone hearing me.

△

Headlines shrieked at me from the News app on my phone.

Six killed in brawl at local football match.

Worst street violence in more than a decade.

Fear of reprisals in ongoing feud with Melbourne street gangs.

Retail staff afraid of going to work.

Police enforcing curfews.

The world was as angry as ever.

I felt like I was watching a movie where all the scenes were so dark that you couldn't really see what was happening. It was all in shadow.

And it was all my mother's fault.

So, what did that say about me?

△

I had been avoiding Jackson for over two weeks. Not responding to his texts or calls. I had made Jet tell him that I didn't want him staying over because I needed space.

And he was not the only one I was avoiding. I had sent Mia a message that I wasn't feeling well and not to come over. The same excuse allowed me to get out of my work shifts, and I was not attending Jet's self-defence training at the gym.

Jet was the only person I saw because he was living in my spare room. I couldn't avoid him. When he came home one day and asked me to contact Jackson, I knew that Jackson was getting desperate. Jet hated getting involved in relationship issues.

"Just tell him I need more time."

As he walked away, I heard Jet mumble under his breath, "I'm not a bloody messenger."

Whatever.

I was feeding into Jet's bad mood too.

Like a faulty electrical switch, I was tripping from anger to apathy, hatred to heartbreak, disgust to despair. It was focused on my mother. And it was focused on myself.

It was also impacting anyone I encountered. Because that's what empaths do.

And that was why I had to stay away from people.

My nightmares were back. The black-haired woman, which I now recognised clearly as my mother, was leading me into the darkness. In the dream I had an urge to follow her through the fire, but I was afraid. I didn't know what was beyond the blackness, and I was afraid of being burned. When I awoke, that fear was quickly replaced by resentment. I was not about to follow Corben anywhere.

Annoyed by my tossing and turning at night, Ripley, my kitten, was spending her nights on Jet's bed instead of mine. She only came to me when she was hungry, and I couldn't blame her. Even I didn't want to be around me.

My life was a complete shit show.

When I looked at myself in the mirror, my face was drawn, my lips were pursed as if I had sucked on something sour, and my eyes were red and puffy.

My own mood swings were making me nauseous.

I was still angry but, most of all, I was now afraid.

Words define a person. Child, daughter, friend, girl-friend, empath. But now my identity had changed. I didn't know what words to use anymore. 'Mum' was an unfamiliar word to me, and 'mother' had become synonymous with something horrible. Something painful and frightening.

Who was I now?

And what was I capable of?

18

There was a knock on the door. I ignored it. Jet could get it.

When he didn't appear, I remembered he was at the gym with Jackson and Han. Jackson was working to advance a belt ranking in Karate, and after a forced rest with his shoulder injury he was doing extra training sessions. At least I knew that it couldn't be him at the door.

There was further knocking. It was getting louder and more adamant.

Then I heard giggling and sensed the gentle warmth of Mia.

There were others with her, and their excitement floated through the wooden door like the large bubbles that kids blow with those plastic wands. When they clashed against the depression and the hostility that I was carrying around, the bubbles burst.

"Nova, we know you're there. Answer the door."

It didn't sound like they were going to leave me alone, so I heaved myself out of the armchair. It wasn't easy. I really should do something about the springs, but it was comfortable when you were sitting in it.

Mia, Imogen, Spencer, and Devon stood on my front porch with tentative smiles. The sun had almost given up for the day, but their energy was like a sparkling string of coloured fairy lights shining in the dusky shadows. They were dressed up to go out.

"This is an intervention." Mia walked past me into the house. "You don't have to see Jackson, but you do have to see us."

"It's a girls' night." Imogen followed her.

"Cheap drinks for students at Club 393," said Spencer. "And I am designated driver." She gently put her hand on her pregnant belly.

"I have to study for my Bio exam." Resisting the guilty twinges that rode through me, I clenched my teeth.

"It's not till Monday and its open book. You have heaps of time." Devon dismissed my excuses with a flick of her hair. She did the same subjects as me, so she knew what she was saying. "And we can only stay out till curfew, so it won't be a late night."

"I don't really feel like it." I looked down at the pyjamas I was still wearing. In fact, I'd had them on for two days.

"What will you remember when you are old? All the times you stayed home studying for your exams or going out with the girls?" Mia pulled at one of my hands and wrinkled her nose. "Come on, we're not leaving until you come with us, so you may as well get in the shower."

Resistance was useless.

When I came out of the bathroom, Imogen was ready to do my makeup. The others were sorting through my wardrobe and arguing about what I should wear.

They chose tight jeans and a slim-fitting, black, long-sleeved shirt. I arched my back in a stretch, realising I had hardly moved all day. The mirror reflected tired green eyes. While the black eyeliner was heavier than I normally wore, it suited my mood. I forced my face into a determined smile.

"Don't forget your student card for the cheap drinks," said Devon.

It was already tucked into the back of my phone case, along with my debit card and licence. I put a lip gloss and the house key into my pocket.

"Okay, I'm ready."

Anger and fear still pulsed within me, but I buried them. Instead, I drew on the friendship and laughter that bounced around me. That gave me the energy I needed to leave the house.

"Let's go, bitches!" Mia pushed us all out the door.

△

Three cocktails later, I floated on a warm buzz. Leaving Mia and Imogen on the dance floor, I joined Spencer and Devon at the table. I wiped the perspiration from my forehead with the back of my hand. The sliders and chips we had ordered had only just arrived. It was a busy night for the club, and the kitchen wasn't coping very well with the unexpected demand.

Even though it was barely 8 pm, Club 393 was pumping. Well, pumping for our town, which was relatively tame compared to Melbourne. Cheap drinks were a big draw card, and young people were tired of hiding away at home. The club set their lockout curfew at 10 pm, so you had to get in early to make it worthwhile.

Giant speakers thumped out a steady rhythm, like a heartbeat for the masses. There was a queue at the bar, and customers yelled their orders above the roar, communicating with exaggerated hand gestures and holding up fingers to indicate the number of drinks. Bar staff navigated through the maze of tables to deliver food and collect the empty glasses.

Jet had come to check on me after he had finished at the gym and was standing outside with one of the security bouncers. In comparison with Jet the bouncer was short, but he was solid in build, and his muscular arms bulged from a black shirt with *SECURITY* plastered across the back. The sides of his head were shaved, and he had a spiky mohawk that became long at the back, like a mullet. A mohawk-mullet, if that is even a thing. He was posturing and puffing out his chest, and I could sense by the clench in Jet's jaw and the shudder that ran through me that Jet thought the bouncer was a dickhead. But he also considered it useful to stay on good terms with the security teams in town.

The vibe was friendly and lively, and I let it filter through me like a cleansing breeze.

Around 9 pm, a large group of young men came in from football training. I recognised a few of the faces, boys from school last year. Mia was also scanning them. She looked relieved that Kenji was not there to crash our girls' night.

Aggression rolled off the football players in sweaty waves as they pushed and shoved and slapped each other on the back. They were well-built athletes, loud and rowdy, and they dominated the space. With a sense of entitlement and arrogance, they elbowed their way through to the front of the bar. People stood aside, but resentment followed them. The party vibe had changed. The room suddenly felt like a pot of boiling water with the lid rattling on top.

A small group of girls were still courageously dancing, but most people watched the footballers with wary eyes, instinctively huddling into closed groups.

One of the footballers lumbered onto the dance floor. He was a big guy and unsteady on his feet, so that when he stumbled into the girls dancing there, it looked almost like he was trying to tackle them. The girls pushed him away, closed ranks, and turned their backs to him. Ignoring the clear message that he was not welcome, he swung his arms around a young Asian girl. Long, dark curls hung around his face, almost covering his eyes, but not the sneer that was stretched across his mouth as he pulled her backside up against his hips. She struggled to get away while he gyrated against her body. Her fear felt like an icy-cold river running down my back.

I stood up with a jerk, accidently knocking over my chair. Her terror had joined with the fury that I had buried, and it was a lethal combination. Both ice and fire.

Mia grabbed my arm, but it was to stand with me, not to stop me, and the other girls were at my back.

"Hey, you! Leave her alone." My voice was loud enough to be heard above the music. "It's pretty clear she doesn't want to dance with you."

"Fuck off, bitch."

"Cole, come on mate. We came here for a drink, not to harass anyone." A tall, red-haired footballer had come up on the other side and was pulling on his friend's arm. He mouthed a "sorry" at the girl and gave a placating smile. I knew him from school, though he was a year ahead of us. His name was Sloane.

Cole turned at the interruption and swung his fist into Sloane's face. There was a squelching sound as blood splattered in a perfect crimson arch across the dance floor. Likely a broken nose.

That was all it took for the pot to boil over.

Fighting broke out between the footballers and the other patrons, but also amongst the footballers themselves. The security bouncers and Jet were ducking punches, hauling people off of each other, and trying to re-establish order. Stools were thrown, glasses were smashed, tables were overturned. Some of the waiters had retreated behind the bar for safety, while others joined the brawl. The deep bass in the music set the tempo for the primal aggression playing out in this urban battlefield.

Cole had a tight grip on the young girl's hair and was pulling her backwards. She screamed. He yelled abuse. I jumped onto his back, while he bucked and tried to shake me off. Devon pulled at his hands, and Mia had her arms wrapped around the young girl.

I blinked away tears when Cole's elbow connected with my ribs, but I hung on.

Then came the sound of gunshots.

As if synchronised, everyone dropped to the floor and scrambled to find cover under tables or behind the bar.

Two guys faced each other across the room, pistols drawn, like cowboys in a gunfight. One of them was Sloane, and his teammates stood behind him with their weapons also drawn. There were mostly knives, but a couple of them had handguns too. They faced the security guard with the mohawk. He had fired the warning shots.

Hostility whipped through the room like a deadly tornado. There was a sense that we were balanced delicately on the edge, just a step away from the path of destruction.

I had been squatting beside an upturned table, watching the stand-off, and was caught by surprise when Cole seized me by the neck.

"Stupid bitch," he growled in a low voice. "This is all your fault."

Pulling and scratching at his fingers, I tried to loosen the tightening grip he had around my throat. I felt as effective as a mouse caught in a trap and struggled to draw a full breath. My body was flooded by his fury, and it just added to the flames of anger that were already riding through me. Part of my brain knew I should be trying to calm him, or freeze him with fear, but it was hard to focus when I couldn't breathe properly.

It took Jet less than a minute to break Cole's grip on me, and then he had him on the floor with his arms cuffed behind his back.

"Nova, are you okay?" Concern coated Jet's voice.

Rage still roared through my blood, and I was breathing hard, but I nodded, not trusting my voice to work. I rubbed at the skin of my throat.

He gestured towards the young girl who was crouched on the floor, with Mia huddled over her and Devon beside them both. "Take her into the toilets with those two, and wait there for me."

I managed another nod.

"Where are the other girls?" Jet was looking around as he spoke, and I followed his gaze to find Imogen and Spencer peering out from behind the bar. "I'll get them out of here."

Spencer was squatting with her hands protectively over her pregnant belly, and Imogen had an arm around her. They were safe.

I ushered Mia, Devon, and the young girl into the bathroom. The walls dampened the noise from the club, but we could still hear yelling and shouting over the blare of a distorted heavy-metal guitar solo. I wished that someone would turn the music off.

Mia was pale, and her fear sent prickles all over my skin, but she was also radiating her usual compassion. "We're safe now," she said to the young girl. "Are you hurt?"

The girl shook her head, but then bolted into one of the cubicles and vomited. Mia was behind her, holding back her hair and murmuring reassurance.

Devon stood silently, with her back pressed hard up against the door as if standing guard. Her anxiety was heavy and made me feel as if I was carrying a sack of potatoes.

My stomach rolled with nausea, I had a splitting headache, and my throat burned. I was holding on, but barely.

There was the sound of a flush, and the girl came out of the cubicle and gave us a weak smile. "He was a creep."

"Yeah, he was," said Mia, and her breath came out in a deep sigh.

"Are you Devon?" The young girl had turned to Devon, who nodded. "I'm Yimo. You're dating my brother, Han."

Devon blushed. "Oh, right. Hi, Yimo." She took off her round glasses to give them a wipe, blinking heavily at Yimo, and gave a small smile.

"Mum and Dad can't wait to meet you. They keep nagging Han to invite you for dinner. He has dated a few guys, but he never brought them home. Now, all he talks about is you. Mum thinks you're the one. She's secretly planning on grandchildren already." Yimo looked at me. "And you must be Nova. I know Jack Lewis. He's Han's best friend. He's so cute. We thought he might be the one for Han for a while, but Jack reckons he was waiting for you. Jack does karate, and I do too. I've been doing it longer than Jack, but Han is the best. I practice with them sometimes. Han is going to kill me when he finds out I was here tonight. I'm not eighteen yet, but my friend got me in on a fake ID."

Yimo was babbling. I figured it was probably shock. There was a tightness to my limbs that I thought came from her, and although Mia was gently rubbing Yimo's back, in a weird way it was soothing for me as well.

The door bumped against Devon, and she let out a short scream.

"It's just me. It's Jet," he called out.

Devon pulled the door open a fraction and Jet put his head through. "The police are here. You girls need to get home. It's almost curfew."

Mia and Yimo moved towards Jet, and he pushed the door back to let them all pass through. With the door opening so wide, it was as if the air was suddenly sucked out of the room and replaced with a surge of dark fury. I felt like I'd been punched in the stomach.

The floor swayed beneath me. I rushed into a toilet cubicle and vomited into the bowl.

It reminded me of the time I'd been given the warrior gene. Those artificial hormones that created aggression had made me physically sick. I flushed the toilet and stood up, but then had to hang on to the wall. The room was spinning.

"Nova, you'd better wait here. Lock yourself in that cubicle. I'll get these girls out, and then I'll be back." Jet's voice was calm and reassuring.

I nodded, returned to the cubicle, pushed the door shut, and turned the lock. The lid was down, so I sat on the toilet seat and hung my head between my knees.

Incoherent thoughts raced through my brain, and I felt like a snow globe that had been thoroughly shaken. There were the things my mother had said, there were memories of Abraham and what he had done to me, Finn being killed, Sage dying, Jackson being stabbed. It swirled around and rained down on me. But it was not like snowflakes; it was more like the burning ash from a volcano.

Cole's words flashed across my brain like a neon sign. *It was all my fault.*

I should not have come out tonight. *It was all my fault.* I was dangerous, like my mother.

These thoughts were not helping.

I shut my eyes and focused on what I could hear, smell, and feel. Okay, not the smell. I was in the bathroom, after all. The music had finally been cut, and there was only a low murmur of voices, no yelling. There were thumps and bumps, and I imagined that the tables and stools were being shifted back into place. I could hear a clinking of glasses and bottles. It sounded like people were cleaning up.

Reaching down, I placed my hands flat on the tiles. They felt smooth and cold, though a little sticky. *Eww.* I placed them on the walls instead and wriggled my toes in my boots, pressing my feet hard against the floor.

My grounding techniques were helping, but both fear and anger still rippled through me in painful shivers. Bouts of vertigo had made me feel unbalanced, off-kilter, lopsided. I had to open my eyes. It was worse with them shut.

I brought up a mental picture of Sage's smiling face. "Stick together?" Her voice was a familiar song in my head. But, somehow, I couldn't bring myself to give the usual reply. Since her death I had been holding it together, mostly, but I wasn't sure that I could keep it up much longer.

"I need you," I whispered to myself, to Sage. "I need you to be here to pick me up. Because you were the strong one." I had always known that.

Tears rolled down my face, and I watched them drip onto the grey tiles, like tiny puddles of anguish.

I was falling apart.

19

My heart fluttered. I felt him as soon as he entered Club 393.

The main bathroom door clunked as it opened and closed. There were light footsteps, then a gentle knock on the cubicle door. I reached up to unlock the latch and sat back on the toilet lid.

Jackson was wearing his new black biker jacket, with the collar up around his neck. Maybe it was because I had not seen him for a while, but with a black t-shirt, blue jeans, and his black biker boots, he looked as sexy as hell. He pushed his messy helmet-hair back from his face and looked at me through narrowed eyes. I could sense his concern, but also a prickle of irritation.

"You've been ghosting me for two weeks." His voice was soft but stern.

"No, I haven't." Anger rumbled through me.

"I'm calling bullshit on that." Jackson raised his eyebrows, but his mouth stayed in a firm line. "Do I get an apology?"

"Sorry." My tone was pure sarcasm, so it was no apology at all.

"Hmm. What's going on?"

I shrugged.

His eyes narrowed. "Can you walk? The girls are waiting for you in the car park."

"What? I thought they'd gone home." I gave a cough to clear my throat. It was still sore. "I thought Jet must have called you."

He shook his head and leaned up against the doorframe. "Nope, and nope. Mia called me. And they wouldn't leave without you. I was at the surgery with Dad. The police asked him to open to treat injuries, but there hasn't been anything too serious."

I sat still, saying nothing, one hand on the wall to keep me steady. The vertigo was almost gone, but I still felt a little nauseous.

"I've never been in here before. Is my name written up somewhere?" Jackson nodded at the toilet door, which was covered with names, initials, hearts, and swear words.

Despite my irritation at him, I felt a laugh bubbling in my dry throat. "I don't think so."

"That's disappointing. Do you have a pen?"

I shook my head and felt the laugh gaining more strength. The hostility that had saturated my body was ebbing away.

"Well, next time I come in here it would be nice to see a heart with our initials in it."

"Oh yeah, and when are you expecting to come back?"

"I'm not sure, but it's cleaner than the men's toilets, so who knows." He shrugged.

A laugh finally escaped through my nose as a snort.

Jackson gave me a wry smile and held out his hand. His eyes were crinkled in the corners with concern. I took his hand and felt the warmth of his love. It seeped into me, surrounded me, settled over me.

Even though I did not deserve it.

I stumbled twice, but his grip on me was strong and solid as we shuffled through the debris. Jet was standing with a security bouncer and a police officer at the bar. He barely looked at us, but I saw a small hand movement. It was waving us to the door. I knew he wanted us out of the way before we drew attention.

Mia, Imogen, and Spencer were waiting in the carpark, behind Spencer's car. Their heads were huddled together, and they stopped whispering as we drew close.

"Where is Yimo?" My voice was still a bit croaky.

"Devon took her home. Jet organised a lift for them with one of the security guys," said Imogen.

"What was Yimo doing here?" Jackson pursed his lips and shook his head. "Han will be so pissed off at her."

"She said the same thing." Mia nodded in agreement, then turned to me. "Are you okay?"

Before I could answer, there was a thumping sound from Spencer's car boot. The girls exchanged a guilty glance.

Jackson frowned at them. "What is going on?"

"Umm, we have a body in the boot." Spencer wore a deadpan expression.

I shivered. "You have a what in the boot?"

"A person, not a body. It's a person." Mia spoke quickly and bumped her elbow against Spencer.

"They're alive," said Imogen in a muffled voice, turning around in a circle, scanning the carpark.

It was empty except for us.

Giant floodlights were reflected in the puddles left by a recent shower of rain. Jackson's motorbike and three cars were parked nearby. Industrial bins were lined up outside the back door to the club.

"Oh shit, do I really want to know?" Jackson put a hand on the boot of Spencer's car.

"It's Griffin. He needs to talk to Nova." Spencer spoke firmly and pushed Jackson's hand away. "We can't open the boot here. It's not safe. He's here about Cooper. And he's bleeding."

"He's been beaten up. But I don't think it's serious. He might need some stitches for a gash under his eye," said Mia, the daughter of a nurse. "We don't trust him after what he did to Nova, so we put him in the boot."

"We should take him to the police station," said Jackson.

Banging came from the boot again.

"No, I promised him," said Spencer.

"We can take him to Dad's surgery then." Jackson gave her a hard look.

There was more banging.

I could sense that, though she was wary, Spencer wanted to hear what Griffin had to say. She wanted news of Cooper. "No. He's afraid of being seen. I don't know what's going on, but I promised I would keep him safe and get him to you, Nova." She looked at me with wide, imploring, trusting eyes. "It's ten minutes to curfew. Can we please go back to your place?"

I shook and then nodded my head in one move.

Mia opened the back car door for me, while Imogen got into the front seat. "Nova is coming with us, Jack. It is still our girls' night out."

Spencer made a small tap on the boot and gave a giggle. "And what a night it has been."

Jackson swore crudely but moved off, alone, to his motorbike without arguing any further.

△

Back at my place, Jackson checked Griffin for any weapons, but he had nothing. Then he and Mia worked together on cleaning and disinfecting Griffin's injuries. They agreed that the deep gash under his eye probably needed stitches, but butterfly strips would do for now.

I messaged Jet that the girls and Jackson were staying over, and that we were all okay. I knew he would stay at his own place to give us space. Jackson was annoyed that I didn't tell Jet about Griffin, but Griffin had refused to talk if I did.

Although I was tired, Jackson's wariness of Griffin kept me alert as well. Mia and Imogen were also on edge, and I could feel the tension crackling in the air.

Spencer, on the other hand, was treating Griffin like an out-of-town relative.

"Coop had made plans to take a few days off and come and see his folks." Griffin held up a hand, cutting off Jackson's protest. "It was a surprise, so he didn't tell you. He was supposed to be coming down this morning and was going to stay on for the weekend. He said he would see his parents today, join his mates at footy training tonight, and see you guys over the weekend."

Spencer gave him a small nod and a smile.

"I had a job in Dandenong, so I drove up after work, and we were supposed to meet at the footy oval. He wasn't there, and he wasn't responding to texts. I followed the footy team to Club 393 and that's when I saw you, Nova, and the rest of you girls." Griffin kept shutting his eyes and swallowing as he spoke.

I got the impression he did not like seeing his own blood on the gauze pads that were piling up beside him. It made me queasy too. Despite the warmth of the central heating, cold chills ran down my spine. I knew it was from Griffin, though he was hiding his fear. This was a vastly different person to the one who had been to my house before. The person who had threatened me with an ice pick.

"Theo knows Cooper is your friend, Nova. Initially, we thought he was your boyfriend." There was a loud sniff from Jackson and then a yelp from Griffin. Jackson was not being gentle with the swab of disinfectant. "Theo sent me here last time. I was supposed to get information about you. I'm sorry about all that." Griffin looked up at me with apologetic eyes. I just nodded and let him continue. "When Coop decided to come to Melbourne with me, Theo had already gone to the Gold Coast. Neo checked in on us all the time, and I thought he was reporting back to Theo. Now, I'm not so sure. Theo got back to Melbourne a few days ago and straight away Neo suggested Coop come back here for the weekend. And he won't let Coop train at the gym with the rest of us. He takes him to that one where your friend has a youth centre. I am starting to think Neo is trying to keep Coop away from Theo. Cooper is a good guy. A really good guy."

Griffin stopped and took a mouthful of water. Jackson and Mia had finished their first-aid treatment. He flexed his hands, which were red and swollen around the knuckles. "Thanks." He looked up at all of us and gave a smirking grin, more like the Griffin I knew.

"You still haven't said why they had to hide you and why you had to see Nova." Jackson glowered at him.

"I finally heard from Cooper just as that fight started at Club 393. I was about to leave, but a couple of guys jumped me. They were serious. They wanted to hurt me. Bad. I managed to get away when that gun went off. And I hid.

Waiting for you." Griffin nodded towards me. "I don't know those guys, but I don't think they are from around here. One of them had the tattoo." Griffin pulled down the collar of his shirt, and low on his neck was a small triangular 'A' tattoo.

I had seen those tattoos before. Abraham's followers had them. Although Theo had taken over from Abraham, it seemed he had not changed the tattoo marking for his gang.

My head was starting to spin again. The room seemed to shift. We were all standing around the kitchen bench, so I pulled out a stool and sat down. Mia moved beside me and placed a steadying hand on my arm. She gave Griffin a glare.

"The thing is, Coop said he'd been asked to do a special paint job in one of the new high-rise offices in Richmond. It was last-minute, urgent, and they were paying double to get it finished over the weekend." Griffin looked directly at me. "I got Cooper on this crew. The jobs always come through me, not directly to him. Coop also said he thought he'd lost his phone, but it was at our flat, on his bed, when he got home. I don't believe that either. He wouldn't forget his phone." Griffin shook his head; the smile had been replaced by fear in his eyes.

I clenched my hands into fists.

"It just seems like someone didn't want Cooper to leave Melbourne. And then there were the guys here. Maybe they followed me, or maybe they were already here, watching you." Griffin's eyes were wide. "Either way, they didn't want me around. I needed somewhere safe for tonight. And, well, Coop talks about you guys all the time. I didn't know where else to go. I can't be on the road after curfew."

"Have you told Cooper all this?" Spencer's voice trembled, and her worry burned in my already sore throat.

"I'll tell him tomorrow, in person, when I get back. It's not a good idea to say too much over the phone."

"Coop should just come home," said Jackson tersely. His frustration felt like sharp prickles rubbing against my skin.

"He doesn't want to come back." Griffin looked from me to Jackson and gave another smirk. "He says he wants a break from being here."

I could taste the irritation we all felt at Griffin's smug attitude, even Spencer, but the concern we felt for Cooper felt like a yawning pit before us.

△

Griffin was sleeping on the floor in the lounge, and he was already snoring loudly. His feet hung off the end of the foam mattress. There had been no other choice but to let him stay.

Although he seemed harmless enough now that he was asleep, Mia eyed Griffin warily. "I'm glad you're here, Jack."

"At least someone is." He looked at me through hooded eyes.

I bit down on my bottom lip and turned away.

"We all are," said Mia kindly. "But I am sleeping in Nova's bed. You can take the couch out here."

I heard a snort from Jackson as he caught the pillow she threw at him. There was a giggle as Mia scampered off into my bedroom, and Jackson gave a quiet laugh at her disappearing back.

Imogen and Spencer had already gone into the spare room, where Jet had been sleeping. They would share the bed in there.

There was another bedroom in the house, but it was my father's room and no one else had ever slept in there. It just didn't seem right. Not yet. I wasn't ready to stop thinking of it as Dad's room.

When I moved into the bathroom to clean my teeth, Jackson followed me.

He shut the door and leaned back against it. His chest was bare, and his jeans sat low on his hips. I swallowed twice, while he gave me a shy smile. "We keep meeting in bathrooms."

His smile did not conceal the anxiety that was evident in the creases across his forehead. I was sure his bare chest was intentional, though. He knew he looked good.

I shut my eyes in a long blink. Self-loathing rose in my throat like bile.

Everything Griffin had said was a reminder that I was dangerous. Violence followed me and hurt the people I loved. I attracted it and I spread it. Like my mother.

I wished that she had not come back from the dead. And that was a horrible thing to say.

But, then again, I was a horrible person.

Jackson deserved someone better.

"Thanks for coming to the club tonight," I said politely. "I'm sorry that Mia made you come out."

His smile disappeared behind a frown. "Don't do that, Nova. We need to talk."

I bit down on my bottom lip again and gave a light shrug. "Whatever."

To avoid looking at his chest, I sat down on the edge of the bath and kept my gaze on the floor.

Jackson shuffled his feet. "You still haven't told me why you've been ghosting me for two weeks."

"I needed time to think."

"Oh yeah, what were you thinking about?"

I gave a deep sigh. "I've realised I'm not a very safe person to be around. Bad things happen to people close to me. It's obvious from tonight. Cooper has joined a gangster cult. Because of me." The words tumbled out in a rush.

"Nova, stop it. You're not responsible for his stupid decisions. If anything, it's because of me."

I studied the neat pattern of terracotta tiles on the floor. It was a perfect symmetry, squares, and lines, until it got to the steel drain in the middle of the floor. The tiles there had been cut into small triangles to fit around the drain, but it was still done with a matching orderliness. It was somehow comforting.

With a deep breath, I looked up to find Jackson's cocoa-brown eyes boring into mine. "I'm no good for you either. You got stabbed. Next time it might be worse. I think it's better if I stay away from you."

He blew out his breath in a loud exhale. His frustration now felt like a wasp stinging my skin. Repeatedly.

"So that's it. You're still overthinking this and you're being ridiculous."

I stood up and glared at him. "I am not. When I look in the mirror, I don't even know who I'm looking at anymore. What if I turn out to be bad like her, like Corben? I have a darkness inside me, Jack. You would be safer away from me."

"No, no way. That's not your decision to make. I decide where I want to be, who I want to be with." Jackson's voice was calm and steady, although he was fuming inside. It was like steam building up. He was always better than me at controlling his emotions. "And stop being a martyr."

"Ouch." I was pouting, but I couldn't help it.

Jackson pursed his lips and looked up at the ceiling. I knew he was composing his words. "You are not Corben. And anyway, she may not have always made the best decisions, but she is not a bad person. Life is not a fairy tale. People are not all good or all bad. Nova, you are the same person you were last year, six months ago, one month ago."

"Am I, though?" I felt like I had been dancing to a different beat these last few weeks, and even then, my timing was out.

"Yes. You are the same girl who would prefer to stay in and watch *The Walking Dead* spin-offs instead of going to a party. Whose favourite colour is green, whose favourite drink is a raspberry slushy, even in winter. The same girl that loves reading, and loves kittens, but doesn't like the smell of coffee. The same girl that loves … me." His voice rose on the last word. It wasn't a question but more like a plea, and resisting it was like fighting gravity.

His next words were almost a whisper. "Nova, nothing is wrong with you. Quite the opposite. You light up the world. I can't see any darkness in you, but even if it is there, I love you anyway."

Jackson took my hand and placed it on his chest. His skin was warm, and beneath I could feel the steady beat of his heart. It was calling to mine. "You, more than anyone, should know how I feel about you. And I am not going anywhere."

His love felt warm, protective, and snug around me. It left no room for my darkness.

"I love you too." I heaved a sigh. The words were too small, too simple for what I felt for Jackson. There was a dramatic shift in my body. It was if everything was slotting back into the right place and I was dancing back in time with the beat.

Jackson took another step and bent his head to kiss me lightly, but then he pulled away quickly. "I'm sorry, I shouldn't have done that. I didn't mean to imply that a kiss makes everything better."

My heart twisted in pain. It had hurt him when I'd told him that, and I had known that it would. I really did not deserve his love. "No, I'm sorry. I shouldn't have said that. It wasn't fair, and it wasn't true."

I slid my fingers up his arms, over the swell of his biceps, across to his chest and rested them on his phoenix tattoo. He watched me. There was a longing in his eyes, and I could feel it singeing the hairs all over my body. I stood on my tiptoes to press my lips against his, and a flare of heat punched through me as I kissed him.

"Nova, I'm here for you. Whatever happens. Promise me that you'll stop pushing me away." He rested against me, his forehead to my forehead, his nose to my nose, our lips not touching but almost. "Say it, Wilson, and mean it."

I hid a secret smile at his use of my surname. It meant he was serious.

"Lewis, I'm sorry for ghosting you and I promise I will stop pushing you away," I repeated quietly.

He pulled me into a closer embrace and murmured against my ear. "Just as well, because I have a feeling this is our epic love."

I chuckled. "That's way too much pressure."

He shrugged and nudged his nose against mine. "Is this okay?" He was asking permission to kiss me again. I really had hurt him.

"Always."

It was a lingering kiss, and I leaned into him. His love peeled away the last of the fury I had been hoarding.

Jackson pulled away and gave me one of his slow, sultry winks. "I have to say, I am kind of diggin' these bathroom rendezvous." He walked out, closing the door behind him.

I stood there, alone, suddenly cold, looking at my reflection in the mirror. The smile dropped from my face.

Green eyes blazed back at me. I could see the desire he had ignited, and my lips were red from his kisses, but the darkness still skulked within me. Jackson may not see it, but I could. Behind my eyes, under my skin.

My chest rose beneath my favourite *Harry Potter* pyjama t-shirt as I took a deep breath.

He was right. People were not all darkness or all light. It was not that simple.

I could be both.

My heart was beating in a steady rhythm, a match to Jackson's. His love lit up the shadow in me with a brightness that was good and pure.

It was clear that I needed him. I needed his light, his purity.

I just hoped I wasn't dragging him into the darkness.

20

The next morning, I loaned out most of my clean clothes to the girls. It was a reminder that I really needed to do a load of washing. Another thing I hadn't bothered with lately.

Jackson had found his own black AC/DC t-shirt that I had borrowed from him sometime last year. I liked to wear it to bed. It was tight across his chest, and it also emphasised the muscles in his arms. I wrapped my arms around him from behind.

"It doesn't fit you. I want that back," I whispered.

He swung to face me with a smug smile and pulled my arms into a lock behind his back. "Don't worry, I'll return it to you."

His love was warm and cosy. I knew he was glad to have me back to normal. If I could ever be called normal.

Spencer cleared her throat and jiggled her keys impatiently. She had already dropped Mia and Imogen home earlier and had returned to take Griffin into town, to his car. I knew she wanted more time with him to question him about Cooper.

"Yeah. Let's go." I broke away from Jackson and pulled on his leather jacket. Another thing I had permanently borrowed from him. I gave an internal smile and felt the joy spread through me.

Jackson and I followed Spencer on his motorbike.

It was only a short ride, but the air was crisp, the sun was out, and it was a beautiful morning. I felt like I was dancing on clouds. Cuddled in close against Jackson's back, my arms were tight around him and we shared our body heat. It was a safe and familiar space.

Griffin's car was parked in a narrow side lane off the main street, around the corner from the ice-cream shop. There was no one else around, but we could hear a gentle buzz of small-town traffic, and occasional laughter or voices that drifted our way from the few people that were having either late breakfast or morning tea at the cafés along the main road. The buildings lining the lane were mostly small industrial storefronts.

"Tell Cooper we miss him." Spencer had a glint of silver in her eyes.

"I will." Griffin gave her a wide smile.

He turned to me, but I just nodded at him and did not return the smile. I was not forgetting the ice pick that quickly.

Griffin shuffled his feet and put his hands in his pockets. "Be careful what you say to Cooper over the phone. After seeing those guys last night, I reckon Theo is having you watched, Nova. I don't know what he has planned, but he doesn't like you. Not at all."

"I know. Thanks." I gave him another nod.

We watched as first Griffin, then Spencer, drove off.

"I'm glad he's gone. Maybe Coop likes him, but I'm still not sure he can be trusted. And he's working for Theo."

Jackson scratched the back of his head and gave me a grin. "What now?"

"I should study. I have an exam on Monday."

"Want some company?"

I nodded. "But we are going to study."

"Of course." He gave me a playful wink as he swung his leg over the bike.

"Nova!" There was a shout from across the street. It was Nigel, who had just pulled up. He was on early shift to open the ice-cream shop.

I moved onto the road, heading towards him. Nigel waited for me next to his car. He alternated between a smile for me and a wary glance at Jackson. I glanced back at Jackson. Sitting astride his large, black motorbike, wearing dark sunglasses, black jeans, and with his leather jacket opened to show the swell of muscles under the tight AC/DC t-shirt, he did give off a threatening vibe. Especially as he was smirking at Nigel. I shook my head and smothered a chuckle. Poor Nigel.

As I reached the curb, Nigel stepped backwards to avoid my 'hello' hug, and both of us turned at the sound of a car approaching. It slowed down. The windows were tinted dark. I watched the front passenger window roll halfway down, and a short, slim pole poked out. There were two loud, sharp cracks. It was like the car had backfired. Then the engine revved and the car picked up speed as it squealed around the corner and disappeared down the main street.

When I turned back to Nigel, he was holding the side of his head. Blood was seeping through his fingers. Then he just dropped into a squat on the cement pavement.

I stared at him, puzzled. "Nigel, what are you doing?"

"I think I've been shot." His voice came out in a croak.

It had been a rifle poking from the car window. And the cracks were gunshots. My brain had finally caught up. I drew my shoulders back and took a deep breath; I knew I had to hold myself together.

Nigel had curled himself into a ball, sitting on the ground with his arms pulled up over his head. He rocked slowly back and forth as if doing a yoga move, and he was crying. There was a lot of blood, all over his face. I wiped it gently with my hands, trying to find the source. There were not any obvious wounds. Just blood. Lots of blood. It was a dull red, thin, and almost watery. The rusty smell caught in the back of my throat. It made me gag. I swallowed firmly and started breathing through my mouth.

"Where are you hit? Where does it hurt?"

Nigel moaned. His eyes were wide and unfocused.

I squatted beside him and rocked back on my heels, wondering what to do. Strong hands pulled at my arms, lifting me up to stand.

Jackson touched my face and wiped at my tears. I had not even realised I was crying. His arms wrapped around me, and he kissed me once, twice, three times. It was as if he was reassuring himself that I was okay.

"Were you hit?"

I gulped as if the air was suddenly thin and I couldn't get enough of it. "No, not me. It's Nigel, but I can't see where he's hurt."

Jackson bent and ran his hands over Nigel's face, arms, and chest with a practiced expertise. "Mate, it's your ear. A bullet has nicked your ear. It's taken a chunk out. I don't know where that wedge of skin is. But you're okay. It's just bleeding."

Jackson was looking at the ground around us. All I could see was blood on the grass, and all over Nigel's face and shirt. All over my clean shirt. And on my hands. I wiped them on my jeans, and the blood made more dirty smudges. My skin felt clammy.

"Everything else seems to be okay. He'll be okay. I'm ringing Dad." Jackson paused as he pulled off his jacket and then the AC/DC t-shirt. Holding this against Nigel's ear with his left hand, he dialled on his phone with his right. He looked at me. "Are you sure you're okay?"

My face was probably a bit green. I gave a rapid nod. "Yeah, I'm fine. What can I do?"

"Call Jet."

△

Jet, Dr Lewis, the police, and an ambulance arrived within seconds of each other. Nigel's ear was bandaged, and he was given a shot of something to numb the pain.

"Do you know who they were?" Jet asked.

"No. It was a black Mitsubishi Pajero. The windows were a dark tint. I didn't get the license plate because I wasn't looking for it. They had gone before I even realized what had happened." Jackson was calm and articulate. He lowered his voice and took a few steps away from where Nigel lay on the ambulance stretcher. "They had an easy shot if they wanted to kill him, so I don't think they meant to."

Jet raised his eyebrows and glanced at me. Jackson gave a small but definite shake of his head.

I knew Jet was asking if they had meant to shoot me.

Jackson kissed the top of my head and pressed the bloody AC/DC t-shirt into my hands. He was wearing his jacket, but his torso was bare underneath. "You said you wanted this back." He gave me a feeble smile.

I nodded but couldn't manage to raise the corners of my mouth. Even breathing through my mouth, I could still smell the blood.

Dr Lewis came over and gave my back a gentle pat before he climbed into the ambulance with the stretcher. "He'll be fine, Nova. Don't worry. Come up to the hospital this afternoon. You'll be able to see him then."

△

Jackson took me home and Jet followed us. The two of them went over every small detail from last night and this morning while I put the washing on.

Jet was fuming that we had not told him about Griffin. He thought it was all connected to Theo. With Sawyer on speakerphone, they discussed what to do about Cooper and the possibility of Theo's men in town, watching me.

Jackson rang Luca to set up a time to talk to Cooper on Luca's phone. I let them make their plans, while I made toasted sandwiches for lunch.

Doing simple tasks held me together, gave me something to focus on.

After lunch, Jackson left to check in on his mum and get some clean clothes. When he returned, Jet took us all up to the hospital.

Nigel's parents were there and showered us with thanks for helping Nigel and responding so quickly. Nigel slept through the whole visit.

It was awkward and uncomfortable. Rather than being thanked, I felt like I should have been blamed for it happening in the first place.

Jackson stayed with me all afternoon, and that night we finally had time to be alone.

We lay on the couch in a comfortable tangle of limbs, and my head rested on his chest.

"This was my fault, wasn't it? That Nigel was shot?"

"We don't know that. It could be random. Besides, the bullet barely nicked him."

"Well then, if it's random, it's Corben's fault."

"Stop it, Nova. Don't go there again. Anyway, you're being too hard on Corben. You can't blame her for every incident. She was not even here."

I shrugged. "Maybe."

It was my fault. The tightness in my chest and the tension in my muscles told me that.

There was a strong temptation to shut down again. Like after Sage. Like when I found out about my mother. To stop feeling. To put my walls up. To push Jackson away.

But I had promised him I would not do that. And I meant to keep that promise.

I let out a sigh.

21

The following morning, Sawyer arrived. He was expected, given the events of the day before.

Corben was with him. She was not expected.

I got the sense that Sawyer had deliberately not asked if he could bring her so that I couldn't refuse.

Jet let them in.

I stood behind the kitchen bench, rising onto my tiptoes then dropping back down as if doing stretching exercises. Which I was not. I was just fidgeting.

"I'm sorry to arrive without notice, Nova. I hope it's okay." Corben was always so polite. "I have something for you. Will you come out the front?"

I looked at Sawyer, who had a broad grin on his face. There was a warm tingling in my chest.

I shrugged. "Sure, I guess."

Parked out the front of the house was a car. A Mini Cooper. It was a deep green colour, with a white roof and two white stripes down the bonnet. There were also white circles around the headlights, so they looked like wide, friendly eyes.

I looked at Corben, who was smiling and nodding. I looked at Sawyer, whose grin was even wider than before, and he gestured towards the car. I looked at Jackson, who shrugged. He was wide-eyed with astonishment.

"What does this mean?" I asked.

"It's for you. Harley was talking with me about getting it for you for your eighteenth birthday. He had even picked the colour. I know it is a very belated present, and I know he is no longer with us, but I am hoping you will accept it from me on his behalf. From both of us. I know he would have wanted that."

I bit down on my bottom lip and felt my eyes well-up. My hand reached out and touched the shiny panels.

"I can't accept this," I said at last.

"I would love it if you did. Besides, I can't really take it back. It's registered in your name. I am kind of hoping it also partly makes up for all the birthdays I missed."

"Is this a bribe?"

"If it is, it's a damn good one!" Jackson was now grinning as widely as the others. He nudged me. "Get in."

I opened the driver's door, and Jackson joined Jet who had opened the passenger door. We all peered in. It was shiny, and it had that new car smell.

"Please get in. Take it for a drive." Corben passed me the keys.

Although I still had no sense of what she was feeling, her voice was pitched a little high as if excited or pleased, or both.

I adjusted the seat and ran my hands over the smooth, shiny dashboard.

Sawyer bent down next to the open door. "Accept it, Nova. She is trying to have a relationship with you. Besides, you need a car."

"I guess I do." He could tell I was coming around. It was hard not to. It was a car. A Mini Cooper. And green was my favourite colour. "Did Dad really plan to give me this?" I asked Corben.

"Yes, he did. I promise."

"Well, then … I guess, thank you, Dad. And thank you, Corben. This is amazing."

"It's so you, Nova," said Jackson. "Your dad did well. Your mum too." He turned to smile at Corben. "So, can I be the passenger on your first drive?"

It only had two doors, and the back seat was tiny, but Jet insisted on squeezing in. I was not sure if he was caught up in the excitement or was doing his protection-detail thing. Regardless, he cheered when I took off down the road.

My heart thumped, and I felt like my excitement shone through the pores of my skin. Jackson laughed as he stroked the upholstery and side panels, as if patting a dog. I giggled.

Maybe there were times when it was nice to have a mother after all.

After I had driven everyone around the block several times, we collected around the dining table. The atmosphere was fun and lively. I kept checking out the window, to make sure the car was still out the front. Jackson and Jet were teasing me about how slow I had been driving, but I just laughed with them. Corben sat quietly, and her smile never left her face. I felt happier than I had in a while.

Sawyer cleared his throat. "Now, after all this excitement, I want to say something. Corben mentioned it the last time we were together. Nova, we believe that you have the capacity to de-activate the warrior gene. That you can make a real difference in this world climate of aggression. Calm it down. Significantly. I've already shown you the statistics

I gathered, showing a much lower crime rate here, and up at Woodside Beach from when you were staying up there. Those statistics have stayed level, even after you left the area." I was starting to protest, but Sawyer held up his hand. "It is true. It's from you. And we need to start making plans for doing something about it. Taking you to other towns, other cities, in Australia and overseas. Soon. We'll keep working to strengthen your skills, but I think we could use Corben's help too."

My heart was beating at double time. Pins and needles burned and prickled in my fingers and toes. This is what I had been afraid of.

Sawyer had indeed shown me the statistical evidence. He'd inferred the lower crime rates were a result of me spreading my empathy. I knew I could influence the emotions of my friends and the people around me. But that was one thing. This was much bigger than my hometown. This was huge; this was massive! And I wasn't sure about Corben. Despite the car, I wasn't sure how I felt about her being around more.

"That's a lot of pressure."

"You won't be doing it on your own."

It felt like there was a warm blanket around me, and I knew it was Sawyer's confidence and belief in me. But underneath that, I was shivering.

I squeezed my hands into fists and wriggled my toes.

"Can I think about it?" The thrill of having my own car was still tingling through me, and I did not want to lose that. Besides, I was an expert at avoidance. "I have to go to work now. We are all doing extra shifts to cover for Nigel."

Nigel was home and doing well, but he'd taken the week off work.

"Do you need a lift to work?" Jet kept a straight face, but I saw a twitch at the side of his mouth.

"Hahaha! No. I can drive myself, thank you." Everyone laughed.

"Do you want to pick me up after work? We can drive to Mia's and then Han's and show them your new car." Jackson sounded like a kid with a new toy. My new toy.

I nodded and let his happiness wash through me. The other stuff could wait. I was good at avoidance.

△

It was a good week. I finished my exams, and four weeks of holidays stretched out ahead of me. The June weather was cold and the days were short, but it stayed fine, which always lifted my mood.

Sawyer had started meeting with me every second day, and when I was not working at the ice-cream shop I was at the gym with Jet and Jackson. It was both mind and body training.

I was enjoying it. Mostly.

Corben often came with Sawyer. She kept up her own emotional shield but showed me how to sense the warrior gene in others and wrap it in layers of calm serenity. We mostly practiced on Jet because he was handy. This meant that he walked around in a permanently good mood. He smiled and made stupid jokes until it almost got to be annoying.

I had reached a kind of impasse in my feelings about Corben. We did not act like mother and daughter but more like polite acquaintances, and that was mostly because of Sawyer.

There were three things that still bothered me. *A lot.*

Firstly, that she had left me. She had disappeared. Chosen to not be in my life. And I had been encouraged to believe she was dead for so long. Dad had lied to me, and that left a stain on my memories, even if he had thought it was better for me. I was angry at both of them.

The second thing was the anger and aggression she had spread, all around the world. Sawyer and Jackson made excuses for her and constantly reminded me that not all people with the warrior gene were violent, that it was a choice.

"Look at Jet and Rayna," they said.

But I still lay the blame on her shoulders.

Thirdly, finally, I was afraid of what it all meant for me, what it meant I was capable of.

Maybe that was not Corben's fault. I knew I had to take responsibility for my own actions. However, the darkness that lived within me was a constant. Sure, I could influence people to be calmer, more cooperative, more peaceful, even joyful. Logically, then, I could also do the opposite. Like my mother had, out of anger, frustration, and pain.

These reservations made me feel like a hypocrite for accepting the car. But I loved it. To the extent that Jackson complained that we never took the bike anymore. I was able to rationalise that it was a gift from my dad as well, not just from her.

The other thing was that Corben made a good impression. Everyone liked her. It was actually annoying how much. Besides Sawyer, I knew Jackson wanted me to have a proper relationship with her. And then there was so much curiosity about the woman who had come back from the dead that I had to arrange for her to meet the girls.

I could feel the way she tugged at the emotional ties that bound us and was able to weave herself into them. They liked her too. Though she kept her own emotions blocked, she was able to read people very quickly. She was quietly friendly, encouraging, and always kind.

As Corben learned about my friends, so did I, and it made me realise how self-absorbed I had been lately.

Imogen and Mia chatted easily with her about our friendship all through school, and the various funny stories that were our shared history. They even told her about Sage.

Ava told her that she had been lobbying for queer and trans rights in private schools. She was writing letters and organising petitions. When she spoke about her rape, I could see that Corben had created a safe space allowing Ava to talk about it. I got to see a strength in Ava that had not been there for a while and guessed it was from Brooklyn's influence.

Spencer spoke about Cooper every chance she had, though thankfully she left out my previous relationship with him. She also talked about the baby.

"It does make me nervous, bringing a baby into this world." Spencer circled her stomach with her hands and heaved a sigh. "Especially being a single mum."

"Don't dwell on that. A baby is the most wonderful gift you will ever get," said Corben, giving me a small smile.

That came from the woman who had walked out on her child. I smothered a snort.

Corben asked Devon about her studies and spoke about her own love of science and research, although she left out the bits about activating the warrior gene and causing world chaos.

Yeah, I was trying to be nice. But it wasn't easy.

I realised that, in a roundabout way, Corben was gathering information about me. My life, my friendships, my studies. It was probably deliberate, as I had been reluctant to share much with her. But she was a good listener. I had to give her that.

With Corben visiting so often, it also provided me with a reprieve. I wasn't bombarded by someone else's emotions. She kept up her solid shield, and although it was frustrating not to know how she was feeling, it was also peaceful. I had not realised how much I absorbed from other people, both good and bad, until there was the lack of it.

I was not changing my mind about her, but I decided I could put up with having Corben around from time to time. Not as my mother, but as if she were a friend of Sawyer or even an old acquaintance of my father. I could cope with that much.

22

The police had no leads on Nigel's drive-by shooting and had stopped investigating.

Jet and Sawyer were convinced it had been a message from Theo. To scare me, or to let me know that he knew where I was. At least he didn't seem to want me dead. Yet. Otherwise, the shooter would not have missed. Nigel had just got in the way of the bullet when he stepped back from me.

While guilt hung heavily in my body every time I worked with Nigel, he was actually strutting around with a whole new level of confidence. He was being hailed as a hero. Somehow a story had spread that he had pushed me out of the way and taken a bullet for me. Jackson was really pissed off about it, but it was close enough to the truth that I let Nigel have the glory.

Sawyer had put Jet on high alert, and he had moved back into my spare room. They were especially wary of any strangers in town and seemed to be running checks on everyone.

Despite that threat, I was happy. Life had settled back into a peaceful rhythm.

Joy echoed through me and, like a pebble thrown into a pond, it caused ripples to spread in all directions, and in increasingly larger circles.

Police reports showed that the violence around town was at a minimum.

Even the news headlines from Melbourne were less alarming than they had been.

Sawyer was quick to give me the credit. Corben backed him up. While I was prepared to accept that I had an influence on my own small town, I thought they were reaching to say that I could make a difference in Melbourne. It was too far away.

"Nova, you need to have more confidence in yourself. You do it so effortlessly that it's instinctive for you," insisted Corben.

Sawyer nodded, with a gleam in his eyes. "It always has been."

He had not yet returned to that conversation about what he wanted me to do. And there was no way I was bringing it up.

Jackson had tried to talk to me about it. He made it sound like a mission, a *Harry Potter* movie, travelling around, destroying horcruxes.

But it was not a movie. It was real, it was serious, and it was frightening.

And so, it was easier for me to avoid even thinking about it.

In the same way that, every day, I ignored the inspirational message on the wall calendar that my neighbour had given me.

Your biggest fear will bring about the most growth.

Pfft.

△

Corben had been going through my father's computer files.

I had not known his password, but she had guessed it. Apparently, he had always used the same one. It was the name of the restaurant in Melbourne where they used to go to celebrate special occasions. Cute.

She found a list of names and addresses he had compiled of other empaths he'd heard about. They were from all around the world. Most were based on newspaper reports, either of a good Samaritan act or sometimes people that were identified as psychic. Sawyer Young was on the list.

Empaths are not psychic, but our capacity to read emotions meant that we were often able to accurately guess what people were thinking as well.

Dad had emailed or phoned a lot of them and had made notes about each one.

Sawyer wanted to contact them all and see if they were willing to help us. He was checking the areas where they lived to see if there was also less violence around them.

It gave me hope. And it took the pressure off me.

I was quick to remind Sawyer that I didn't actually know what I was doing.

Which I didn't. So maybe these empaths were better options.

Sawyer just smiled and went ahead with organising for Corben to do 'empathy training' with me. That is what I had started to call it. We worked on my emotional control, creating a peaceful environment around me, sensing others, sensing the warrior gene, and trying to de-activate it.

Although Corben maintained her emotional walls, I was very aware of her empathic strength. She was extremely accurate in reading my feelings and guessing my thoughts.

"Nova, focus! What are you thinking about?"

"Nothing specifically." I felt the heat rise in my face because I had been thinking about Jackson.

Corben raised her eyebrows and shook her head. She looked just like a mother.

"Well, this is not just about having nice thoughts about Jack. Concentrate on what you are sending out."

I tried harder. It was what worked best for me though. When I thought about my friends, wave upon wave of joy and contentment spilled out of me.

There was laughter from next door, and I could hear children having a game on the swing at the end of the street.

"That's good, but you need to give out both a stronger and wider influence. Dig deeper inside yourself." Corben's mouth was set in a firm line.

I gave her a dirty look. "I am."

But I was not. There was stuff deep inside me that I did not want to come up. The darkness I carried after Abraham, the stain from taking someone's life. I certainly did not want to let that loose.

"You have to own it," Corben said quietly. She was good at this cognitive empathy gig. "Accept it, and in doing that you will take away the power it has over you."

"Is that what you have done?" I heard my snarky tone.

It was frustrating that she could read me so easily and yet she was a closed book. Except for that tiny glimpse of rage she had let slip, I'd never sensed any of her emotions. And she clearly had her very own darkness inside. She had admitted that already.

Corben was biting on her bottom lip. I knew that I did the same when I was holding something back.

"You need to share yourself," she said at last. "Let your emotions flow, let them echo out like giant sound waves. That is what will change people. Your compassion, your joy, will remind them of the good in themselves, in others. That is what will stop the violence." She patted my hand. "Relax and try again."

I let out a heavy sigh and shut my eyes. Leaning back in the chair, I stretched out my legs and crossed my ankles, rubbing the scuffed heels of my boots against each other. The air had a fresh smell, the scent of a recent shower of rain. There was the melodic sound of children's laughter from the end of the street. I let my mind wander outside the walls, beyond the streets and the houses, until I imagined myself lying on a beach. It looked a lot like Woodside Beach. The sun was warm on my face and the sand formed a soft mound beneath me. My toes dipped into the water, which sent an invigorating chill up my legs.

It was my happy place, and I let that feeling echo through me, around me, beyond me. The echoes rolled out further and further.

"That's good."

I could hear the smile in Corben's tone, but I kept my eyes shut. My breathing was even and calm. I imagined Jackson lying beside me. He reached out his hand …

"And we are back to Jack." Corben's voice was edged with frustration.

I blinked my eyes open as the heat rose in my face. It was not my fault that he was such a big part of my happy thoughts.

For the next hour, Corben had me exploring different emotions, finding out where I held them in my body and then concentrating on the sensations in that area.

Anger seemed to ride in the top of my chest but also deep in my stomach. I could slow down my breathing to soothe my chest, but the pitch and roll in my stomach was harder to calm. Stress was held in my shoulders, and it definitely helped to rotate them as a release.

I carried joy and love in my heart, of course, but also in my face, around my eyes and in my smile. It was hard for me to separate those two emotions; they felt so much the same to me.

"Thank you for allowing me back into your life," Corben said politely at the end of our session.

I shrugged, not sure how she expected me to answer. It wasn't like I had a lot of choice.

"I was dreaming about you for months before I reached out to Sawyer."

"Oh yeah?" I was running the zip of my hoodie up and down, fidgeting.

"You were trying to lead me out of the darkness. You were standing in fire, and it created a broad path of pure light. It was beautiful. You were holding out your hand to me. But I didn't know how to step through the flames. They weren't burning you, but I was afraid they would burn me."

Corben looked at me with raised eyebrows as if waiting for me to respond, but I just shrugged and didn't say anything more.

Her dream was eerily similar to the nightmare I had been having, but in reverse. She was the dark-haired woman, leading me into the fire, into the darkness. It seemed clear that we were sharing the same dream somehow, leading us towards each other. I didn't want to share that information with her. There was still a long way to go before I would trust her, and I wasn't sure what it was all supposed to mean.

Fire and darkness. Was that who we were? They were both so destructive.

△

Jackson was quietly thoughtful when I told him about both dreams later. My trust in him was easy.

"I reckon she reached out and you responded. The darkness and light make sense. She recognises the darkness in herself. You have so much light in you."

"It's not light, it's fire in my dream. And anyway, I have darkness too." I placed my hands flat on the kitchen bench.

"Yeah, so you keep saying. The rest of us don't see it."

I shook my head, and then sucked in a breath as I scratched my fingernails against the stone benchtop. "Jack, I don't know if I can do what they want me to do. I'm scared."

He moved in and looped his arms around me from behind. "Of course you are. We all are."

"What if I can't do it? That fire in those dreams, I think it's the anger, the violence. And I am terrified that it will consume me. It took my mother."

Jackson swung me around to face him. He pulled down at the neck of his jumper to expose the phoenix tattoo on his chest. "Nova, do you know why I got this tattoo?"

I shook my head. "No, but Han and Jet seemed to be in on some private joke about it."

"Forget them." He locked eyes with me. "I got this tattoo to represent you. You are like a phoenix. You don't need to be afraid of the fire. Or the darkness. You can walk through them both. Nova, you will rise from the fire and out of the darkness." His voice was both playful and sincere.

There was a tingling all over my body. I knew that Jackson loved me. It was in the way he looked at me, the way he said my name, and now it was in this tattoo on his chest.

I gave a silly grin. He bent his head and kissed my forehead.

"But why were Han and Jet being weird about it?"

Jackson's mouth twitched as if he was holding back a smile. "Well, it's what Sawyer and Jet call you."

"What? What do you mean?"

"They call you the Phoenix, like a code name, instead of using your name. Sawyer made it up."

"What?" My eyes narrowed and I put my hands flat against his chest. "Like the president? Like, 'the eagle has landed'?"

"Well, not quite." Jackson snorted but then gave an apologetic laugh. "But, yeah, sort of, I guess."

"Why didn't I know about this?"

He shrugged.

"How do you know about it?"

"I heard Jet say it a few times and I asked him what he was talking about." Jackson pulled me in against his chest.

"So, you got the tattoo because of a stupid name they call me."

"Hey!" His eyes were deep brown pools of warm cocoa. "I like the name. I like the symbolism."

There was a slight stiffness in my jaw. I was annoyed, but I knew it was mainly because no one had told me about it. Phoenix was a good name.

I wondered why Sawyer had chosen it.

Jackson was attaching a special meaning to it, and that sounded like a lot of pressure.

"Don't try to make me into something mythical. I'm just a girl."

"I know you're just a girl." His hands were now roaming up and down my back in taunting, teasing strokes as I arched against his chest. "And I am just a boy."

I knew where this was leading, and I wanted it too. My pulse sped up and my breathing deepened, matching his.

"So, what were you saying? That I am trying to make you into ..." Jackson's voice trailed off as his lips pressed against my forehead before moving down the side of my face.

I giggled. "I can't remember."

His answering chuckle vibrated against my ear. Jackson bent his head further and scattered soft kisses across my neck and up to my chin, until his lips met mine. His kiss was soft, yet passionate.

It stole my breath, but only for a moment.

When I exhaled, the stone that had been sitting in my stomach for days, for weeks, weighing me down, simply floated away.

△

I spoke to Jet about the phoenix name the next day.

"It's just a security thing. A military thing. Pick something else if you'd prefer." He shrugged dismissively.

I stood for a moment, thinking. I didn't even know where to start. And phoenix was a cool name.

"No, it's okay. I just wish someone had told me."

"The point is that people don't know about it."

"Jack and Han knew."

"Yeah, well Jack has big ears and a big mouth. And now he has some fancy ink across his chest." Jet narrowed his eyes in assessment, then raised his dark, bushy eyebrows until they almost met in the middle, and gave me a wide grin. "Maybe we should change it."

He turned away. The conversation seemed to be over. I followed him out of the room.

"Wait, what would you change it to?"

He just laughed and shut his bedroom door behind him. Shutting me out.

△

Mia had made girls' night a weekly commitment. Thursdays at Club 393.

The crowd were all young people, as families and older people were less likely to venture out at night these days. It was a comfortable, easy-going vibe, especially since the football team had been banned after the fighting. At the bar, people waited their turn without complaining. They shared small talk or chatted each other up, hoping to exchange numbers.

The small dance floor was crowded. Mia kept requesting feminist anthems because she and Kenji were arguing again. We shouted out the lyrics while we bumped against each other with a crude coordination.

We danced, we drank, and we laughed.

Jet was out with Rayna in a restaurant down the road, close enough to keep checking on me. The bouncers probably had him on speed dial anyway. He was a favourite among them, especially whenever there was trouble.

Towards the end of the night, one of the bouncers approached our table. He was tall, muscle-bound, and perfectly bald. There was a slight shade of stubble where he shaved the areas of his head that still grew hair. "Nova, there's a guy outside that asked if you were here. He looks like a football player so I'm not letting him in, but he asked if you could come out." He shrugged. "He said you know him. His name is Griffin. I can call Jet if you want."

"It's okay. I'll come out."

"I'm coming too," said Spencer. A veil of worry dropped over her face and, combined with the butterflies that swirled around in my stomach, I knew that she was wondering if it was news about Cooper.

Spencer had told me that she and Cooper were texting each other most nights, so we knew he was okay. Jackson had also been keeping in contact with his brother through Luca. Cooper did weekly self-defence training with Luca and Magic Mike.

In the end, all the girls came out with me. We were still very wary of Griffin.

He was leaning up against his car door, parked on the opposite side of the road. With a small salute of recognition he stepped forward, but then he paused as a black four-wheel drive came down the street.

I had a vague sense of déjà vu but, before I could process the feeling, it was over.

There were three loud, sharp, snapping sounds, almost like slow claps.

The car drove by, and Griffin had crumpled onto the road.

Dark liquid was spreading over his chest, and it took me a moment to realise that it was blood. Under the streetlights, it looked like black paint. There was also a small, dark mark on his forehead.

Griffin's eyes were open, but I knew that he could no longer see.

I could not sense him. When I reached out, there was nothing. And I knew what that meant. There was a void where I should have been feeling his emotions.

I stood still, both numb and nauseated.

Death. Shock. Disbelief. I had been here before.

Spencer was crying.

Mia was muttering words of comfort to her.

Imogen and Devon had gone to get the bouncers.

It seemed only a few minutes later that Jet was beside me, a steady arm around me. An ambulance came for the body. Griffin was loaded onto a stretcher and wrapped in white.

Rayna was looking after Spencer. She herded us into a side room at Club 393, where the police took our statements. There was not much to tell. We barely knew Griffin. It was another drive-by shooting, and this time it was fatal.

None of us knew what sort of car it was, besides being black, with dark-tinted windows. It could have been the same one that had shot at Nigel.

Griffin had been there, and now he was not.

We did not get to find out what he wanted to say.

Jet had contacted Jackson, who was trying to get hold of Cooper.

The peaceful rhythm that had been forming was shattered.

23

The clothesline stood on a slight lean amongst the long grass and overgrown weeds. A hedge that had grown far higher than the tall wooden fence and provided too much shade made a delightful border of green. Leaves of various autumn colours were scattered across the lawn like blobs of paint in a child's picture.

I held my head to one side, listening. There it was again, low voices and a giggle. It had woken me up. I had not slept much, and I still felt groggy and tired.

The ground was soft and soggy and, even in my gumboots, my footsteps did not make much sound as I made my way to the tall Japanese maple tree in the corner. There were a few hardy leaves that still clung on to the craggy branches, but the foliage provided little cover.

Two sets of eyes peered down. One set were a slate-grey colour and a little bloodshot, but they sparkled with mischief. The other set were a clear, brilliant blue, though they stared a little to the side of where I stood. I shut my own eyes and counted to five, giving this hallucination ample time to disappear. When I opened them again, Bellamy scratched the top of his head, sending his messy blond hair into more of a tangle, and gave me a pleasant "Mornin'!"

Okay, so it was real.

Bellamy and Maize were in my old treehouse.

Many of the wooden boards hammered across the branches now dangled from rusty nails, but enough of the floor was still intact to provide a stable platform. The two remaining walls and a rickety roof would have kept out most of the drizzling rain but given no protection from the cold.

A vision of Sage in her pyjamas, whispering from the sleeping bag next to mine, flittered across my memory. I pushed it aside, into one of my mental compartments.

"Oh my god, you two must be freezing! What on earth are you doing here? Come inside."

Bellamy was wearing a long, black trench coat, like a cowboy would wear. He had probably scored it in a vintage clothing shop or off someone's clothesline. It swung about his legs as he climbed down. Above him, he guided Maize's feet onto the wooden rungs that had been hammered into the tree trunk. Maize skipped the last two rungs and jumped to the ground, landing with perfect balance. It was so easy to forget she was blind. She wore a dark-blue puffer jacket and thick leggings. Yet, despite their warm clothes, they were both shivering.

In the kitchen, they huddled over the central heating duct while I made hot chocolate, then we sat around the dining table.

Mia joined us, woken by the noise. She had stayed the night with me. I made the introductions.

"Okay, now spill. How did you get here? And why were you in my treehouse?"

"I drove Neo's car." Bellamy was smiling broadly as he warmed his cold fingers around the hot mug.

I choked and spluttered on my drink. Bellamy was only fifteen.

Maize turned at the sound and nodded. "Neo sent us. He told us not to be seen, so we went around the back. And you guys were still asleep, so we waited in the treehouse."

"Neo's car," I repeated slowly. "But, Bellamy, you're too young to have a licence."

"Well, I can't drive at night; it's too dark." Maize gave a sarcastic smirk and flicked back her hair.

Bellamy chuckled.

"Wait, what? Why did Neo send you?" This was far too confusing when it was so early, and on so little sleep.

"He sent Griffin first, but that was ... well ... fatal." Maize's voice dropped an octave, and I felt a slight tremor run through my body. It was more from pity than fear because it was hard to imagine Maize being afraid of anything. "That's why he told us to stay out of sight."

"Neo sent Griffin. And he knows what happened?"

"Nova, keep up." Maize's tone was permanently on sarcastic. "Neo said to tell you that Cooper is on the Gold Coast, in Queensland. They left with Theo late last night. Theo is joining with a bikie gang up there. It's been too hard for him to keep operating in Melbourne. The cops have been all over him."

"Why did Cooper go with Theo? Isn't he a bad guy?" Mia was still rubbing the sleep from her eyes and, like me, she seemed to be having trouble keeping up.

Maize shrugged. "Neo said to tell you that Cooper will be fine. He'll try and work out a way to send Cooper home. But the main thing he wanted to tell you is that Theo still wants you, Nova. Badly. And Neo said whatever you do, don't follow them up to the Gold Coast."

The warning was like an ominous clap of thunder.

"I'd better let Jack know about Cooper. And Sawyer. Maybe he can do something."

Jet had stayed the night in the spare room, but I had heard him leave early this morning to check in with the police regarding Griffin's death. The images of last night flashed through my head and my stomach lurched.

"Jack will want to go up to get Cooper," said Mia, interrupting my thoughts.

I nodded. "I know he will." That is what worried me.

While I made the phone calls, Mia made bacon sandwiches for our guests. Bellamy did not talk much, but Mia kept up an easy conversation with Maize. They were talking about rappers and song lyrics, agreeing that they preferred the ones that told a story.

Bellamy and Maize were both naturally wary of strangers, which was not surprising given their homeless lifestyle, but Mia's natural kindness broke through their barriers with a comfortable ease. I could sense the ties of genuine friendship she was offering them, and which they were happy to receive. She even got Bellamy to do some rapping, and they all laughed together.

I smiled at her, and she grinned back. Mia may not have been an empath in the same way that I was, but if there was an empathy gene, I knew that Mia carried it. That was what the world needed more of. People like Mia. She drew out the goodness in people.

Something lit up in my brain and there was a flutter of excitement in my chest. It was the beginnings of an idea, an epiphany, flashing through my mind. But it was too quick, and I was too tired to hang on to it.

△

Jackson, Jet, Sawyer, Mia, and I sat around the dining table, while Bellamy and Maize sat on the couch. They had been a lot quieter since Sawyer had arrived, but I knew it would not take long till he won them over too.

They were still eating. Luckily Sawyer had brought pastries because I had run out of bread, bacon, bananas, juice, and almost every other food item in the fridge or pantry. To be fair, I did not have a lot to begin with. I still tended to rely on junk food. The healthier stuff belonged to Jet. I would have to replace it.

There was an undercurrent of anxiety in the room, and it twisted through my stomach. I knew it came from everyone's concern for Cooper. As predicted, Jackson wanted to leave immediately for the Gold Coast and bring his twin brother back home.

Cooper had not responded to any texts or calls from Jackson, nor from Luca, who was also trying to contact him on our behalf. He had at least sent a message to his father, though. It just said that he was at Surfers Paradise for work and that he would ring home tonight.

"I will find out where and how he really is, Jack. I do not think you should go up until we have more information." Sawyer spoke with a quiet authority, and I could feel him working the room to keep things calm.

Jackson nodded reluctantly.

"Nova, do you think Neo will talk to us?" asked Sawyer.

Maize snorted. "No way."

Sawyer nodded as if he knew that would be the answer. "We have other contacts who can find out. At least give me a couple of days." He was reassuring, but I was not sure if it was just an act for Jackson. Sawyer was good at hiding his real emotions when he wanted to.

We stayed in for the entire day. Bellamy and Maize took Neo's warning seriously and did not want anyone to see them. Jet went out to get burgers for lunch, and then later went for some pizza for an early dinner. Maize and Bellamy ate and drank continuously. Mia put on *House of The Dragon* and Bellamy narrated between the dialogue for Maize.

Jet, Sawyer, and Jackson talked in circles about the little we knew and the concerns we had, until Jackson left to go home and wait for Cooper's call.

Sawyer was going to drive Bellamy and Maize back to Melbourne, in Neo's car, under the cover of darkness. Along with the other young people that attended the drop-in centre, Luca had been giving Bellamy an occasional driving lesson, but he would have a fit when he found out that it had given the fifteen-year-old the confidence to drive all the way here, on the highway, at night. I wondered if Neo had realised who would be driving when he had offered Maize his car. Mind you, he had offered it to a blind girl.

I shook my head which made my headache worse.

Jackson returned just before Sawyer left.

"Cooper phoned Dad. He said he was fine. The weather is warm, and he reckons he'll go surfing after work. He has heaps of painting work and his own apartment in the complex where he is working. Dad told him to be careful and to stay in touch. I hadn't said too much to Dad, just that I thought it was a bit sudden for Cooper to take off like that. But Dad has enough on his plate with Mum. I don't want him to worry about Cooper as well." Jackson sighed. He looked pale and tired. "When I got on the phone, I told Cooper about Griffin. He had already heard about it. He did sound pretty cut up. And then he just said he had to go. I didn't want to mention Theo's name after Griffin's warning about being careful on the phone. I didn't know what else to say."

"Leave it with me for now, Jack. Please. Give me another day or so. Stay in touch with Cooper as much as you can. But keep it light and friendly. Don't say too much more." Sawyer gave his shoulder a squeeze, and Jackson winced. It was the side where he had been stabbed, and it was still a little tender. Sawyer lifted his hand immediately, looking mortified, but Jackson just nodded.

$$\triangle$$

Before bed, I did a bit of stretching to help slow my heartbeat and calm my breathing. Jackson lay on the bed with his hands behind his head, staring at the wall opposite where I had strung up a single strand of fairy lights. His worry and frustration rode through me like churning waves. There was also a chill in my body, and I knew he was annoyed at Cooper.

"Do you ever feel like we're on the *Titanic*, steering straight into that giant iceberg?" Jackson looked at me with a grim expression.

"All the time." I stopped my exercises and climbed up onto the bed, next to him. "But if we hit the iceberg, then we'll just get into the lifeboats."

"There were not enough lifeboats. That's the whole problem."

"Well, we will find a floating door and wait until the rescue boat arrives."

Jackson gave a snort. "You know Jack could have easily fit on that door with Rose."

"Easily. Heaps of room."

The sound of his laughter loosened the knots in my shoulders more effectively than my stretching had done.

His nose nuzzled against my ear, and he started humming 'My heart will go on'.

24

It was the third time we had argued about this.

"I told you. It's a brother thing. I have to work this out with Cooper on my own."

That was just an excuse. It was really about my safety. Jackson took it just as seriously as Jet did. But at least Jet was leaving this decision up to me. Of course, if I was going to the Gold Coast, he would be coming with me.

"But the invitation included me."

While we couldn't get him on the phone, Cooper had sent a text suggesting Jackson and I join him. An invitation to have a holiday on the Gold Coast while we were on university break.

"Neo said you shouldn't go up, and you said you trust him." Jackson shrugged, and I could feel his cold resolve. Suddenly he agreed with Neo. "So, you're not going up."

"But I'm worried about Cooper too. And we are better as a team. You said we belong together." I could hear the persuasion in my voice, but it just seemed to bounce off his stubborn back.

Jackson shook his head. "Not this time."

I picked up a pillow from the floor and threw it onto the bed with more force than was necessary. "You're taking Han."

Jackson shrugged again and focused on straightening the doona. I knew it was to avoid looking at me. He was never this neat.

I twisted my hands. There was one last plea, but I knew it would totally piss him off.

"I feel like I need to be there. I can go on my own if you won't take me," I said quietly.

This time, his eyes locked with mine in a glare. They were dark brown and mesmerizing.

I could imagine the conflict going on in his mind, behind his frown. Both warmth and cold flooded my body. He wanted to protect me, but he also knew I was as stubborn as he was. I would go up on my own if left with no other option. There seemed to be a strange compulsion pulling at me, and I really did feel that I needed to go. I didn't think we would get Cooper back otherwise, despite what Neo had said. After all, it was my fault Cooper was there in the first place, and I was not going to let Jackson deal with that on his own. Especially if Theo was there.

I pulled back my shoulders and could feel the steel that ran down my spine.

"You don't really leave me with much choice, do you?" Jackson's voice was harsh, and I felt like my skin was rubbing up against a cheese grater.

There was no need to answer him. I drew in my bottom lip, holding my breath.

Finally, Jackson let out a loud sigh. "If you come, we're not taking any risks, and you have to promise to stay away from anything or anyone that might link to Theo."

I jumped across the room with an awkward leap into his arms. His grip was strong and steady, as always. I hugged him tightly, feeling the tension drain from both of us, until he gave a gasp.

"Umm, trying to breathe here."

I giggled and loosened my hold a little.

Jackson pulled away and held me at arm's length. "I mean it, Nova. You stay in the background. Let me work things out with Cooper. Hopefully Theo won't even have to know you're there." His voice was firm and unyielding.

"Yes, sir!" I was nodding like a bobble-head doll.

Jackson shook his head at me again, but now his smile was as broad as my own. "I'm going to regret this, aren't I?"

I shook my head vehemently. "No way!" My excitement bubbled and fizzed as I jumped from one foot to the other.

"Road Trip!" Mia yelled as she, Devon, and Han tumbled through the doorway. They had been eavesdropping in the hallway.

Jackson groaned. "Really? Everyone? I am already regretting this."

"But we are not taking the Mini," said Han, and he bumped his arm against mine. "I feel like a pretzel getting in and out of that car."

I laughed. "I'm easy."

Jackson put both his hands up to rub his forehead, as if he were getting a headache. He probably was. "Wilson, you are anything but easy." But he laughed when I poked my tongue out at him.

△

As the road trip plans grew bigger, Jackson's impatience gnawed through my stomach like hunger pains. I knew he wished that he had just left with Han and kept it simple.

Sawyer had wanted Jet and Rayna to come with us, which meant we had two DOVE jeeps for the trip, and more planning. Everyone had to organise things within their families and request time off work. I had to arrange for Mia's mother to look after Ripley.

Corben came over the night before we left. Unannounced. It was becoming an annoying habit of hers. Probably because I never invited her over.

"Jack, are you sure it's a good idea to be taking Nova on this trip? I don't think it's safe."

"I could not agree more. It's certainly not my idea. Your daughter can be exceptionally stubborn." His mouth was drawn in a thin line, and he shook his head in my direction.

I shrugged and gave him a placating grin, but I stopped myself from giving Corben the finger.

"She probably gets that from …" When Corben paused, I narrowed my eyes. My father had been the opposite of stubborn. He was a pushover. "From me, I suppose," Corben finished with a sigh.

That made more sense. I could attribute all of my flaws to my mother.

"Both of you, please, be very careful." She placed a hand gently on my arm.

Although her emotions remained firmly shielded, her voice was soft with concern. It made me feel a bit guilty about my previous thoughts. But, then again, she'd managed to forget about me for years, so worrying about me now seemed a bit redundant.

"We will." Jackson gave Corben a smile, but I just nodded.

He seemed to find it easy to have a normal conversation with Corben, and I knew he liked having her around. As did Sawyer. It frustrated me that they just accepted her role as my mother. I ground my teeth together in a hard clench.

When Corben left, we sat down to a dinner of toasted sandwiches.

"Your mum is right; it might not be safe. Why are you really coming?" Jackson pushed his plate away. He pressed his lips together and looked at me.

A tightness gripped my chest, almost like indigestion. I decided to skip my smart retort about Corben having no idea and focused instead on his question. "What do you mean? I'm coming to help."

"I feel like Cooper is always getting between us." He rubbed the back of his neck, but I could feel the stiffness in my own.

"No, he's not." My voice carried my surprise.

"A part of me has enjoyed Coop being in Melbourne," he said quietly. "I haven't had to listen to all the snide comments he makes about him being better for you than me."

My jaw dropped. "Does he say that?"

"All the time. It gets under my skin." He looked at me with large, soft eyes and I felt my stomach clench. "I know you're worried about him. But I can't tell if your feelings run deeper than that."

"Jack, no. I'm going to the Gold Coast because it's my fault that Theo is doing this." Jackson opened his mouth to protest, but I kept going before he could interrupt. "My feelings for Coop are only as a friend. They are surface-level. I didn't make a choice between you and Coop. He was my path to finding you. He's not between us. My feelings for you are so deep, there's no bottom to them. You are what I need, what I want, who I love. You are the best thing that has ever happened to me." I unclenched my hands and laid one on the table, palm up, fingers splayed, inviting him to hold it. His palm was warm, and we linked fingers in a tight clasp.

"You really mean that?"

"I do."

"Ditto."

I smiled and he smiled back.

Our love felt like threads of gold which wove us together and tightened around us. They were strong, and they were permanent.

△

Three days after Cooper's text, we were finally packed and ready. Sawyer had come to see us off.

It was just after dawn, as we wanted an early start for the long drive that lay ahead. Wishful thinking meant that we had packed our summer clothes for Queensland, but Victoria was reminding us that it was mid-winter and giving us a frosty send off. Our breath came out in puffs of steam, and we were all rugged up with scarves, gloves, and beanies.

Devon wore a black woollen hat with a couple of enamel badges on it. One read *We are all mad here* and the other *Stay Weird*. I made her and Han pose for a photo, while Jackson paced nervously.

The undercurrent of worry was heavy in my heart, but the excitement of a holiday still rippled through my body.

Kenji was dropping off Mia, and he arrived at the same time as Rayna. With him came an impenetrable cloud of resentment. Mia had not invited him on the trip. His fists were clenched at his sides, and I felt a stiff ache in my arms and legs. Mia reached up to give him a hug and whispered in his ear, but Kenji barely responded to her.

"So, can we go now?" Jackson was either oblivious to Kenji or deliberately choosing to ignore him. I couldn't tell which.

Jet slapped Jackson on the back and motioned to the Jeep he normally drove. "Do you want to drive that one? I'll drive Rayna's."

Jackson nodded.

Kenji sidled up to him. "So, you're taking both cars. I thought there was only room for the five of you."

Mia had the grace to blush when Jackson gave her a dirty look. "Mate, the five of us are in one car, that one is just for them." He waved a hand at Jet and Rayna who had climbed into the second Jeep.

Kenji turned to Mia. "Well, have a good time, then." He spat the words out as if they were distasteful and turned away to his own car. Fury rolled off him like peals of thunder.

Mia's guilt sat heavily in my chest, but her natural empathy still fluttered over to Kenji like the soft wings of a butterfly. I drew on my own empathy, deep within my body. It was such an integral part of me, and when I joined it with Mia's I could almost see it, glittering and dancing like diamonds sprinkled over those butterfly wings. Stretching out to Kenji, our combined compassion tugged on his heart strings.

It was dissolving his anger as easily as jelly crystals in hot water.

That was it.

As suddenly as I had forgotten it, I realised what the epiphany was that day when Bellamy and Maize had arrived in my treehouse. Mia was showing me the way. Again.

I had to be an empathy echo. Join mine with other people's to make it stronger.

With Corben, with Sawyer, and even in my own exercises, I had been going about it all wrong. I had been trying to turn off the warrior gene, trying to change people's anger and aggression. That was too hard. It was like swimming against the tide. Instead, I needed to draw on the good feelings people already had, their own compassion, their own concern, their own love for each other. Combining it with my own empathy, I could echo that back to them in stronger, more powerful waves. I just had to build on what was there, even if it was hidden or buried or had not been used in a while. It was turning with the tide, not against it. They could flick the switch back themselves.

My heart leapt with a sudden conviction, with hope.

I knew it meant assuming that there was good in everyone to be echoed back. But there was. I had to believe that. I did believe that.

A wide grin had spread across my face.

Kenji turned around as he got to his car. His scowl had been replaced with a smile. He blew Mia a kiss and gave us all a wave.

We waved back.

"That was so awkward," said Jackson quietly.

"Yeah. I'm sorry, guys. My bad. I told him there wasn't room because I didn't want him to come." Mia's tone was apologetic, but there was excitement shining in her eyes.

My body was already flushed with her natural compassion and the added thrill of anticipation lifted me even higher. It felt like I was floating on clouds.

Devon shrugged. "It's your call." She gave a broad smile, as the excitement had spread to her as well.

Han waved the girls towards the back seat and slapped Jackson on the back. "I'm in the front with you."

Sawyer put his hand on my arm. "Nova, hang on a minute." He drew me aside and spoke quietly, his words just meant for me. "I just want to say that I'm sorry I got you into this, with Abraham and now with Theo. I should never have brought you into DOVE last year." The painful ache of his regret sliced through my happiness like an icy wind, and I knew he was thinking about Sage, as well as Cooper. At the same time, his compassion was as warm as the thickest winter coat.

"Sawyer, it's not your fault." I kept my voice low but made sure the sincerity rang clear. "It wasn't then and it's not now. You do everything you can to protect us. You always have. I have learned so much from you."

"Thanks, Nova. That means a lot." He gave a half smile and we stood in silence for a moment, enjoying the bond we shared and valued. "Now, I get that you feel you need to go up there, but I'm relying on you to stay safe. You need to keep everyone calm and level-headed. Jet and Rayna will be looking out for all of you, so don't make it hard for them. I can fly up if you need me, and I'll pass on any information we get about Cooper."

"Of course." I reached out to embrace him.

He held me tightly for a moment. His concern was like a shadow clinging to his usual bright warmth. I knew he cared deeply about me, about all of us.

"Oh, I've had an epiphany," I added. Mia's empathy was still sparkling inside me.

Sawyer gave a small laugh. "Tell me later. If you don't get going Jack will have a fit."

I nodded. It already felt like a large stick was prodding me in the back.

"I'm coming, I'm coming." I climbed into the back seat next to Mia and Devon and wiggled my fingers at Sawyer, in a wave. "See ya."

Jackson heaved a sigh, and then grinned at Han and started the car.

Finally, the time had come. We drove off down the street, following the other Jeep. Past friends, past neighbours, through the town we knew so well.

It was a community of respectable homes owned by hardworking, friendly people. Most residences were well-maintained, if a little shabby, and all of them were now fitted with security doors and screens and recently-installed alarm systems.

Scattered throughout were also a few stand-alone houses that had been neglected and vandalised. Broken windows and doors, graffiti across the walls, overgrown gardens, burnt-out cars. Tragedy and violence had left its mark.

Gradually, these weathered buildings, suburban streets, and parked cars gave way to an open expanse of greens and browns. The rolling hills and fields were split only by the black motorway lanes and white lines.

Despite the concern about Cooper and what we might find at the Gold Coast, we were like young children released early from school, and our excitement jumped up a notch with every bump in the road.

25

Mia, Devon, and I were still in the back seat. Han was driving, and Jackson was in the passenger seat. Our tyres gave off a monotonous hum on the rain-drenched highway, which stretched out like a shiny, black ribbon.

There were not many cars sharing the road with us, but we had been overtaken by several gangs of bikers. They rode by in single file, or sometimes two abreast, and were spread over a kilometre or more, but the gang membership was clear from their jackets and vests. We counted twenty-five in one group. The outlaw biker gangs were back in force and heading north. They looked mysterious and dangerous, with their dark helmets and huge, black bikes. Initially, Han and Jackson watched them with a lively interest, but this was soon replaced with a cautious vigilance.

At regular intervals, huge semitrailers thundered past in convoys, making their deliveries to outlying regions. Jet had told us armed guards accompanied them, and they would not stop for anything or anyone.

As it was my turn to pick the music, hits from the eighties and nineties played quietly through the speakers. It was the playlist I had created with my father, his music, and what I had grown up listening to.

Han used his thumb to flick down the volume. "I feel like we're the Avengers, setting off on a rescue mission."

There was a chorus of laughter as our lazy mood lifted.

"So, who are you?" Devon asked Han.

"Tony Stark, of course."

"I'm the Black Widow." Mia tried, and failed, to speak with a Russian accent.

Devon placed the book she had been reading face down in her lap. She looked at me over the round frames of her glasses, which were perched on the edge of her nose. "I'll be the Hulk."

I raised my eyebrows, worried she was making a reference to her body shape.

"But the Hulk is a guy," said Han, glancing back at us in the rear-view mirror.

"Surely we're not getting caught up in gender roles here," I said pointedly.

"Of course not!" Jackson muttered, and he turned to give me a mischievous wink.

"Devon, you can be whoever you want," Han quickly qualified, and I felt the swell of his affection for her.

"Bruce Banner is the scientist. And that's me." Devon used her thumb to point at herself.

"True." I dropped my head to her shoulder for a moment, relieved it was not about her body size.

"Nova, what about you?" Han asked.

"Hawkeye," I said firmly, as if it was obvious. "He is the best Avenger."

That started a lively debate between Tony Stark, who was supposed to be concentrating on the road, and Bruce Banner, beside me, about who was the best Avenger.

"Jack, who are you? Thor?" Mia interrupted them.

"Nah, I'm Loki." He turned to face us with a cheeky grin.

"Isn't he a villain?" Mia teased.

"A villain and a hero." Han slapped his hand on the steering wheel. "Good choice, dude."

"And what about Jet?" I asked. He and Rayna were in the car behind us.

"The Black Panther," said Han.

"That's always his choice in the game," said Jackson.

"Then Rayna has to be Captain Marvel."

We were all giggling now.

"Sawyer can be Nick Fury," said Jackson.

"Yes!"

"We don't have a Thor."

"We can pick up Chris Hemsworth from Byron Bay on our way through."

"I'm definitely up for that," said Mia, with an emphatic nod.

"Me too," said Han.

Devon giggled. "Me three."

Jackson's laugh was loud and hearty.

$$\triangle$$

We had stopped for petrol, toilets, and snacks.

Jet had not wanted to take any risks by staying the night somewhere, so we were driving all the way through to the Gold Coast. There were enough drivers to change regularly and avoid fatigue. Jet and Rayna had already mapped out our stops, based on the safest options.

The old guy behind the counter looked us over warily. I smiled and let my happiness float through the shop like soft flower petals waving in a light summer breeze.

Beside me, Jet was paying for the petrol in both cars, courtesy of Sawyer.

"Hey, Nova, what do you want?" Jackson called to me.

The attendant's eyes flicked to Jackson and Han, who were looking in the drink fridges.

"A raspberry-Coke slushie, please."

Jackson laughed. "Of course you do."

"It's minus degrees out there, Nova. You're nuts." Han gave a loud chortle.

Mia and Devon were still in the bathroom. Rayna had stayed outside. She was casually leaning up against the car, but I knew she was on alert. There were a couple of large trucks parked in the bays to the side, but I couldn't see their drivers anywhere. Maybe they were sleeping in their cabs.

The attendant had relaxed, happy with his assessment of us, and he returned my smile. "I thought at first you were recruiting these young ones for the Army or something." He nodded at Jet and ran a hand over his own short military-style haircut. "But you seem like one big, happy family."

"Yeah, something like that." Jet grinned, and it lit up his whole face.

In line with my epiphany, I was drawing on the affection and compassion I sensed in each person and reflecting it like a mirror. It made for a general atmosphere of harmonious wellbeing, which followed us around.

"You timed it right, then. This feels like a good day," said the man.

"Oh yeah?"

"Every day for over a week we've had bikers coming through, heading north. It doesn't take much to set them off. It's dangerous to end up in the middle of their disputes. Knives and guns. They are more brutal than they ever were in my day." The attendant looked over at Han, in his black leather jacket, but seemed to be reassured by the easy camaraderie between him and Jackson.

"We've passed a lot of them on the road. I hope you're not on your own here. Are these monitored?" Jet nodded at the surveillance camera behind the counter and another in the corner.

"I'm not alone. There is a whole bank of monitors out the back. And armed security." The attendant moved one hand to rest under the counter, probably to a rifle hidden there, and with the other hand he gestured towards a frosted glass door. "But I've got a good feeling about today. I don't reckon we'll need them." He placed both hands back on the countertop and smiled again.

The attendant continued to laugh and joke with us as we purchased our food and drinks.

I really hoped it would continue to be a good day for him.

△

I was driving. Mia was in the back seat, asleep, with her head back against the headrest and her mouth wide open. Han and Devon were in the jeep behind with Jet and Rayna. Harry Styles was singing through the speakers, from Mia's playlist.

Jackson had his seat pushed right back, his knees bent, and his feet resting against the dashboard. He was staring at me and smiling. His contentment vibrated softly through me, just like the motion of the car.

"What?" I glanced at him, then back at the road ahead.

The tarmac rolled away underneath the car. White lines marked the way. Scrubby bushes and red dirt blurred on both sides.

"Nothing. I just like watching you."

I laughed self-consciously but kept my focus on driving. "You're weird."

"You're beautiful." His voice was low and throaty.

"You're distracting me."

"Sorry, not sorry." He gave a smile that was both lazy and affectionate.

I felt his gaze travel over my body, and my cheeks burned. "Stop it."

"Stop what?" he teased, and I could feel the desire electrifying his body.

I knew his eyes were lingering on my lips, just as I knew he was thinking about kissing me.

"Actually, I need to tell you something important." I spoke quietly, not wanting to wake Mia.

"Okay." He shifted on his seat and chuckled.

I knew he thought I was going to say something flirty, so I shook my head. "I've had an epiphany. I haven't had a chance to tell Sawyer. I don't want to text him, and it happened just as we were leaving."

"Okay, tell me." His voice held a more deliberate tone.

"I think I can do something about stopping the anger. Well, maybe not, probably not, but it feels better than what I've been trying to do. I mean I doubt it will make that much of a difference, like, in the world, but maybe just a little bit. Maybe if other empaths can help. It's not turning back the warrior gene, but maybe it will stop people turning it on in the first place, or the second place, or something." I shrugged, suddenly lacking confidence in my idea.

"Nova, you are barely making sense."

"Well, it was actually Mia. She gave me the idea."

"Mia? What did she do?" I could see out of the corner of my eye that he was watching my face, and I could feel the curiosity bubbling through him, but I had to keep my eyes on the road.

"I've been doing it all wrong. I've been trying to turn off the warrior gene, trying to turn back people's anger. A bit like how Sawyer calms people down. But that's too hard. The anger causing this violence is a powerful emotion. I can't turn it off. Not really. Not easily. Even Corben said it's easier to ignite the warrior gene than it is to stop it once ignited."

Jackson interrupted me. "Nova, you are stronger than you think. Sawyer and Corben think you can do it."

"No, listen. I've got a better way. Mia has a natural compassion for people, and I realised I can piggyback on that. Not just Mia, but everyone. It's easier to go with things than against them. I can draw out the good feelings people have, their friendships, their love for each other, their community spirit. I can echo that back to them. Make it stronger, more powerful than the anger. I just have to use what's there, and I think they'll turn off the warrior gene themselves. I think I have more chance of making this work. Stopping the anger by pulling out people's own compassion, combining it with my empathy. Does that make sense now?"

"It makes a lot of sense." I heard the reverence in his voice and felt the surge of admiration from across the car. It lifted me like a burst of sunshine on a cloudy day. "By reminding people that they care about each other, you will get them to stop being angry and violent."

"Well, yeah, maybe. Sort of. That's the idea, anyway. It's not really me. People do it to themselves. It does mean

I have to find the good in everyone. I'm sure in some people its hidden under a lot of horrible stuff. And, I mean, maybe it won't even work."

"It will work. You can do it; I know you can." He reached over to squeeze my knee. "You can change the world."

I gave an embarrassed laugh, but I felt energized. It was like an electrical current ran through me, but in a good way. For the first time in a while, I didn't regret who I was and what I could do.

△

We crossed the border into Queensland just after dawn. It had taken us twenty-two hours. Although we were exhausted by the long car trip, the last part of our journey brought us brilliant sunrise views over the ocean. It had restored our excitement.

As soon as we were off the main highway and amongst the towering Gold Coast holiday apartments, however, I felt my chest constrict. It was the same feeling I'd had in Melbourne, under Abraham's rule. There was an underlying hostility, hidden beneath the bright lights and neon signs. An underbelly that felt putrid, noxious, and oily.

Sawyer had organised our accommodation in one of the smaller high-rises, a street back from the ocean and south of the main shopping area of Surfers Paradise. A three-bedroom apartment for us, and a neighbouring two-bedroom for Jet and Rayna. I was fairly sure that Jet and Rayna only needed one bedroom and, if I sensed it, Sawyer must have, but I guess they wanted to keep up professional appearances.

Our apartment was a riot of scents. Sunscreen, fresh air, and salt water mixed with the smell of sausages and bacon cooking on a barbeque below somewhere.

It was clean, secure, and roomy. The kitchen opened straight onto the lounge, with a giant television screen and comfortable couches. Double glass doors led out to a large balcony, with a round table and chairs, but no ocean view because of the large high-rises between us and the beach. A small hallway led from the lounge to the bathroom and the three bedrooms. One of which had an ensuite. We played off for that room with a game of rock paper scissors, and Mia won.

Jackson collapsed onto the bed in our room. His weariness weighed heavily in my body. I rolled my shoulders. They were stiff and sore.

He had not told Cooper that we were coming. Yet. The less Theo knew about us, the safer we were. Jackson wanted to be in and out before Theo even realised that I was here.

That was the plan. And I hoped it was not just wishful thinking.

26

We walked up the beach to the centre of Surfers Paradise, and it felt good to stretch our legs and be out in the sun.

A flock of noisy seagulls scattered as we went past, but then resettled on the beach as if they were marching in a parade.

School holidays were dwindling to an end and only the bravest of tourists were out and about. In front of the flagged swimming area, a few striped cabanas crowded together. Children, inflatable toys, and stressed parents spilled out onto the sand and into the water.

Cavill Avenue offered a large, open, pedestrian area, surrounded by cafés and bikini shops. I had expected more of a holiday vibe, but the people were solemn and stern.

We chose a café at the beach end of the mall and crowded around a small table.

Jet and Rayna sat close by, but separate to us, and I knew it made it easier for them to do their security thing. There had been a change in them ever since we had arrived. It was not just about them providing protection detail, it was the general feeling of the place.

Anger seemed to hang in the air. It gave me a headache, but in Jet and Rayna it also tugged at their warrior gene. It put them on edge, and it tested their control. I could feel the tension in their muscles.

Breakfast came and restored our fading energy.

"Is it just me, or do you guys also feel like we're sitting in a *Home and Away* scene? Everyone here looks shiny and beautiful. And blond. And really skinny." Mia gestured towards two girls passing.

They were both tall, very slim, and blond. One had long curls that gleamed like gold, while the other had straight hair that danced across her back as she moved past us. Long legs rose from high-heeled sandals to the short skirts they wore. Their make-up was exquisite. I nodded my agreement. They looked like supermodels prancing down the catwalk. But neither of them looked happy about it.

"I get what you mean." Devon nodded towards a guy sitting at a table in the café next door to ours.

He definitely looked like an actor from *Home and Away*. Slim, but toned and muscular. His brilliant white shirt was unbuttoned across his tanned chest and hung loosely over tight, ripped jeans. His curly hair was bleached blonde with dark roots, and still a little damp, suggesting an early morning surf. His face was also deeply tanned, and his chin darkened further with a designer stubble. Sunglasses were perched on his head and he scowled at his phone, slowly sipping his coffee.

"They're all too skinny." Han spoke dismissively. He leaned back in his chair, his solid frame taking up a lot of space, as he pushed aside an empty plate that moments ago had been piled high with 'Charlie's big breakfast' and Belgian waffles on the side. "Do you really want someone that only eats carrot sticks? I prefer some curves."

Jackson groaned. "Be careful what you say, mate. Damned if you do and damned if you don't."

"Hey, hang on. I want to hear it," said Mia. "Curves just on girls, or guys too, Han?"

He shrugged. "Both."

"Me too," said Devon.

"Babe, do you like curvy women? Is there something you haven't told me?" Han teased, while Devon blushed a deep shade of red.

"I just mean there's too much pressure on girls to have a skinny body, and on guys to have muscles." Devon shrugged and hung her head.

"I don't mind the muscles." Han flexed his own large biceps. "But I want someone with curves that you can cuddle up to. I don't want some bony arse sitting on my knee. And mostly, I want someone that has opinions. Someone that I can talk to, that teaches me things and listens to my stuff. This is my perfect partner right here." Han swung an arm around Devon and pulled her into his chest. She was still blushing, but she gave him a warm smile.

"That's so lovely." Mia smiled at Han and then turned to Jackson. "Your turn, Jack. What do you want in a partner?"

He took a deep breath. "Okay, then. I prefer brunettes for starters. Someone not afraid to eat junk food. Someone who looks sexy in my t-shirts. Who doesn't care about putting on a lot of makeup or styling her hair. Whose body fits right up against mine on the bike. I want to feel those curves when I'm riding." He wiggled his eyebrows suggestively and Han reached forward to touch fists with him.

"You're just describing Nova. That doesn't count," said Mia dismissively.

"Hang on, I care about putting on makeup and styling my hair." I reached up to smooth back the strands that had escaped from my hastily-assembled ponytail and licked my lips. My breakfast had erased the lip gloss I'd put on before we came out.

"No you don't," said Mia and Devon in unison. I poked out my tongue at them.

"You asked me what I wanted in a partner. That's the description. Why don't you describe your perfect match, Mia?" Jackson challenged.

"Taller than me. I don't care if he has muscles; I just don't want him to obsess over them. Nice eyes. Soft lips. Someone gentle, kind, interested in what I want to do. Considerate. A good sense of humour. He can be assertive, but doesn't get moody when he doesn't get his own way." Mia rested back against her chair and gave a sigh.

"Sounds like the complete opposite to Kenji," said Jackson sarcastically, but then he shrugged when I elbowed him in the ribs.

Mia just gave a serious nod and didn't respond.

"Yeah, well, it's not just about appearance, is it?" said Han lightly. "That might initially get your attention, but it doesn't hold it."

"Nova, what about you? And you can't just describe Jack. That's boring." Mia held up her middle finger, in a rude gesture, at Jackson.

"I guess, for me, it's more about what I sense about a person."

"Do you look for auras?" Han asked.

"No, I can't see auras." I shook my head.

"Just as well. Jack's must be black," Han said with a smirk, reaching forward for another fist bump, which Jackson returned with a grin.

"What do you see?" asked Mia.

It felt like I was encircled by inquisitive meerkats, sitting up on their back legs, watching me, waiting. Jet and Rayna were also quiet and seemed to be listening in.

"Well, I don't see anything. It's just a feeling in my body. Sort of what they're feeling in their body. But I guess it brings up a picture in my mind. And it's just what that emotion is right now. It could be quite different in an hour. Like that girl." I flicked my hand towards another tall, blonde, slim girl, walking past in a pink, long-sleeved crop top, a short, white skirt, and white stiletto ankle boots. She wore sunglasses, so we could not see her eyes, but her mouth was twisted in a pout. "She's unhappy, maybe grieving. It sits in the pit of my stomach. Umm, it makes me think of a rose whose petals are falling off."

"Oh my god, Nova. That is so sad, and so amazing at the same time." Mia was jiggling on her chair. "What do I feel like?"

"You ... well, you make my heart feel warmer, lighter, softer. It makes me think of a summer day, ice-cream, and lots of laughter."

"Oh, I love you, Nova." She leaned over and kissed my cheek. "I wish you could tell the future." She let out a deep sigh, and it felt like a stone was resting on my chest. I knew she was thinking of Kenji.

Jackson took my hand. "And me?" he asked quietly.

"At the moment? Umm, a bit on edge. Like fingernails scraped down a chalkboard." I shivered. "But you also feel like one of those cosy weighted quilts. Warm and safe. That's what I feel from you most of the time."

He smiled and rubbed the inside of my wrist with his thumb.

"Pfft." Han scoffed. "Surely I'm a fire-breathing dragon."

"You make my hands feel both steady and soft. It's like … Tony Stark." I giggled. "Strong and sarcastic on the outside but sweet and generous inside."

Han puffed out his chest, which was quite expansive already.

Devon stretched an arm around him and looked adoringly into his eyes. "You are like a cuddly teddy bear to me."

Han looked at her with wide eyes and a mock frown. "Don't say that out loud. You'll ruin my tough biker reputation."

Devon shook her head and laughed. Jackson snorted.

"And what about Devon?" Mia patted her arm.

"She feels solid and dependable. It's a feeling that sits comfortably across my shoulders. Sorry, that doesn't sound as exciting. It's like a calm sea. Or the answer to a question."

Devon nodded firmly, and her eyes sparkled. She seemed pleased with my analysis.

I realised Devon and Han gave me similar sensations. They both had strength but a softness at the same time.

"What about you, Nova?" Han winked at me.

"After all this," I laughed awkwardly, "happy in my heart to be here with you guys. Drained and tired in my bones as well. I'm like a page of messy scribbles."

"Wow. You're incredible." Mia's voice held a new level of awe that made me blush.

I shook my head in protest.

"I never realised how exhausting it must be for you, Nova." Devon looked at me with wide, sympathetic eyes.

Jackson leaned in and spoke quietly. "When we get back to the apartment, can I wrap your tired, messy scribbles in my cosy weighted quilt?"

"That's one of the nicest things you've ever asked me."

We both giggled. Jackson placed his hand on his chest, his heart, and gave me his special wink intended just for me. I nodded at him and put my hand on my heart as well.

"Stop it, you two. Or I will honestly vomit up my breakfast." Mia pointed her fingers towards her mouth and gagged. "You lovebirds better not make me feel like the fifth wheel in this trip."

"Well, you did invite yourself," Jackson muttered under his breath, earning himself a glare from Mia but laughter from Han.

Jet appeared beside us. "I've paid the bill. We should move. You lot are laughing so much you're attracting attention. I don't think they're used to happy people here." He looked around with a wary eye.

"But we haven't heard about Devon's perfect man," said Han.

"She'll just describe you." Mia stood up and waved a hand in dismissal.

"Actually, I was going to describe that hot blond guy." Devon held her hand over her mouth, as if hiding a smile.

"You were what?" Han jumped to his feet, looking like a deer in headlights, until we all started laughing again.

This time I noticed the other people staring, and I felt the animosity like daggers being thrown at our backs.

"Come on." I ushered everyone forward to follow Jet.

Rayna brought up the rear. Jackson and Han walked on either side of us girls, and I knew they were also being protective.

We stopped at the supermarket on the way back to collect some staple food items, and Mia bought blue hair dye.

"It's time for a change," she said when I raised my eyebrows in a silent question.

$$\triangle$$

That afternoon, we went for a swim.

The water temperature was freezing, but we were Victorians in Queensland. Regardless of the season, regardless of how cold it was, we had to go for a swim. It was like a rule or something.

"It's refreshing," said Mia, as the waves circled our ankles.

The water was icy cold. She was lying.

I was not sure whether it was better to go in slowly and let your body adjust, or to get it over with quickly. Once I got used to it around my ankles, I took another step. That just meant the iciness splashed up to my thighs. The ocean floor was like corrugated iron, with little hills and dips which made it very uneven. The worst was when I dropped into a dip and the water hit my stomach.

There were screams and squeals from Mia and Devon, who were taking it very slowly, while Jackson and Han ploughed through the smaller waves and swam out until just their shoulders and heads bobbed above the water.

I knew it would not be long before they targeted us girls, so I did a shallow dive under the next wave. The cold took my breath away, and I came up gasping.

Jackson laughed at me, but he came over to wrap his body around mine. I was hoping for his usual warmth, but it was like hugging an iceblock.

Han was already using both hands to splash water over Devon and Mia until they finally relented and dived under.

The five of us jumped over or ducked under the waves until Han and Jackson caught a wave and body surfed into the shore.

"Can we go in, before they get back out here?" Devon eyed the boys, who were already returning to us.

I nodded. My teeth were chattering, and I was not sure I could talk.

"Yeah, we've had our swim." Mia's lips had turned blue.

Han and Jackson stayed in longer, body surfing, and Jet joined them.

Rayna had a quick dip, but then lay with us girls, in the sun, gradually warming up.

I stretched back on my striped towel, courtesy of the apartment, as the droplets of water on my stomach and legs dried into little dabs of salt. The sand was warm on the surface but cooler if you dug your toes in.

The waves were not big, but they travelled fast from the deep to the shallow water, and they were dumpers. The boys had to time it right to pull out and avoid a face-first plunge into the sand at the bottom. There was a joy in watching them. The swell building, the curl of the wave just as it broke, the splash of spray high into the air.

Although tanned in comparison with my fairness, Jackson looked pale next to Jet's dark skin and Han's golden colour. But he looked completely at ease in the water. His phoenix tattoo moved as he turned and stretched, as if it were alive and about to take flight.

△

Just before sunset, Jet took Han and Jackson to have a look at some addresses that Sawyer had sent through. They were hoping Cooper would be home by then. Jackson didn't want me to go, and Jet backed him up. They were not hopeful, as Cooper had not been sighted, but they were checking out buildings that were known to be undergoing painting and renovation.

Devon and I helped Mia dye her hair. She just wanted the tips coloured blue. It was quite a process. Mia's hair was shoulder length and a little frizzy. We had to be careful to keep the colour to just the ends and not get any dye on any of us, or the white bathroom tiles. We used a stainless-steel bowl from the kitchen to hold the dye, and placed that in the sink. Mia sat on a chair in front, with her head held backwards over the sink and the bowl. There was only one set of plastic gloves, so Devon wore those and dipped the ends of Mia's hair into the dye mix, while I tried to hold her head still. I had prepared strips of Alfoil, and Devon wrapped these around the hair strands. Then we waited the required thirty minutes.

"So, now it's just us girls, are you going to tell us what is going on with you and Kenji?" Devon had the courage to ask Mia what had also been on my own mind.

"Well, I guess it's a lot of little things. And, basically, I think I deserve to be treated better."

Devon and I nodded vigorously in support, even without knowing any details. That is what friends are for.

"We always do what he wants to do. I go to all his footy matches and club nights, but he doesn't ever think of taking me out to dinner. He never wants to just hang out at my house. We never go out alone; some of his mates are always with us. I ask him about his work, but he never asks me about my work or my studies. He is always late picking me up. He's too tired to come over, but never too tired to go to the footy club. And he takes ages to respond to messages." Mia paused, her eyes wide and glistening with unshed tears. "Do I sound petty?"

Devon shook her head.

"Of course not." I sent Mia soft waves of compassion and friendship.

"It hasn't been good for a while, but then last Saturday night, at the footy club, Jimmy was drunk and being stupid, and he got the DJ to make an announcement that Kenji and I were getting engaged and having a baby. Everyone had been drinking. It was supposed to be funny, I guess. Lots of people cheered and came to congratulate us, and of course I was saying that it wasn't true. Anyway, Kenji was really mad. Not at Jimmy, but at me. He thought I had put Jimmy up to it, which I hadn't. Then Kenji said he wouldn't marry me even if I got pregnant."

Mia was hurting. It felt like my heart was in a vice.

I put my hand on top of hers. "Oh, Mia. That's a shitty thing to say."

"It's not as if I would ever do that. I don't even want to marry him or have his children. He should be so lucky." Mia's lips formed a defiant pout, but she rubbed at her eyes as the tears finally escaped.

I reflected again on how self-absorbed I had become. Mia had been struggling for a while and I had not even noticed. So busy with my own issues, I'd closed in on myself and pushed everyone away when I should have been reaching out.

We needed each other. Our friendships made us stronger. I had learnt that.

"You do deserve better than that." Devon was rubbing Mia's back.

I drew on the bonds I could feel between the three of us and let them fold around Mia, providing layer upon layer of acceptance and understanding.

When Mia's phone alarm went off, she disappeared into the bathroom to wash out the hair dye. She reappeared with a towel wrapped around her head.

"Okay, let's see the new you." I smiled at her.

Mia swept off the towel with a flourish. "New and improved." Her auburn brown hair ended in brilliant blue tips. It did look good, and it really suited Mia, who had always had a zany style of her own. She did deserve better.

"New, maybe, but there was no need for improvement. You have always been strong and beautiful." Devon had a knack for saying exactly the right thing.

We moved into a group hug, a circle of safety and love.

26

The following day, Mia managed to talk Jet into letting us girls go shopping at Pacific Fair, while he took Han and Jackson to scope out a few more potential locations for Cooper. Mia wanted some new clothes to go with her new blue-dipped hair. Devon wanted something new too. We were all going out to the pub for dinner.

"Stay together. I need to be able to see everyone at all times." Rayna was on edge.

Jitters ran down my spine and I was clenching my jaw. I knew that Rayna carried a heavy load of guilt for what had happened with Sage in Melbourne. Although she had only left us for a short time to report to Sawyer, it was long enough for Abraham to arrive and kill Sage. Rayna blamed herself. There was a lot of that going around. She was not going to make the same mistake ever again.

I drew a deep breath in through my nose and made a conscious effort to ground myself, noticing what I could smell and see around us.

Freshly made cinnamon donuts. It was a tantalising smell. People, quite a lot of people, wearing light-coloured clothes. In Victoria, during winter, we all tended to wear dark colours, but here, it was like a European landscape painting in which people were dressed in pastels and carried parasols. But without the parasols.

It was time to try out my new idea. I wanted to draw on the goodness in others and send that out in larger echoes. That should influence the emotional climate all around the shopping centre.

Pulling on the little pockets of affection that Rayna hid amongst her layers of professional self-discipline was relatively easy. I let it spread through her and ease her anxiety. Despite that, the sense of responsibility never left her, and she remained alert and cautious. I wouldn't have wanted it any other way.

Mia and Devon were even easier. Their caring natures spilled out of them requiring little effort from me. It seemed to make a difference. We were greeted with smiles in the shops and even from people we just walked past. I created a cheerful bubble that floated around us.

Although it was working, I knew it would not take much for the aggression to rise to the top. People here were angry and scared. More so than at home. And an hour of me sending out good vibes wasn't enough to change that. There were still raised voices, arguing about prices or lack of service. Threats were made when someone was accidentally knocked aside. And I heard the cries of a child who had been scolded for dropping their ice-cream.

We moved cautiously and slowly between the clothes shops, and eventually everyone made a purchase, including Rayna. The retail therapy had worked wonders.

△

Devon came out of the apartment's bathroom. She wore her new black top, which stretched across her large chest. The deep neckline revealed her substantial cleavage. Han raised his eyebrows and gave a wolf-whistle. Devon blushed and hung her head.

"You look gorgeous," said Mia. She wore a layered, dark-blue, peasant dress, which totally set off her new hair.

"Are you sure it's okay?" Devon's face and neck were still a deep red.

"Definitely." I nodded with a wide smile.

Han swung his arm around her. He wore his usual black leather jacket, but with a new white shirt that Devon had bought for him. "Better than okay." He whispered some more words against her ear, which just made Devon's blush deepen.

We walked the few blocks to the pub. There were some people eating at the cafés in Cavill Avenue, and I knew Jackson checked them all in case we accidently came across Cooper. Everywhere that he had tried today had been another dead end.

The tables were well-spaced in the pub's dining room, and most of them were occupied. Everyone looked like … well, like normal people, quietly talking, sometimes even smiling, but I could still feel the now familiar, ugly undercurrent. I knew I had to copy Sawyer, and work at keeping things calm and peaceful.

Mia and I waited to be served at the bar.

The bartender came over and lined up a couple of shot glasses. "These are from him." He nodded towards a thick-set guy in a light blue shirt, standing at the end.

The guy was talking with two other people, but he stood a little apart from them, giving the impression that they were a couple but he was on his own. When the bartender poured out the two shots of vodka, the guy smiled at us and raised his own glass in salute.

"Thanks, but we can't accept these," I said. "Can we?" I turned to Mia.

She shrugged and giggled. "We've seen them being poured, so I don't see why not. We need to let loose a bit." She turned to smile at the thick-set guy as she picked up one glass and drained it.

He smiled back and moved through the crowd towards us. "Hi, I'm West." He held out a hand for a formal hand-shake, and Mia shook it, with another giggle.

"I'm Mia. And this is Nova."

West had dark grey eyes, which crinkled at the sides with his smile. As I shook his extended hand he turned his wrist, so my tattoo showed beneath my sleeve. "Nice tattoo."

Before I even had a chance to respond, Jackson was at my left shoulder and Jet was at my right.

"Take your hand off my girlfriend." Jackson's voice was harsh, and a protective heat surrounded me.

Jet's suspicion was much colder, but more lethal. It sat between my shoulder blades like a large lump of ice.

West flinched and quickly pulled his hand away. He took a step backwards.

"Sorry. Sorry, just being friendly."

I probed West's emotions. There were no pockets of darkness, and I could sense an innocence that reminded me of a playful puppy. He seemed harmless, and nice.

Mia was watching me, and I nodded in reassurance. "It's okay." I turned to Jet and then to Jackson. "He's okay."

Mia smiled at West and moved a step closer to him. "Sorry about them; they can be a little over-protective."

"I totally get it. You can't be too careful these days." His broad smile had returned. "So, what about you? Are you here with your boyfriend?"

"I'm not. I'm here on my own." Mia reached up, smoothed back her blue-tinged hair, and adjusted her nose ring.

Jackson murmured under his breath, "Umm, Kenji?" But if Mia heard him, she ignored it.

I nudged him. "Don't. It's complicated."

"Hmm." I could tell Jackson didn't approve, but he didn't say anything further.

West and Mia had their heads bent towards each other, asking and answering questions. Jet had moved away as quietly as he had arrived.

When I looked up at Jackson and smiled, there was a shift in him, as if he'd finally loosened tight shoes that he'd been wearing all day. He picked up the full shot glass that had been intended for me and passed it to West, with a nod and a half smile. "You should have this one." Then he signalled to the bartender for two more. When they came, he passed one to me. "Can I buy you a drink, beautiful?"

"Are you flirting with me?"

"Most definitely." A smile played around his lips.

"And does that line normally work for you?"

"I've never tried it before."

Jackson downed his shot, and I did the same. It had a strong bite that caught in the back of my throat, but in a good way.

I was wearing my new cropped hoodie, and a small area of skin was bare between my jeans and my top. Jackson reached forward and rubbed his knuckles across my bare stomach, flesh against flesh. It sent a tingle down my spine. His fingers were warm and silky as they slid around me, and his thumbs moved in slow circles up my back, under my hoodie.

"So, did the line work?" he asked.

"Most definitely."

He gave a hoarse chuckle. "Good to know."

△

Mia organised for West and his two friends to join our table. They were up from Melbourne, also on holidays from university. Preston was reserved, and with his thick, black glasses and a permanent frown of concentration, he had the look of a studious nerd. His girlfriend, Farah, was also quiet and shy, but I could sense a gentle nature and warm heart. They were both very wary of Han and Jackson initially, but gradually relaxed as Mia wove her usual magic in making people comfortable and I kept up my calming vibes. All three of them were studying engineering, and they compared subjects and assessments with Han.

The soft music playing in the background was overlaid with our chatter and quiet laughter. The meals came out with inviting aromas, and drinks were clinked together with a holiday cheer.

Our joy spread around the room, and occasional laughter drifted across from the other diners. It seemed like we were breathing cleaner air, less polluted by the anger that rode through the streets outside.

The exception was a small table behind us. It was given a wide berth by staff and customers alike.

People could not help but notice the man sitting there. His black leather jacket marked him as belonging to one of the biker gangs, and he wore a white bandanna around his neck. He had a facial tattoo, but not one of those tribal ones.

It was a snake, which wound around his cheeks and chin, with a forked tongue rising above one eye.

The woman wore a red dress and stood out as particularly attractive. They were talking quietly, drinking heavily, and sharing a plate of hot chips. When he smiled at her, I saw two of his teeth had been filed to a point, like fangs. As such, he never looked particularly friendly, but they seemed to be on good terms. I sensed a connection between them. Not intimate, but more like there was between siblings.

So, when he pulled out a small axe and, in a single slash, chopped off her fingers, the ones that were reaching for some chips, it was a shock, to say the least.

Everyone in the pub leapt to their feet as if we were part of a synchronised flash mob, about to start dancing. But there was no dancing, and instead we froze. A game of statues when the music stops. But it hadn't. An old rock song droned in the background, and it was suddenly loud and garish.

The couple had remained seated.

Jet was instantly by my side as if he had been there the whole time. He had a hand on Jackson's arm, and I saw his knuckles turn white. He was making sure Jackson did not move to help the woman. Rayna stood behind Jackson, with her hand on his other arm. I sensed that she also wanted to help, like a medic's urge or something, but had decided it was better to hold back. Although Jet and Rayna were both outwardly calm, the adrenaline that flowed through them felt like a car revving at the start of a race.

Han was behind Rayna. He had one arm around Devon and the other around Mia. His mouth was set in a firm line, while Devon's hung open. Mia's eyes were wide, and I knew her heart was pounding. As was mine. As was everyone's.

West and his two friends had taken a few steps back away from our table, away from the couple.

The woman was moaning. Her pain lashed across me like the strikes of a whip, and, just like a wild animal caught in a trap, I knew she was struggling to make sense of what had happened. She clutched at the stumps where her fingers had been with her good hand, using paper napkins to try and stop the flow of blood.

The man didn't say anything. He sat back in his chair and laid the axe down on the table between them. It was a small one that you used for chopping logs into kindling for a fire, but not big enough for cutting down trees. Next to that were the two finger ends. They looked like the plastic severed finger toys you bought in a joke shop for Halloween. The same, but different. This was a hideous reality.

The fight-or-flight response had kicked in for the pub crowd, and people were turning to look for an exit or pulling out their own weapons to arm themselves. Fear surged across the room like a tidal wave.

The woman finally stood up, demanding the spotlight as if she were the star of a show, and everyone froze once more.

She reached for the axe and raised it above her head with her good hand. Her arm shook, and the axe quavered with it, but she managed to keep it high.

The man smirked at her. "You haven't got the guts."

Her mangled hand hung at her side. Blood dripped onto the floor with a steady regularity from the two red knuckle-stumps. She swayed for a moment and looked about to fall over. Then she raised the axe even higher.

She gave a smirk of her own. In one swift stroke, she brought the axe firmly down on his head.

The axe sunk into his skull. It made a sound like a knife slicing into a slab of meat, and then cracked when it hit bone. My stomach lurched and bile rose to the back of my throat. It was sour and harsh.

The biker fell forward onto the table, into the bowl of chips. His head was caved in the middle, looking like a valley through a mountain. Blood swelled up around the axe blade like a red river bursting its banks, and chunks of skin, or maybe brain, hung loose out the front like large boulders. His blood mixed with the tomato sauce on the chips.

There was a scream and the sound of someone vomiting, followed by a deathly silence. Chills ran through me.

"We need to get out of here." Jet's hand was firm and steady on my arm. His strength flowed through that touch, and I stood up a little straighter.

"I'm scared," said Mia.

I reached for her hand and squeezed it.

"Don't be." Jackson's voice was low, but steady.

"Why not?" Mia looked at him with wide eyes.

He gave a quick shrug, but he also reached for her other hand. "It doesn't help."

I stifled a hysterical giggle. Mia gave a huff, but I sensed a lightening of her fear.

People had blocked the closest exit. Pushing, shoving, all trying to get out. There was shouting, and a few guns were being waved about with threats from those at the back. Against this rush, I could see the grey uniforms of the security guards pushing to gain entry inside. They were not having much success, and they were far too late.

The woman in the red dress had sat back down on her chair. She was whimpering. I could not make myself look at her companion again but I knew his body was there, half in his chair and half across the table.

Rayna still had a hand on Jackson's arm, and she pulled at him while pointing towards the kitchen at the back. "This way."

Jackson pulled Mia behind him, following Rayna. Han and Devon moved in behind Mia and I had to let go of her hand to let them in.

Jet was close behind me, bringing up the rear. He bent his head low, next to my ear. "Nova, are you okay? Can you try and calm people down?"

Others were feeding into my panic, so it was not going to be easy, but I took a deep breath and blinked hard. I found myself reaching for Jackson, but he was too far ahead of me, so I clutched at Jet's hand. "Can we just stop for a minute?"

Jet stopped and moved me behind his body, shielding me from the table and the throng of people. Rayna and the others were moving away but I focused on the back of Jackson's head, imagining his face and the smile he reserved for me. His eyes would crinkle in the corners. They were a deep cocoa-brown. It filled me with warmth and comfort.

I was still holding Jet's hand, and now that I had calmed my own emotions I was letting his steady courage pulse through me and echo around the room. It moved through people like an invisible wave, and the results were noticeable almost immediately.

A man took a step back and helped up a lady that had fallen over. Two girls stepped aside so a child could pass by them to reach his mother. Another man that had been threatening someone with his gun apologised and let the person stay in front. With each act of kindness, I worked on amplifying that person's compassion and sending it out in waves.

The chaos was subsiding, and the crowd finally parted enough to let the security guards and the police through. Behind them came two tall men with crew cuts. They were not in uniform, but they had the look of the military.

One of these guys approached us, and while no words were exchanged, he and Jet touched fists. I realised he must be SAS too.

"That was good, Nova. Thanks. It made a difference." Jet spoke quietly against my ear. "Let's go now. The police can take it from here."

Jackson and the others were waiting for us in the kitchen by the back door. It opened into an alleyway behind the pub. A few other people with the same idea had come through the kitchen too, but the majority were being directed by the police to leave through the main doors.

Devon was pale, and her mascara was smudged as if she had been crying and rubbing her eyes. Mia's eyes were still wide with fright. Han had both arms wrapped around Devon, and I knew it was as much for his sake as hers. Jackson did his usual visual body scan of me, checking for injury, and I felt the stab of concern when he saw Jet and I still gripping onto each other's hands.

Jet shook his head at the unasked question and passed my hand into Jackson's like it was a formal ceremony. "She's fine."

Jackson pulled me close against his chest. Relief swam through the both of us, as sweet as honey.

"Where's Rayna?" Jet asked.

Jackson gestured towards the alleyway, just as Rayna's head appeared around the doorway.

"Come on," she said.

The alleyway was dim and dirty. Crates and boxes were stacked in precarious piles next to huge dumpsters that smelled, predictably, like garbage and rotting food.

Rayna led us out onto the main street, which was bright and clean in comparison. A large crowd still surrounded the front entrance of the pub, huddled under the streetlights. The glass doors had already been cordoned off with police tape, but people jostled gently against each other to get a view of what was happening inside. I could almost smell the morbid curiosity.

Local television news vans were parked up on the footpath, and the reporters and camera crew were busy recording comments from anyone who had witnessed the violence and wanted their few minutes of fame. It had not taken them long to get there.

"Vultures circling to pick at the scraps." Han shook his head in disgust.

"Let's go home," said Jet.

28

Rayna and Jet stayed with us for a few hours once we got back to the apartment and encouraged us to talk about what had happened. The shock was gradually subsiding and sharing our versions had a cathartic effect, but the abhorrence at the violence we had witnessed was still rattling through us.

While aggression and crime had become daily occurrences, there was something especially horrific about what we had seen.

When we finally went to bed, no one slept very well. Fear wafted through our dreams like whispers of cruel gossip that could not be ignored.

I woke when Jackson thrashed against me. He tumbled from the bed and ended up in a crouch on the floor. His shoulders shook with loud, gasping sobs, and it felt like the breath was being squeezed from my own lungs.

Eventually he looked up and gave me a weak smile. "I'm fine. It was just a dream. A nightmare."

I nodded. "Do you remember what it was about?"

He gave an embarrassed shrug. "Kind of predictable, really. It was dark, there was a guy in the house with an axe.

He was killing people. I could hear the sounds the axe made, and people's moans." Jackson took a deep breath and seemed to shudder a little when he let it out in a loud hiss. "But I hid, and I didn't go out to help. I was too scared."

I could sense the shame in him. It sucked at all my energy, and my heart dropped to the pit of my stomach. "Come here," I said gently.

He looked up at me but did not move.

"Please."

He unfolded himself and stood up.

"Closer."

He sat on the edge of the bed. His cocoa-brown eyes still shone with silver. They were like bottomless pools, inviting me to dive in. I draped an invisible veil of love and compassion over him.

"You might have been afraid, but you're not a coward." I was talking about what had happened at the pub, not his nightmare, and he knew it.

Unsure if he was ready to be touched, I reached out a tentative hand, but instead he pulled me into his arms and we lay back onto the pillows in a tight embrace.

"Thank you," Jackson said quietly.

I felt a smile lifting the corners of my mouth and snuggled against his chest.

We must have drifted off because when Mia had a nightmare and started screaming, it took me a good few minutes to work out what was going on. The easiest thing to do was to spend the rest of the night in her bed.

△

We were a subdued group the next morning. No one had much appetite for breakfast, except for Han. We lay about on the couches in the lounge room, watching the morning shows on TV, reluctant to leave the safety of the apartment. I was weary, both from a broken night's sleep and from absorbing everyone's fear. Rayna and Jet were the easiest to be around because they had already reverted to their cool, well-controlled emotional baseline.

Jet had been out early to talk with the police and his SAS buddy.

The man and woman from last night were brother and sister. She was secretly dating someone from a rival biker gang. Cutting off her fingers was a punishment. Clearly, the brother had not expected her to react as she had. The sister was in custody and under police protection. They were worried about repercussions. Biker gang violence was rampant on the Gold Coast, and it was well known that the gangs had police on their payroll. The woman was not safe, even in custody.

When there was a loud knock at the door, we all jumped. Han and Jackson rose from their seats in fight mode, ready to move into action, while Mia and Devon seemed to shrink back into their chairs. They all looked to Jet, waiting for his direction. I stayed where I was. A familiar and welcome serenity had already settled over me. Jet exchanged a glance and a short nod with Rayna, and I knew they had been expecting this visitor.

"It's okay." Jet waved a hand at the boys, gesturing that they should sit back down, while he stood up to open the door.

It was Sawyer, and he was followed by Corben. She, I had not expected. I was still sensing nothing from her.

Sawyer got an update from Jet and Rayna, although it was clear he had already been thoroughly briefed. Like a concerned and protective big brother, he checked in with each one of us, spreading the calm tranquillity that was an integral part of his very being.

Corben sat to one side, not saying much, not giving away any of her feelings, just smiling politely.

"So, none of those addresses I sent for Cooper panned out?" Sawyer asked Jackson, who shook his head. The heaviness returned to my body. Sawyer nodded and put a hand on Jackson's forearm. "I think it's time to text him and tell him that you are here. Set up a time to meet."

"What about Theo?" asked Jackson.

"I'm quite sure that, after last night, Theo will already know you're all here. There will have been a lot of talk about what happened and who was there to witness it." Sawyer looked over at me, his eyes crinkled with worry.

Jackson sent a text to Cooper. *I'm in Surfers. When can we meet?*

He got an immediate reply. *I can do today, after work.*

They exchanged more messages and planned to meet at a café off Cavill Avenue. The relief that ran through Jackson was palpable.

However, Cooper's last message caused a bit of a stir. *Come alone.*

"I don't want you going alone." Sawyer's voice was firm. "Jet and I will come. We'll keep out of the way."

"I'm coming with you too," said Han.

I knew they would not want me to go to the meeting, so I stayed quiet. But I was glad Jackson would not be alone. Theo's influence with Cooper was still an unknown factor.

△

Sawyer and Corben had brought some food with them for our lunch, and I offered to help Sawyer make the sandwiches.

It was a chance to talk to him, to tell him about my epiphany and that I'd been trying it out – on the drive up, at the shopping mall, and then at the pub last night. I would have preferred to talk privately but Corben stayed in the kitchen, which meant she was part of the conversation too.

"So, rather than turning off the warrior gene, you're drawing out people's natural empathy and then they turn it off themselves. Nova, that's a brilliant idea. I think you're right. That works better for you. You do it instinctively already. Enhancing what is already there, the good things. It's turning on the empathy gene, if there is one, rather than turning off the warrior gene. And I think it'll work. I think it'll really change things." Sawyer gave me a broad smile.

"Well, yeah. I guess." I was pleased that he thought it was a promising idea, but the grand expectations he had of me made me uncomfortable. "I know I can't stop the aggression in people. I just can't. It's okay with Jet and people I know. They trust me, they're open to me, but strangers are resistant. They protect their little pockets of darkness. Besides, with things like last night it just happens so fast. I can't stop that."

Corben had been cutting tomatoes while she listened. She put down her knife and placed her hand next to mine on the bench, not touching, but almost. Her expression was solemn. "Nova, I know you blame me. Both for leaving and for causing this spread of violence around the world. And I'm not trying to let myself off the hook for either of those things. But, with the violence, you need to know that I was not doing it intentionally. In my job I was solely focused on the warrior gene, and I was immersed in all that aggression. Because I was not looking after myself, in the end I was angry all the time. Without meaning it to, my anger reached into other people and drew on the darkness inside them. I pushed at that darkness. I fed it with my own. I activated the warrior gene." She paused and gave a small nod. "I'm only saying this to point out that your idea is a valid one. To reverse this, you don't need to do anything special. You just need to be yourself. Happy, kind, and full of love." She gave a small smile and glanced towards the lounge where Jackson was sitting with the others. "Instead of the anger that I fed, you will be feeding people's compassion. Drawing out and activating their empathy, just as Sawyer said. That will stop the violence. Not completely, of course. Humans can be horrible sometimes. But they are also capable of love, of generosity, and of acts of charity. And that's what you'll be inspiring, without doing anything except being yourself."

Wow. It was quite a speech. "Umm. Thank you, I guess. But I'm not sure it's that easy. I will probably just disappoint you all."

"You could never do that." She sounded like a mother.

A warmth swam through me at her words, despite the resistance I still felt towards her.

$$\triangle$$

We all went to the beach after lunch. There was an offshore wind and quite a swell. The waves were over a metre high. Sawyer had managed to get hold of three surfboards, and he went out with Jackson and Jet.

Jackson had often surfed at Woodside Beach and could hold his own. Jet was naturally athletic, and he rode his board with a graceful balance. But Sawyer was the surprise. His timing and choice of waves was perfect. He perched on the edge of the swell, the wave curling behind him, and carved his way across the ocean. It was like watching a professional surfer.

The three of them came in at last, relaxed, laughing, and pushing at each other in good-natured friendship. Jackson dropped onto the towel beside me and shook his hair, so that drops of icy water sprinkled across my bare stomach. I gave a little squeal and he laughed. Then he glanced warily at Corben before he dropped a light kiss on my lips. Neither of us were used to having my mother around, and I knew he was not sure how affectionate he could be with me. His lips were cold, and he tasted salty.

Corben looked up from her book and gave Jackson a friendly smile. She had probably sensed his self-consciousness.

The book she was reading looked like an airport-bought crime novel. A boarding pass was wedged between the pages as her bookmark. Something caught my attention and, when I looked closer, I noticed the pass bore an unfamiliar name.

"Who is Esther Allen?"

Corben gave a small smile. "She was my high school netball coach."

"Who? What?"

"It's Corben," Sawyer said. He had also shaken out his wet hair, and it now hung in a shaggy, blond mess. The top of his wetsuit was pulled down to his waist and hung around his hips. He was tanned and muscular, and looked like he spent all his spare time in the ocean. Mia, Devon, and Han all gazed up at him in admiration. "We used another name for the flight. The U.S. Department of Defense knows she's working for the Australian Government now, but we're trying to keep her whereabouts and movements off their radar."

"Huh, that's cool," said Han. "Nova, will you get a secret name when Sawyer takes you away?"

Sawyer shook his head and sucked in his cheeks as he lifted his eyes to the sky. "Does Jack tell you everything?"

"I didn't. Well, I mean … I just said …" Jackson broke off. He was blushing a deep shade of red, and he glared at Han.

"It's okay. Really." Sawyer gave him a playful kick and grinned. "I don't think there are any secrets within this group. And that's a good thing. That's how friendships should be. And no, Nova will not need a secret name."

"Where are you taking Nova?" Mia wanted to know, annoyed that she had been left out of the loop for once.

"Do you want to explain, or shall I?" Sawyer was still grinning at Jackson, who shook his head and gestured back at Sawyer. "I want to take Nova on a trip around the world. Visiting the cites and countries where the violence is especially bad. We'll be away for a couple of months. I think she can help turn off the violence by spreading her empathy."

"Oh my god. How did you not tell me this, Nova?" Mia looked at me and then at Devon, who smiled and shrugged. Han had clearly told her.

"Well, it's not definite. It was just an idea Sawyer had. I don't think it will do any good, anyway. And it won't be for ages," I said.

Sawyer looked at me sheepishly. "Actually, I'd like to leave just after we get back to Victoria."

I swallowed and felt my stomach twist, despite the calm vibe Sawyer was spreading.

"We can all go! We can help too. Can we? Pleeease." Mia had lifted her face up to Sawyer with an angelic smile.

He laughed. "I wish I could take all of you. I know it would help Nova." His voice was warm and kind. "But I'm afraid that's not in my budget. It will just be Nova and Jack."

Jackson squeezed my hand.

"Why does he get to go?" Mia pouted, and Jackson poked his tongue at her. She turned to me. "Nova, take me instead." I tried to smile as Mia's excitement nudged at me. It was like a persistent puppy wanting me to throw a ball. But my self-doubt had already reared up like a giant stop sign and smacked me in the face. Nausea churned through me.

"That soon? I'm not ... I can't ... I don't think ... I'm not even ready." The words tumbled out of me.

"You're ready. You just need to be you." Sawyer sent me another wave of comfort. "I'm not expecting you to do anything that you don't already do."

"Nova, you can do it. Although you would be better if I was there. For support." Mia grinned up at Sawyer, who grinned back but shook his head.

Devon was nodding emphatically. "Empathy is your superpower."

"You're ready." Jackson squeezed my hand again.

Their confidence was like a gentle breeze across the top of a frothing volcano of anxiety. Helpful, but not really.

"What about uni?" I asked. "And Jack has lab classes this semester. He has to go in to Melbourne for them."

"You can still study," said Sawyer. "Classes are online. I can organise a private tutor for both of you if you like. And we'll make the arrangements for any laboratory sessions Jack needs to do."

Jackson nodded, and I got the feeling they had already discussed this.

"You'll have my help," said Sawyer quietly, sensing my angst. "We'll meet with the other empaths from your dad's list and ask for their help too. No one is expecting any miracles. We'll just see how it goes."

"But is it safe?" I wasn't really concerned about safety, but it sounded like a good excuse not to go.

"Don't worry, kiddo." Jet reached down and ruffled my hair. "I'll be with you too."

It sounded like a done deal.

I took a deep breath. *You can do it, Nova.* I knew I would be well supported. *We'll just see how it goes.* Positive thinking.

But, after last night's trauma and a lack of sleep, I just felt sick.

And, right now, we still had to focus on getting Cooper back home. That was the reason we were here.

29

Jackson and Han went to meet Cooper. Jet and Sawyer followed but kept out of sight. The rest of us stayed at the apartment and waited.

I paced the floors and kept checking my phone for the time. Devon sat on the edge of the couch, jiggling her legs. Although Mia had the television on, she barely watched it. I knew I was feeding into their anxiety.

Shivers ran through me although it was not cold, making the hairs on my arms and legs stand on end. My hands were clammy, and I squeezed them into fists and then stretched out my fingers. It did not help. I was starting to get a bad feeling about Theo's part in all this.

Corben and Rayna sat at the dining table drinking tea and chatting quietly about the books they had both read. Rayna exuded a calm composure, and Corben was still a blank. It was quieter being close to them, so I sat at the table too. For about thirty seconds. Then I resumed pacing.

"Sit down, Nova," said Rayna at last. "I'm sure they'll be back soon."

I nodded and sat down for another thirty seconds.

Rayna snorted and shook her head when I stood up again. "I have to check my phone. I might have missed a text."

"Unlikely," she muttered under her breath.

After what seemed like an eternity, there was the sound of keys in the door. Sawyer came through first and gave a quick shake of his head. Jackson followed him, and his disappointment swooned through my body.

"Coop didn't even show," Han said. "We waited for an hour."

"Then a text. It just said *I told you to come alone.* For god's sake. What game is he playing?"

"Or more like what game is Theo playing," I said, and then regretted it when Jackson swore again and dropped into a chair.

"So, what now?" Devon spoke quietly to Han, but Sawyer answered her.

"Jack has sent Cooper another text, so we just have to wait."

I let out the breath I had been holding and felt the bitterness of Jackson's frustration in the back of my throat. He hated waiting.

$\triangle$

Although there was extra security posted around our building, the trauma of the night before was still fresh, and we decided to stay in for dinner. Sawyer left straight after, to attend meetings with the other DOVE teams that were working on the Gold Coast. Corben also left, saying she wanted to have an early night. They had rooms in the apartment block across the road from ours.

Rayna and Jet stayed to watch television for a while, but it was not long before they also retired to their own room, next door.

Everyone was tired and feeling a little low. I probably should have used my skills to try and lift the energy, but it was too much effort.

When Jackson stood up and announced he was going to bed, I went with him.

"I'm sorry, Jack." I sat on the end of the bed and flopped backwards so I was lying down.

"Thanks, but it's not your fault." He dropped down beside me.

"Mmm." *It actually was.*

I figured this whole thing with Theo was a direct result of me shooting Abraham. As it had been covered up to protect me, Theo probably didn't know for sure what had happened, but he still blamed me for Abraham's death. And he wanted payback. That made all this my fault.

I didn't say all this aloud, but I didn't have to.

"It's not, Nova. Coop put himself right into this. He was warned about the people he was hanging out with." Jackson's tone was angry, but it was also layered with the anxiety I could feel wringing through his body.

I didn't bother arguing with him. Neither of us were up for it.

"So, we're going to be leaving for overseas when we get back home," said Jackson after a few minutes of silence. "To save the world." The change of subject and his flippancy were supposed to lift my spirits, but I would have preferred that he not remind me of it.

"I doubt that we'll be saving the world. It'll probably just be a waste of Sawyer's time and DOVE's money. He thinks

I'm much more capable than I am. I'm barely able to sense what people are feeling half the time, so I can't see how I'm going to stop them being angry and violent."

"Don't do that, don't minimise it." His voice was sharp. "You have a very special ability."

I shrugged. "The truth is, I don't think I do, Jack. I don't think I can do what Sawyer wants."

Jackson sat up and leaned over me. He took my face between his hands. His eyes crinkled at the corners. "Sawyer said he just wants you to be yourself. And the truth is that you are more capable than you give yourself credit for. Devon's right, empathy is your superpower. Anyway, you have to do this, Nova. If there is even a small chance that you can save the world, as cliché as that sounds, you have to try."

I was silent for a moment thinking over his words. He was right. If I could draw out people's kindness and compassion, switch on the empathy gene, if there was such a thing, it might make a difference. I might be able to make that small difference. Maybe. Stop some of the anger, stop some of the violence. So, I had to try. But to do that, I needed Jackson. For, even as I doubted myself, I believed in Jackson, I believed in us. As Corben had reminded me, all I needed to do was draw on the love I felt for Jackson, and the love he returned. After all, that was what had set off my ability in the first place. And Sawyer knew that too.

"You're right. I can try. And I will try." I sat up and put a hand on his chest. "But the only way I can do any of this, is if you're with me."

Jackson's eyes were rich and soft as he gazed at me. "I would not miss it for anything."

His thumb rubbed small circles across my fingers as he brought my hand up to his lips.

△

It was late when the text alert sounded on Jackson's phone.

I had been asleep, or at least in that stage where I was almost asleep and not sure whether I was dreaming something or if it was really happening. It took me a full minute to orient myself after Jackson had elbowed me in the ribs and squashed me into the mattress as he climbed over me to get to his phone. I rubbed my eyes.

Jackson had read the message and was looking at me. His mouth was a straight line, as if he disapproved of something, and he was breathing heavily through his nose.

Uh-oh. I could sense his indecision.

"Is it Cooper?"

He nodded, but he did not look pleased, or relieved, or … hopeful.

"Well?" I lifted the corners of my mouth in what I meant to be an encouraging smile, but I was still drowsy so it may have looked like a grimace.

He heaved a sigh. "He wants to meet early tomorrow. 6 am. I guess it's before he goes to work."

"Okay. That's good. Isn't it?" I knew there was something else he was not saying.

"It says … for you to come too. This time. But no one else. Me and you."

"Okay." I kept my voice even, knowing that Jackson would not want me to go but knowing that I had to. We simply had to get Cooper away from Theo and back home. "Can I have a look at the text?"

He narrowed his eyes but passed me his phone.

I can meet you tomorrow, 6 am. Come with Nova. But no one else.

There was a tingle down my spine, and I knew it was partly fear and partly the thrill of danger. I was fully awake now. "So, then, what do you want to do?"

Jackson was biting on his lips.

"Do you trust me?" I asked.

"Of course," he said, but I could sense his hesitancy.

"Then let me come. It's the only way to get Coop home. And you shouldn't be going alone."

"But Theo might be there."

"Yeah, I know." I had a strong feeling that Theo would be there, and that was why the text specified for me to come. "But we have to get this over with."

Jackson looked up at the ceiling, as if looking for guidance from a higher power. I knew he was conflicted. Both scared and hopeful. I knew because I felt it too. The hope was a light flutter in my heart, while I had to roll my shoulders to loosen the fear that rested between them.

I waited.

"Okay, we'll both go." He let out another sigh and looked straight at me. His deep brown eyes were solemn. The decision was made. "But I'm not telling Jet or Sawyer this time. I don't want them to come with us, and if they know we're going they won't let us go alone. I'm not going to take the chance that Coop is a no-show again. And this time he is coming back with us, even if I have to drag him here."

Jackson sent Cooper a text asking for the address and got an immediate reply. It was an apartment building a few blocks away.

"The security outside is watching for people coming in, not leaving, so we can leave through the garage. And you know Jet and Rayna go to the gym at five, so they won't even be in their room when we leave. They won't even know we're gone. And everyone else will still be fast asleep. No one will realise for at least an hour."

"And, by that time, we'll be back."

"With Cooper."

"Yeah." Jackson pulled me up against his chest, and we lay back on the pillows. "You have to promise me you'll be really careful."

"I promise."

We held each other with a desperation that bled from the anxiety pulsing through us.

△

The hallway was narrow. Jackson walked in front at a fast pace, as if he were in a race. I knew he was worried about bringing me, and it was almost like he was trying to leave me behind.

We reached the door. 1402.

Jackson knocked twice. There was no sound from inside, so he turned the handle. It was unlocked.

He looked at me with raised eyebrows. "Are you ready?"

I nodded. As ready as I could be.

My heart was pounding, but my back was straight.

There was a sense of inevitability about being here. I had a strong feeling that today I was finally going to have to answer for taking a life. Abraham's life. Regardless of who he was and what he had done, I regretted that day with everything in me. I didn't know what payment Theo would demand, but I would not let it be Cooper.

"Please don't put yourself in any danger," Jackson murmured.

"I won't. It's alright." I gripped his hand, drawing on his strength and courage and sharing my own. "I'm not scared."

"I know you're not. That's what worries me." He looked me up and down, gave a weak smile, and then opened the door.

The apartment was empty.

Jackon heaved a sigh of relief, but then he started pacing.

I moved towards the windows and looked out at the beach, fourteen stories below. Concentrating on that while we were waiting would help me stay calm.

30

Today

Theo stood quietly, watching us. Two of his men remained in the hallway, but one trailed after him into the room. It was Neo. He closed the door and stood against it, barring our way out.

I forced my face into a composed smile and swallowed. *Breathe.* My legs felt like jelly, barely holding me upright. I was not sure if it was just from my panic or from Jackson's as well. While he couldn't feel Theo's strong need for revenge in that same way that I could, he knew we were in terrible danger. The fear ricocheted between us and around the room like the small, silver ball in a pinball machine. I clenched my hands together, as if trying to catch that rebounding ball and contain it there.

"Hey, Coop. How's it going?" Jackson's greeting sounded light and friendly, and I marvelled at his self-control.

"Hi, Jack. Nova." Cooper nodded in acknowledgement.

His tawny blond hair was cut short, which made it look darker and closer in colour to Jackson's. The familiar brown eyes, also lighter than his twin's, were wide, and his mouth was set in a straight line. As Cooper's eyes met mine, his emotions punched through me. Heat flared in my cheeks as if embarrassed, and my stomach twisted with regret. There was also a warmth in my heart – the love he felt for his brother, and for me. But overriding all of that was something that made the hairs on my skin stand up. Icy cold tendrils wove around my neck and down my back. Cooper was frightened.

"Hey, Coop. Theo. Neo." I gave an involuntary laugh at the rhyming names, which came out as half whimper, half snort, and my cheeks burned even hotter.

"Hello, Nova." Theo's face was expressionless, but his need for vengeance burned beneath his skin, and mine. It was consuming him.

"We came to see Cooper," Jackson said firmly. Then he added quietly, "I hoped it could just be us, bro."

"Me too." Cooper turned to glance at Theo and took a step closer towards us. "I'd like to talk to my brother alone."

"Fine. You two can go into the bedroom. Nova will stay here with me." Theo spoke confidently, but he lacked the air of natural authority that Abraham had always displayed.

"No chance," said Jackson loudly, as Cooper also shook his head.

I felt the bond between these twins. It was as strong as ever. I was certain that, despite the black t-shirt and jacket, Cooper was not part of Theo's crew.

Theo turned to Neo and gestured towards us. "Check them for weapons."

Jackson did not wait for Neo, though, and pulled his handgun from the waistband of his jeans. "I don't think so." Holding the gun steady, he kept it pointed at the ground.

Theo also pulled out a gun. It sat comfortably in his hand, aimed at me, like an extension of his fingers.

A sick feeling jumped around in my stomach. This situation was quickly spinning out of control.

"Are you prepared to shoot me? Have you ever shot someone before? I know Cooper hasn't." Theo was looking at Jackson, but kept his gun aimed at me. He gave a sinister smile. It was almost theatrical. "I have. And I don't hesitate. Nova would be dead before you even took aim."

"You would never get away with that. Killing her." Jackson's voice rose on the last two words, as if he were asking a question.

Theo laughed, and it was an ugly, hollow sound. "Violent crime is a commonplace occurrence on the Gold Coast. Random shootings, domestic disputes. There would be no evidence that we were even here."

I knew he was right. With Theo's connections, it would be hard even for Sawyer to prove anything. I tried to swallow, but my mouth was dry and my tongue felt thick.

"But I just want to talk." He held up his arms, with his weapon now pointed at the ceiling, as if surrendering.

I sifted through the emotions in the room. The air felt dense and dark. My blood was cold, and my spine crawled with the fear that stretched between Jackson, Cooper, and me. While Theo was not afraid, he was wary, and his uncertainty prickled against the back of my neck. He was not sure what I was capable of.

There was also churning rage, hot and painful, in the pit of my stomach. The warrior gene was active in Theo, and it was lethal.

At the same time, I felt like my heart was wrapped in a soft, protective cocoon, and I knew that came from both Jackson and Cooper.

As if sensing my probing, Jackson turned to me and gave me a weak smile. His courage was a solid foundation beneath my feet. It was also a reminder that I should be doing something. I had skills; I could change the emotional climate in a room, draw out people's empathy. As if I were building a house of bricks, I drew on the kindness and compassion that was so much a part of both the Lewis boys, and I worked at creating layer upon layer. A calmness settled over me and spread around the room.

Cooper gave a sigh.

Neo had been avoiding making eye contact with me, but now he glanced up and raised his eyebrows. That small action generated a warmth between us, and I recognised the link of friendship.

"Let's put the guns away." Theo dropped his arms and held out his palms, facing up. His pistol hung loosely between two fingers. "I'd like to talk to Nova in private."

"That's not going to happen." Jackson shook his head and tightened his grip on his handgun. The barrel was still pointed at the floor, and I was reminded of Jet's warning not to aim a gun at a person unless you intended to use it.

Theo turned to Cooper. "You said you could arrange it for me."

"Nova, he said he just wants to talk to you. No one will be hurt." Cooper's voice was a plea, but he lacked conviction. He was in over his head.

I put my hand on Jackson's arm before he could protest again and looked directly at Theo. "Okay. I'll talk to you. In private. No guns. Jack and Coop can go into the bedroom and talk there. Neo can go out into the hall."

"Neo will go into the bedroom too." Theo's gaze was just as direct, and his tone was sharp. He didn't like being told what to do.

I shrugged. Although Neo was being the obedient follower, I was relying on those ties of friendship I had sensed. He had helped me once before. At risk to his own life.

Theo took two steps forward and placed his revolver on the kitchen bench. He nodded at Neo, who pulled a gun from his shoulder holster and put it beside Theo's.

"You probably have more weapons hidden somewhere." Jackson's voice was loaded with suspicion.

Theo shook his head. "That's all we have."

Jackson added his pistol to the collection on the bench. Cooper shook his head; he was not carrying a weapon.

"Neo, pat them down," Theo ordered, looking directly at me.

I could tell Neo was not being gentle as he ran his hands over Jackson's legs and around his arms and body. The shoulder injury still gave Jackson twinges of pain, but he did not even wince. Neo ignored Cooper, as if they already knew he didn't have any weapons. When Neo moved towards me, Jackson put out his hand. "She doesn't have anything."

"I don't," I confirmed.

Theo studied me for a moment, then nodded and waved Neo away. Neo huffed, probably just to bait Jackson who was still breathing loudly though his nose. I put my hand on Jackson's arm again and squeezed it gently. His fury felt like a coiled spring, just moments away from exploding.

"Nova can check us. That's only fair." Theo held up his arms while he continued to study me.

I moved forward and ran my hands lightly down his sides and around his ankles. Then I did the same with Neo. No weapons.

"That wasn't very thorough. I might have something hidden between my legs," said Neo, with a smirk.

Jackson snorted. "She's not that desperate."

"Enough," said Theo firmly.

Neo's eyes glittered with an intensity that did not match his teasing smile.

Theo gestured towards the bedroom, and Neo moved over to hold the door open for Jackson and Cooper.

Jackson took a step, but then stopped and turned back to me, raising his eyebrows as a question.

I nodded and gave him a false smile. "It's okay. We're just going to talk. I'll be fine."

Jackson backed into the bedroom, his eyes still on mine. "I'm just in here."

His concern shone like a beacon. But he trusted me, and that's what I was relying on.

Them being safe. Neo, too. I didn't want any of them hurt. Maybe there was a way out for them. Because I didn't think there was a way out for me.

I knew Theo didn't want me leaving this room alive.

31

Theo moved to shut the bedroom door behind Neo, Cooper, and Jackson.

"Hey!" Jackson exclaimed.

"This is a private conversation," said Theo.

I could hear Jackson's objection through the closed door and a murmur from Neo. Then I heard Cooper's voice, and I knew Jackson would be pushing him for information. Theo moved to the kitchen bench and rested his palms flat on the counter, fingers splayed, as if proving he was not going to draw a weapon on me. He watched me through narrowed eyes. The guns were in a pile at the other end of the bench, out of arm's reach.

I pressed my hands together to stop them shaking and watched him in return.

The boys had gone quiet in the bedroom. They probably had their ears to the door.

Theo was of medium height and quite stocky. He had thick arms and big hands. They looked strong. His hair was short, shaved at the sides and spiky on top, which emphasised the square shape of his head. He had a prominent nose and chin, and his forehead was lined in a permanent scowl.

"I hear you were at the Surfers Pub the other night. Did you enjoy the show?" From his mocking tone, I knew he was baiting me.

"It was horrible," I said as calmly as I could.

He gave a coarse laugh. "Yeah, well that's the sort of justice we deal out here." If he was trying to scare me, it was working.

"I thought it was a thing between the biker gangs."

He shrugged. "They're my people." Based on the information Sawyer had, Theo was probably exaggerating his importance. But it did not make him any less dangerous.

"You said you wanted to talk. What do you want to say?"

Anxiety twisted through me, slimy and slippery, and it slowly sucked away my courage.

I will not be afraid. It was the mantra I used to repeat with Abraham. I said it over and over in my head. *I will not be afraid.*

"I want to hear what happened to Abraham. I want the truth. I know you were there."

"If I tell you, will you let us leave here? No one gets hurt. And Cooper comes with us."

"Yes."

I knew he was lying. His eyes were dark and hooded, and I felt my jaw tighten in an involuntary clench.

The darkness swirled in me, and I could see it inside Theo too. I felt like I was walking a tightrope above a bottomless chasm.

I inhaled and held my breath. Then I exhaled.

I will not be afraid.

There was a deep, dull ache in my heart, alongside the fury that burned there. These were Theo's emotions. He was angry, but he was grieving too. And when my knees trembled, I realized that the bench he was leaning on was also holding him steady. These were immensely powerful emotions. And he was blaming me for them.

"Tell me about Abe," he said.

I took another breath, held it, counting silently, and then let it go. *In with the good, out with the bad.* There didn't seem to be any alternative other than to tell him what he wanted to know. At least some of it.

"Well, after I escaped from that room above the gym, I was living on the streets for a couple of weeks." As I started to talk, I felt the instant relief. It was like ripping off a bandaid. "I was afraid of putting my friends in danger, but eventually I had to go back to them. That's when Abe found me. He came to our apartment."

I paused. It was hard for me to talk about it. About Sage.

Theo tapped impatient fingers on the kitchen bench. His face wore a contemptuous sneer, but I knew he was listening to every word.

"Abe held a gun on us and demanded that I come with him. My friend – my best friend – was not going to let him take me. She had a gun. I didn't know that she had one. I didn't know that she would point it at him. I probably would have just gone with him if she hadn't had that gun."

As if he had taken off a mask, Theo's face had lost the expression of controlled scorn he'd held before. His eyes were wide and watery. The corners of his mouth drooped, and he had sucked in his cheeks. He looked grey.

It was a face of deep sorrow.

I suddenly realised that Abraham had been more than his boss, more than his friend. Theo had been in love with Abraham. It explained the painful ache in my heart.

This changed things.

I had been ready to give him the official version, that an SAS officer had pulled the trigger, killed Abraham, protecting me. And while it may not have guaranteed our safety, it was probably the best option I had. But suddenly my guilt was like an oil slick; sticky, greasy, and coating everything in darkness. Theo deserved to know the truth. For his love, for his loss.

I had to come clean. My mouth opened and then shut again, without me making a sound.

All I could do was flood him with empathy and hope for the best. I searched for the good in Theo. His love for Abraham. That was his good. He was capable of love, of compassion.

Just pretend you are brave. My new mantra.

"When Sage raised her gun, Abe shot her. He killed her. She died." I paused again. "She was my best friend."

There were tears in my eyes. I could feel them, drops of water resting against my eyelashes. When I closed my eyes in a hard blink, they squeezed out. I sniffed and wiped my hand across my face.

Theo's forehead was furrowed. He made a whimpering noise like an animal in pain. Pity swirled through me. I had to put him out of his misery.

"So, I shot him. I shot Abe. And he died. I did it, and I wish I hadn't."

There was a strangled cry, and my heart felt like it had been ripped in half. An impenetrable darkness bled through me.

The bedroom door slammed back against the wall, and Jackson and Cooper burst through. They stood beside me, cautious, distrustful, not exactly sure what was going on. Neo moved to Theo's side, at the kitchen bench.

Theo thumped his fists on the counter. He shut his eyes for a few seconds and sucked in his lips. I could see he was composing himself. Then he moved his hands to his crotch, as if adjusting his pants.

But instead, he pulled out a gun.

Of course he had kept one hidden. So much for me checking him. Neo's flirtatious comment about me checking between his legs had been a warning, but I had missed it.

The gun barrel was pointed straight at me. Again. His hand was surprisingly steady.

"Theo," Neo said quietly. He put a hand on Theo's arm and looked as if he was going to try and take the gun.

"Get out of the fucking way." Theo flicked Neo's hand away and pushed the gun up against his chest. "I knew you would lead me to her eventually. She got under your skin. And you betrayed him." Theo gave a small moan.

Neo glanced at the bench where his own gun lay, but he held up his hands and backed away.

"I want her to know what it feels like." Theo turned the gun back on me. His eyes pierced through me like darts thrown at a dart board.

"I do know what it feels like. Abe killed my best friend, he killed ... Sage." I stumbled on the last word, and it came out as a croak.

"That's not the same. That's not enough." Theo turned to Cooper. "I thought it would be you. You were easy for us. But it's not you. It's your brother that she loves."

Jackson placed one hand on Cooper's shoulder and the other in the middle of my back. His eyes were wide, and while I could feel his fear, I could also sense his strength. The clench of his jaw showed that he was weighing up our options, looking for an escape.

With his touch, I was able to borrow some courage and use it to calm myself. I let the stillness echo around me, towards Cooper and Neo, but I knew I had no hope of keeping Theo calm.

"You said if I told you the truth you would let us leave. You said no one would be hurt." My voice sounded childish as I made the desperate plea.

"I lied." Theo looked between the three of us. There was a cold calculation in his eyes, and I could tell that his heart had hardened into steel.

Theo was the only one holding a gun. The front door was behind him, too far from us. Neo was closest, but Theo could turn that gun on him in a heartbeat if he made a move. I couldn't see a way out, and I doubted that Jackson could.

Cooper shuffled forward to stand in front of Jackson and held up his hands as if surrendering. "This is my fault," he said quietly. "I'll stay. Let them go."

His courage was like glass, strong if handled with care, but also fragile and easily shattered. All it would take would be a stone. Or a bullet.

"Don't come any closer. I don't want you." Theo's eyes raked over Cooper, and there was a cruel smile on his face. He could smell the weakness, the naivety, as I could. It was sickly and sweet, like toffee. Cooper did not believe that Theo would pull the trigger.

But I knew Theo could. Probably would.

For months, his grief had slowly stoked this burning fire of hatred and revenge. And we were all caught in it. Because of me.

"I killed Abe." My voice held a cold brutality that I didn't recognise, and didn't feel, but that I knew would draw Theo's attention back to me.

I moved to stand in front of Cooper. At the same time, Jackson grabbed my arm and pulled me back. I should have expected it. He stepped out in front of both Cooper and me, protecting us. Protecting me. But it meant that Theo had the three of us lined up, almost single file. Frozen for those few seconds. It was long enough.

There were two sharp bangs. I had heard those sounds before.

Loud snaps, like whip-cracks in the quiet room.

At first, I thought Theo had just fired warning shots. That no one had been hit. But then Jackson hunched forward. He dropped to his knees on the carpet. His hand reached up to his chest.

It was like a repeat of Sage.

Bullets that were meant for me.

I bent down, pulling on Jackson's shirt where sticky, red blood was forming into rivers. The rivers were joining up. There was too much blood. I couldn't find the wounds. My hands moved over his chest and stomach, searching. I knew I had to press on the holes, plug them to stop the bleeding. His shirt was a slippery, wet mess.

"Jack, what do I do?"

There was a moment of contact, of recognition, but then his eyes rolled up into his head and he fell backwards.

I knelt and stroked his face, making more bloody smudges, willing him to respond.

My head was spinning.

I looked around for help, needing someone. Needing Jackson. He was the medical one.

Cooper stood above me, still frozen. His mouth hung open, but his expression was blank. He was clutching his chest, just like Jackson. Neo moved over and put an arm around Cooper. His eyes met mine. They were soft with a helpless sympathy.

I turned to Theo, who was still standing across the room behind the kitchen bench. His gun was still raised. There was a predatory smile of satisfaction on his face. I gulped in air.

It was surreal. This couldn't be happening. Not again.

"Help him. Please. I can't lose him. We need some help. Please." Words spilled out of my mouth, but no one responded.

It felt like I was standing on a trapdoor in the floor, waiting for it to give way.

This couldn't be the end. There were so many things I needed to say to Jackson. And I knew he couldn't go without a final joke, a sarcastic comment, or at least a wink.

But there was nothing. Just lots of blood. It was now forming a puddle on the floor. Dark red.

Life leaking out. Love leaking out.

I shut my eyes. The pain in my chest was unbearable.

Nausea pitched in my stomach, and I gagged at the smell of his blood.

An emotional whirlpool whipped through my body, fragments of memories flashing past too fast to hold on to. The sweetness of laughter, the ache of sorrow, the warmth of joy, and the rigidity of fear.

I could hear voices yelling in rage, screaming in pain, crying in terror. Maybe it was just my voice. I wasn't sure.

My heart pounded, raced, then slowed. Raced again, then slowed.

I was hot, then I was cold.

A brilliant white light filled me, lifted me, and I flew with it. Higher and higher. It was Jackson's love, and I cherished its purity.

Then, suddenly, it was gone. I reached for it, but it was like trying to grab hold of the wind. The floor was crumbling away beneath my feet, and I was falling.

There was no pain. I couldn't feel Jackson at all. There was nothing.

I found myself on the ground, amongst the rubble of my own heart.

32

Darkness stirred deep within me. It was all I had left. And, like a wild beast, caged and pacing, it was waiting to get loose.

I sat up and opened my eyes when the apartment door burst open, crashing back against the wall. Theo's look of surprise was recorded somewhere in my fragmented brain as he turned, swinging the gun with him.

Jet came through the opening first. He and Theo faced each other, guns drawn, like cowboys in a movie scene. Rayna was behind Jet, shielding Sawyer and Corben.

I looked into Corben's eyes and saw them flash wide. Then she dropped her shield.

The response was intense.

Like a mother dragon, protecting her baby, Corben was breathing fire. Her rage roared through the room, and found Theo. She wanted to burn him to a crisp.

I piggybacked on her anger and went along for the ride. Both darkness and fire surged through me. The lethal combination. This is what I was capable of.

Theo cringed under the onslaught, hunched over like an old man. Corben's fury on one side, mine on the other. Together, we consumed him.

Sawyer's efforts at calming me were as effective as a cup of water thrown at a blazing fire.

My eyes glazed over, my blood boiled, my skin was burning, and my mouth was dry. I could hear a jet engine roaring in my ears. It was my own rage.

Then I heard Jet clear his throat.

That tiny, simple sound distracted me.

I let go of my emotional grip on Theo. Just for a second.

It was enough for Theo to straighten his back and take aim with his gun. At me.

I stayed still for another second. I wanted him to shoot me. I willed him to pull on that trigger.

When I shut my eyes, a picture of Finn flashed through my mind. I knew it was from Jet.

Finn, his friend, my friend, who had been killed by Abraham while doing his duty to protect me.

I opened my eyes. Despite the emotional turmoil that seethed around him, Jet stood perfectly composed, a true professional. He watched Theo line me up in his sights and he reacted as he had been trained. Two loud cracks.

Jet's aim was true. It was his tribute to Finn.

Theo dropped to the floor.

He was dead.

I knew because the burden of his grief had lifted off me and floated away in that instant.

People started moving around the room, but I couldn't hear a sound. It was like being in a silent movie.

Jet moved to check on Theo. Rayna knelt beside me and held Jackson's wrist in her fingers. Sawyer bent down behind her, one hand on her back and the other on Jackson's leg. Rayna was looking for signs of life and so was Sawyer, in his own way.

I felt Corben's arms drape around me. She was holding me, but she was also draining me. I felt numb. She was absorbing the anger, the fire, the darkness; she was taking it all from me.

Then I felt her walls go back up, and there was nothing again. She let me go, and sat on the floor with her arms wrapped around her knees and her head resting on them.

Sawyer's arms replaced Corben's. His compassion was soft and soothing, but it was too little, too late. The carnage was all around me.

Jackson lay in a pool of blood. Corben sat in a heap behind me. Cooper was hunched over on his knees, opposite me, his head in his hands.

Theo was flat on the floor, closer to the door. There were two small, dark holes, one in his chest, one in the middle of his forehead, and they seemed to suck away the light. Jet stood over him.

The rusty smell of blood made my nostrils flare. My throat was raw. My eyes stung.

Weariness rolled through me and I sank into an empty space in the back of my mind that I never knew was there.

My chest rose and filled with air, and then I exhaled again. But it was too much effort.

I didn't want to keep breathing. Not without Jackson.

33

I rested my hand on Jackson's cheek. His face was rough with a light stubble and still warm. I ran my finger over his lips. They were soft.

But there was no spark.

I couldn't feel him. I couldn't feel any emotions.

Jackson was dead.

I wished it were me. It should have been me. Again. Just like with Sage. That should have been me.

I was a giant, cosmic, bad luck charm.

Jackson was dead.

Corben had taken the anger from me, but I was left with a gaping hole. A void. It was waiting to be filled. I was probably in shock. Or denial. And it would not take much for me to find that anger again. I could probably do all the stages of grief in one go.

But not acceptance. I would never accept this.

Jackson was dead.

I wished it were me instead.

Rayna leaned across and put her hand on my arm. Her touch was soft and tender. "Nova, can you move back so I can check ..."

She didn't finish her sentence.

I nodded but I didn't move. My fingers touched the bare skin at the base of his throat, where a pulse should have been. This should have been me. Theo should have shot me.

I squeezed my eyes shut. Take me instead.

A new fire was building in me, smouldering, waiting to be fanned, to be fed. And I knew this time I was going to let the flames consume me.

I needed him. My heart was in spasms. I couldn't let him go.

Jackson was dead.

34

Nova, climb out of the fire.

My eyes flashed open. These were not words from my head.

His lips didn't move, and his eyes were shut. I had imagined it.

"Jack." It was a croak.

No response. Nothing. It had just been in my head.

Then I felt a tiny flutter of ... something.

"Jack, I can't do this without you." I whispered.

His lips moved. The tiniest little bit. His mouth opened a smidge and then shut again. A tiny breath.

"Holy shit!" It was Rayna's voice but my words, my thought.

I had not imagined it, then.

His eyes were still shut.

Rayna reached across me, and her fingers replaced mine on Jackson's throat. She waited. I waited.

"I think there's a faint pulse."

Jackson opened his eyes. Those dark, warm, cocoa-brown eyes. I blinked, hard. Twice. I could barely see him for my tears.

"Hey. Hey. Hey." It was stupid, but I couldn't help repeating this one word, waiting for a response.

Jackson gave a weak smile and shut his eyes again.

I could feel his pain. It was like a vice tightening across my chest, and it was excruciating. But I welcomed it. It meant Jackson was alive.

Jackson was alive.

Cooper was making loud, exaggerated breaths, as if he were trying to keep his brother breathing. Maybe he was. "Hold on, bro. Please hold on." He was gasping, smiling, and crying all at the same time.

Rayna pushed me out of the way. She ripped through Jackson's shirt, and I watched as she wiped away blood, both cleaning and examining him at the same time.

"Rayna?" Sawyer didn't say any more words, but I knew what he was asking.

She kept one hand on Jackson's chest and looked from me back to Sawyer. She spoke softly. "There seems to be only one entry wound, and the bullet is still lodged in his chest. His heartbeat is very faint, but it's there."

I reached for Jackson's hand, and his grip was surprisingly firm. The Phoenix on his chest rose and then fell again, as if it was trying to stretch its wings. It was only a small movement, but I could not take my eyes off it, willing it to continue.

Sirens wailed from the street. The ambulance had finally arrived.

I was climbing out of the fire.

Jackson was alive.

35

I rarely left his bedside. It was partly selfish. Away from Jackson, I felt empty and hollow.

The darkness inside me was gone. Corben had taken it, and she continued to carry it for now. The fire was gone too. I had no more rage, no more anger, but the memory of it still scared me.

Jackson had spent hours in surgery at the hospital. The bullet had been removed. It had missed his heart.

His parents had flown up and rented an apartment nearby.

Along with Cooper, they practically lived at the hospital. Jackson had a private room, with its own bathroom and an extra bed for a family member to stay over. A combination of Jackson's father being a doctor himself and Sawyer pulling some strings through DOVE.

Jackson was asleep. I sat quietly beside him, listening to his breathing, watching his chest rise and fall. Watching him breathe. I could do that all day. Every day.

The chair moulded around my body in a comfortable, cosy way. I had slept in it on several occasions. It was one of those white, cushioned armchairs for patients to sit in when they got out of bed. But other than taking short walks to the shower or down the hallway, Jackson had rarely been out of his bed.

There was a quiet knock at the door. Cooper poked his head in. "Can I come in?"

"Of course." I smiled.

Cooper's face was thin and drawn, and there were dark circles under his eyes. I knew he had carried Jackson's pain in the same way that I had. They had that twin connection.

There was also a heavy weight that draped itself across my shoulders as if I was carrying a backpack full of bricks, and I knew it was Cooper's guilt.

He dropped into the chair on the opposite side of Jackson's bed and we sat quietly, letting Jackson sleep. Cooper rearranged the water jug and cup and then sorted through the three *Get Well Soon* cards on Jackson's bedside table, though I was sure he had seen them all before. He kept giving me sideways glances and then a small smile when I looked up. I had the feeling he wanted to say something, but I let him take the time he needed.

He offered me a mint and squeezed it out of the packet onto my palm.

Cooper's hair was too short, but he moved his hand as if pushing the hair back from his eyes. It was the same gesture that Jackson did all the time.

"You saved his life, Nova," Cooper said at last.

It was not what I was expecting, and I felt the heat rise in my cheeks and across the back of my neck. "No, I didn't. He saved mine."

"Well, yeah, he saved both of us." Cooper's eyes were glistening with silver. "But that's not what I meant. He died.

I felt it. I know you did too. Then you brought him back. I don't know how. I don't care. But I am so, so grateful."

I shook my head and opened my mouth to protest, but he held up a hand.

"You did, Nova. And I told Mum and Dad what I felt. There was nothing, a blankness, an emptiness, like I'd lost half my heart, and then there was Jack, back with me again."

I felt the tears brimming in my eyes at the memory. Cooper reached across the bed to take my hand.

"I didn't want to listen to Jack's warnings about Griffin and the others. I thought I was really clever, really independent. Getting myself a job, moving to Melbourne. But Theo was orchestrating everything, using me to get to you the whole time. I'm so sorry."

I started to protest again, but Cooper squeezed my hand and kept talking.

"I'm glad that you two are together. I get that this is what you do, Nova; what you need to do. And Jack can help you. He's crazy enough to want it too. I'm happy for you both. I truly am. You are better with him. I know that now. And I'm sorry I was making it so hard for both of you."

There was a tightness in my throat from Cooper admitting a difficult truth, but my heart was full.

Jackson's hand emerged from under the sheet, and it clamped over Cooper's and mine. It was a strong grip, firm and warm. Alive. Jackson was awake.

"I love you, brother." Jackson's voice was deep and clear. He had heard us.

"I love you too, Jack."

And then they were hugging, crying, and hugging again.

My stomach tightened, and a tingle spread through my whole body.

I laughed with the simple joy of it all.

△

It had been two weeks. Jackson was no longer at risk, but they were keeping him in the hospital for a few more days.

There had been no shortage of visitors, but everyone was finally returning home.

Corben had returned to Melbourne as soon as she knew Jackson was okay. Mia, Han, and Devon had left yesterday, and Cooper took his mother on the same flight. Rayna accompanied them. She would stay in town until the rest of us returned. I was waiting for Jackson to be cleared to fly, and Dr Lewis and Jet would accompany us.

Sawyer put his head around the doorway. "How's the patient this morning?" His voice was bright and cheery.

"Pretty good." Jackson's smile faded when Neo followed Sawyer into the room. "What's he doing here?"

"Neo is collaborating with me, working with DOVE now," Sawyer said. "I made contact with him just before … before everything went down."

Jackson's nostrils flared and he looked at me. I nodded. Sawyer had already told me.

Jet gave Jackson a pointed look and slapped Neo on the back. "He was the one who alerted us to where you were that morning. It was lucky that he did. We owe him for that."

I felt the muscles across my back tighten with tension, and Jackson shifted on the bed. His distrust of Neo was not going away any time soon. He gave Neo a curt nod.

"I'm glad you're okay," said Neo. "I might go and grab a coffee from downstairs. Anyone want anything?"

Jet left with Neo. I could tell that those two were becoming fast friends. Jackson was not going to like that either.

"How did that happen, then?" Jackson's voice was still loaded with resentment.

"I just presented Neo with an opportunity that he preferred to the ones he'd had with Theo." Sawyer held out his hands in an exaggerated shrug. His naturally calm, compassionate style flowed around all of us. "To be honest, Nova started the change in him back in Melbourne. You know what she's like. She brings out the good in people."

The heat rose in my face and I shook my head.

Sawyer bumped shoulders with me and smiled.

Jackson gave me a half-hearted glare, but then sighed with resignation. "As long as he won't be hanging around us."

Sawyer shrugged. "I'll be keeping him close to me, both for his knowledge and his own protection. But I'm sure you'll like him when you get to know him."

I sucked in a breath, but Sawyer just gave a wide grin and his eyes danced. Jackson shook his head, but he couldn't help laughing. Sawyer's empathy was working its usual magic.

$$\triangle$$

The planning had recommenced for our overseas trip. There had been long conversations with Jackson's parents at the hospital while we waited for his medical clearance. Sawyer was still keen for us to leave once we returned to Victoria, as soon as Jackson felt up to it.

Until then, Sawyer had allocated another project to me. He wanted me to work on Corben. She was not coming with us overseas, but he wanted me to at least make a start.

"She's closed down again. Buried herself under a mountain of guilt." He gave me an encouraging smile. "She needs help, Nova. And I think it could be good for both of you."

Corben had layers to her shield. We had both seen them when she had dropped it. It would mean working through one layer at a time. And it would not be easy, or fast. I couldn't just take on all her anger and guilt as she had done with mine. She had drained all that darkness from me – my guilt over Abraham, my anger towards Theo. I didn't want that back. And I didn't want whatever load Corben was carrying. Sawyer wanted me to draw out the goodness, her empathy, her love, and build on that until she was strong enough to let go of her own darkness. That was my skill set.

I grimaced, but I gave him a reluctant nod.

A part of me felt like I owed her. She had taken away those shadows that I had been storing deep inside myself, and now she was carrying them. And so I would help her. For that, and for Sawyer.

But I was not ready to have a proper mother. Not yet.

△

I slowly pushed open the door of Jackson's room and peeked inside to make sure he was alone.

He was lying there, staring up at the ceiling with a broad grin across his face.

"Hey," I announced myself.

He blushed a deep shade of red, lifted his knees, and pulled one of his pillows down onto his lap.

"What are you up to?" I had the sensation of being flooded with warmth.

A muscle twitched at the side of his mouth, but he continued to stare at the ceiling. "Just thinking about you."

"Really?" I smiled. "What about me?"

"Well, actually, I was imaging being naked with you, in bed. In this bed." He adjusted the pillow again and gave me a suggestive wink. And a big grin.

"Oh. *Oh.*" The heat rose in my own cheeks now. "I don't think I would fit in that bed with you."

"Can we try?"

"Jack, we are not … we can't …"

"I know. I know." He made a face and then laughed. "I just want to lie next to you. It's been so long."

"You must be feeling a lot better."

"Oh, I am."

Jackson shuffled over in the bed, and I snuggled in beside him. It was cramped, but it was nice. More than nice.

"God, you're beautiful."

I felt the warmth flush through my face. "Maybe your eyesight has been affected."

He smiled and gave a slow shake of his head. "You know, I heard what Cooper said to you the other day. Do you think I'm crazy enough to be with you?"

"Well, you stepped in front of a bullet, so I'd take that as a firm yes!"

He laughed, and it made his body bump gently against mine. "And you brought me back."

"I did not. Please don't say that."

"Okay, love brought me back."

"Oh my god, that's even worse." I laughed.

His eyes dropped to my lips, then back to my eyes. I knew what he was thinking. His mouth lifted at the corners. "Can I?"

I nodded.

He wriggled sideways to face me, and we lay head-to-head, sharing a pillow. With a gentle nudge, he kissed me. It felt like home. I kissed him back.

It was not enough. A hunger rode through us like wild horses. We met in a deeper kiss, a passionate kiss. Electricity sparked off us, lighting up the room, probably the entire building.

I pulled back. "Jack, don't hurt ... you'll stretch ... it's probably not ..."

Jackson put a finger on my lips. He smiled and it was like the sun shone from that smile and gave it's light and warmth to the whole world. I felt like I was falling in love all over again.

"Jackson Lewis, thank you for coming back." I spoke quietly.

"Nova Wilson, I will always come back to you."

36

We clustered in a small group, a little reluctant to say our goodbyes. Our luggage was checked in for our flight to Los Angeles and through the next door was security, the duty-free shops, and then the departure gates.

It had been a busy month since we had returned from the Gold Coast.

Sawyer had planned our itinerary with Dr Lewis, who had taken an active interest in the whole trip and even provided Sawyer with some contacts he had in the US and Britain. They were not identified empaths, but they were doctors and medical researchers that he believed would have a strong interest in what we were doing and might be able to help. Sawyer had contacted them, and almost all the empaths on Dad's list, setting up meeting times. We were travelling to most of the places Corben had visited, which were the countries that had a U.S. Army base. Sawyer had made sure to include some sightseeing, and these were the only days I looked forward to.

Dr Lewis had also been a persuasive voice in encouraging both Jackson and me to defer from university for the semester. He thought we had enough to occupy our time and wanted us to enjoy the trip without worrying about assessments and study. It was a bit of a relief, to be honest.

The month had given Jackson further time to recover, though he claimed he was back to normal. He had started doing a light workout with Jet and Han again, and Cooper joined them as well. The others held back when fighting with him and treated him with a caution that matched the concern we all felt. The anguish we had been through was still too raw. Of course, it annoyed the hell out of Jackson, which left me feeling prickly all over my skin after each session. I didn't care; I was simply happy to be feeling any of his emotions again.

Sawyer had continued with my 'empathy training', which, despite his other commitments, he made a priority. Corben had often come along as well, and when she let us, Sawyer and I tried to peel back her layers. He flooded her with a calm compassion, while I delved deeper for her own emotions, drawing out the positive ones she had buried beneath the anger and the aggression that she had absorbed in her military work. I felt the warmth curl around me and a lightness in my chest in those small moments when she let us in, when she let her feelings out. It was like a shower of rain on parched earth, or the sun breaking through dark storm clouds; something you needed, even if you didn't know it. And the love that she held within herself was all directed at me.

I couldn't help but slam down my own protective barrier after a while. I needed to keep a wall between us, to avoid becoming too close. Sawyer shook his head at me at those times, but his kindness still shone from his eyes and wrapped around me. I knew he understood. He had told me she would forgive herself if I forgave her. But I was not quite ready. Ten years of being dead is a long time.

Corben had also offered to house sit while we were away, and she was going to look after Ripley, my kitten. Along with everyone else in my life, Ripley had taken quite a shine to Corben, and she loved to curl up on Corben's knee. The traitor!

Everything had been happening so quickly that I'd hardly had time to think about what this trip meant for me.

And now here we were, at the airport, ready to go.

My throat was dry, my skin was itchy, and my limbs felt stiff.

Sawyer stood a little to one side, with Jet and Rayna. They didn't have anyone to see them off. As always, a gentle calmness floated around Sawyer, covering all of us.

"I wish I was coming with you," said Mia, as she hugged me tightly. There were tears in her eyes, and waves of affection and friendship spilled over me. "You guys are going to have so much fun."

"I don't think it's supposed to be fun." The weight of expectation was heavy across my back, and the butterflies in my stomach were doing frantic laps.

"But you're travelling to so many exciting places."

"Yeah, that will be good, I guess." I lifted the sides of my mouth, trying to look more enthusiastic.

"It will be dangerous too, Mia," said Imogen, moving in for her turn at a hug.

"Not with Jet looking after her." Mia gestured towards him, and he gave her a friendly wave.

"Have you got everything you need for the plane? Passport, phone, neck pillow, a book?" Imogen sounded like the school captain she had been last year, but I envied her natural self-assurance. I straightened my back, trying to borrow some of that confidence.

"Send us lots of photos." Devon held me firmly but gently, and then stepped back. She was just as awkward as I was with these displays of affection, but I could feel her kindness and her strength, and I drew on them both.

My heart felt like it was being wrapped in sheets of soft tissue for safekeeping.

I looked over at Jackson, and his mother was holding him in a close hug. My shoulders drooped under the worry she carried. Tears ran down her face as he murmured quietly in her ear. Mrs Lewis was still grieving for her oldest son and recovering from the shock of Jackson's recent near-death experience. This goodbye was particularly hard on her. Dr Lewis moved in and put his arm around her, encircling Jackson with his other arm.

"Stay safe. Look after Nova." I heard him say. "We want updates every couple of days."

Jackson nodded in reassurance.

"Nova, you look after our boy too." Dr Lewis turned to me with a brave smile, and a swell of gratitude rode through my heart.

"I will. I promise."

Cooper put one arm around me and the other around Jackson and pulled us in to a three-way embrace. "I'll miss you both." There was a croak in his voice, and I felt my throat constrict as tears welled up in my eyes.

"We'll miss you too, Coop," I said.

"Look after Mum," Jackson said quietly to his brother.

Han pulled on my hand and drew me into a giant bear hug. "Stop all this mushy crap; you two need to hurry up and go save the world." He gave a loud, hearty laugh. "We'll take care of things here till you get back."

Jackson laughed with him, and I felt the lightening of his mood. "I'm relying on you to do just that," he said.

Spencer moved in and hugged me gingerly, across her large, pregnant stomach.

"I'm sorry I won't be here for the birth," I said.

"Doesn't matter. He won't remember it anyway. But you're making this world safer for him; that's what's important."

"No pressure," I muttered under my breath.

Sawyer either heard me or knew what I was feeling. "It's not just on you, Nova. I'm helping, and so will every other empath we meet." He had come to stand beside me, a subtle hint that we needed to get going.

"You've got this." Jackson reached for my hand and gave it a squeeze.

"Jack, this is on you too." Sawyer put a hand on Jackson's shoulder. He was smiling, but behind the smile I could sense the concern and guilt he still held, like a residue, left over from Jackson's gunshot wound. "Nova will be drawing on your love, your own empathy. That's what we are spreading. The kindness and compassion we can draw from each other, and from others.

"We want to dissolve the anger, the aggression, and instead draw out the humanity in people. If we can tap into their empathy and share that, we will rebuild the connections that promote harmony and acceptance. And the healing can follow. Kindness is an extraordinary force. It can soften an angry heart, soothe pain, dissolve hostility, and even calm fear. Compassion, too, is an emotion of great strength. It takes courage and an immense effort to rise above the anger and find understanding. Our empathy will have a ripple effect. I know it will. So, this is on all of us."

There was a silent collective cheer. We had inadvertently crowded around Sawyer during his small speech, and I felt the hope that blossomed in the hearts of my friends. Sawyer stood like a beacon before us, a lighthouse in a storm, and we were the boats being guided to safety.

Jackson grinned. He stuck out his chest and stood a little straighter. "We've got this. All of us."

As I looked into his eyes, the butterflies in my stomach stopped fluttering. My heart still galloped, but just to match the excited pulse I could sense in Jackson. There was a comfortable tingle all over my skin and I felt my muscles relax, letting go of all the tension I had been storing there.

Jackson met my gaze and squeezed my hand again. The other hand moved to rest over his heart, over his phoenix tattoo. He smiled and gave me a small wink, the one he kept just for me. The one that meant he loved me. The one that kept me safe.

The one that would change the world.

Epilogue

It was mostly dark, but tiny slivers of pink light peeked around the curtains, so Jackson knew it must be dawn. He leaned away from Nova, moving carefully so as not to wake her, and picked up his phone to check the time. For a minute or two he considered going for an early surf before the beach became crowded, but then he decided it was too early to get up. It was the last week of holidays before the university semester started and, after all the travelling they had done, he just wanted a week of lazy days.

He pressed on the News app, and the screen lit up with the headlines.

PM says no more curfews.

Salvation Army gives thanks for the most generous Christmas donations ever.

AFL clubs already preparing for coming season.

Retired gangland boss surprises senior community residents with brand new shoes.

He smothered a laugh and made a mental note to tell Nova about that last one. She would love it.

He scrolled down to the international news.

Twenty-three-year-old cat in the UK celebrates birthday with salmon cake.

Portugal and Denmark competing for title of safest place in the world.

Stricter US gun control laws passed at last.

Canadian teachers educating students in important life lessons beyond schoolwork.

He put the phone back down on the bedside table and shifted over on the mattress. Delicately sliding one arm into the space between the pillow and Nova's shoulder, he wrapped it around her and pulled her gently up against him. Her head moved instinctively to rest on his chest, and her arm moved across his stomach as she snuggled into his side. A wash of contentment floated through him and he knew it was from Nova, but she did not wake up. Jackson loved to sleep with her in his arms. She made him feel safe and secure. He wanted to be the one protecting her, but he knew she was the real warrior.

Carefully, he tugged on the straggly strands of her hair that stuck out over her ear. He looped them around his fingers as he pushed them back from her face. Then his fingers gently traced her cheek bone and down to her soft lips. Her mouth twitched as she slept. He was tempted to kiss those lips, but he knew she would be really pissed off if he woke her up this early.

Jackson brought his hand back to his bare chest, and it rested on his phoenix tattoo for a minute before he shifted it across to the left. His fingers hovered above the scar from his bullet wound, barely touching it. It was a raised lump, and still a deep red colour. He moved back to the tattoo and could feel his heartbeat beneath, steady and strong. It was a song of love for Nova, his phoenix.

The warmth and comfort of the bed created a pleasant drowsiness that tugged him back towards sleep.

There was the gentle sound of the waves spilling onto the beach, down past the dunes.

Closer to home were the reverberations of someone's soft snoring. It wasn't Cooper; he was arriving tomorrow. It sounded too faint to be Han, who could challenge the roar of a motorbike engine with his snoring. He and Devon were in the bedroom next door. Jackson wasn't sure whether West snored. He and Mia were across the hallway. Of course, it could be one of the girls snoring. He wasn't one to assume it had to be one of the boys.

Jackson smiled to himself and shut his eyes.

Acknowledgements

This is the sequel to my first book, and it was much harder to find the time to write and edit when I was also working – in a real job. So, I want to acknowledge and thank all those people who kept asking me when this one would be ready, because they enjoyed my first book. It was sometimes annoying (only because it put the pressure on!) but mostly it was heart-warming and encouraging to hear that you were so invested in my story. You kept me going when my energy was fading. Thank you so much.

There are a few extra special people I need to acknowledge – for their help and patience with this book. My first readers and unofficial editors are always my kids – Jordan and Brodie, whose feedback and opinions at all stages of writing, editing, and publishing are invaluable to me. They also look after my social media and my website. I need to add in thanks to my husband, Graeme, who lags behind the kids in reading my book, but gets there eventually. All three of them make the effort to read and re-read manuscript drafts, review back cover blurbs, appraise front covers designs, and generally just respond to any of my questions and requests for help and support.

I also want to thank my sister, Loueen, and my brother, Mark. They were great for further confirmation on the areas where I had doubts and just needed a second and third opinion.

As with my first book I drew inspiration from some of my escapades with my high-school friends, quite a few of whom I'm still in contact with. Sally and Lyn – you are two of my biggest supporters, thank you. Dean is the stand in for my best friend, Debbie – thanks Deano for your encouragement.

I also want to make special mention of an old high-school friend who asked me to put him in this book – as a blind, female character. Maize is for you, Brendan. I like her and I hope you do too.

And finally, I want to thank the team at Brisbane Self Publishing Service who make the publishing process easy with their guidance and professionalism.

It's been fun!

Lyndal Hennell

About the Author

Lyndal Hennell grew up in Melbourne, Victoria. At high school, her friends were nicknamed 'the young doctors' because their escapades were like a soapie drama.

Lyndal currently lives on the Sunshine Coast in Queensland. She loves cats, drinking hot chocolate and walking on the beach.

When she is not writing, Lyndal works as a registered psychologist, providing counselling support to young adults.

Climbing Out of the Fire is the sequel to her first novel *Flying Close to the Sun*.

www.ingramcontent.com/pod-product-compliance
Lightning Source LLC
Chambersburg PA
CBHW070531120726
47909CB00007B/2099